Challenging the Doctor

Challenging the Doctor

A Marietta Medical Romance

Patricia W. Fischer

TULE
PUBLISHING

Dedication

To Gaby
"She believed she could, so she did."

Acknowledgements

I am forever grateful to the incredible women of Tule Publishing for giving me the opportunity to write Jade and Edmund's story. It has been difficult to bring together two people who've had their worlds turned upside down by those they trusted, but I hope you enjoy reading their journeys as much as I have writing them.

My heartfelt thanks to Meghan, Sinclair, Jenny, Lee, and of course our fearless leader, Jane.

To my writer peeps at San Antonio Romance Authors who always inspire me and help me feel like being a writer is a totally normal form of employment.

A great big thanks to my hubs, Steve, and our children Emma, Katelyn, Alex, and Sophie, who believe in my storytelling ability.

Finally, I want to thank the readers out there. Your belief in the power of words and happily ever afters keeps writers like me, at the keyboards.

Much, much appreciation.

Sincerely,
Patricia W. Fischer

Chapter One

NURSE PRACTITIONER JADE Phillips never believed in fairy tales.

The mere idea of a helpless princess waiting to be rescued angered her beyond reason, because Prince Charming and knights in shining armor didn't really save those who wouldn't save themselves.

She'd learned that lesson the hard way at fourteen when unspoken signals for help to teachers and counselors went unnoticed.

Desperate, Jade confided in her best friend, Thomas McAvoy, about her situation at home. She thought he would give her a safe place to stay.

Instead, he called the police.

After her mother and stepfather were taken away, child protective services called her stranger of a father, Harlan Carter, and put her on a plane here, to Montana, where she'd finally grown up with a parent who truly cared about her.

And now, he was gone.

A crisp morning breeze danced in through the open living room windows, bringing in the sweet smell of summer wildflowers into the bare kitchen as Jade packed up the last of the cookbooks. The top one caught her attention. The one her father used almost constantly.

A binder that had "Food" written across it in black Sharpie pen.

The worn edges and ripped cover brought a sad smile to her face as she remembered her dad opening this very book to make her dinner the first night she arrived over fifteen years ago.

"Man, was I angry for being here." Her fingers gently ran down the short list of ingredients for French toast before seeing her father's secret ingredient written in the margin—vanilla creamer. "I think this is all I ate for four weeks and he made it every time I asked."

During the first months of her life in this mountain town, she quickly discovered Harlan's wonderful sense of humor, his good nature, and his loving heart. Her gentle giant father could bring an adversary down with a strong discussion. If that didn't work, he had an incredible, rarely used, right hook.

He empowered her by teaching how she could defend herself, use a gun with pinpoint accuracy, and drove her to therapy sessions as she learned to trust again.

When the weather allowed it, they'd hike the beautiful trails of Copper Mountain without a compass where he taught her how to pack, navigate, and survive on every level.

He'd not only been her protector and teacher, but a strong example of what a good man should be and the only reason she had ever healed.

So why had she chosen so poorly when it came to a husband?

Correction.

Make that late husband.

"Spaghetti and meatballs." Instead of answering her own question, she flipped the pages of the binder, focusing on the happy memories of the meals eaten in this very kitchen. "Practically perfect pancakes. Italian wedding soup. Macaroni, cheese, and bacon. Bacon, lettuce, tomato, and avocado. Potato soup with bacon, James's favorite."

Along with her father, she lived with her older brother James, who was a carbon copy of their dad and younger brother, Junior, whose devil-may-care attitude always landed him in trouble.

Even though it had been well over a year since her father's death, rereading more examples of how hard her father worked to be a good parent both warmed and broke her heart.

After coming here there was no more worrying about her mother's lies and denial.

No more sleeping with one eye open, waiting for her stepfather to visit her during the wee hours of the morning.

Her life here became normal. Comfortable. A sanctuary.

A few tears dotted the recipe pages, but she defiantly wiped them away with her hand. "Enough, Jade. He was hurting. It was time."

Being a nurse practitioner, she'd seen her share of death. In her practical mind she knew heart disease had made her dad a shell of a man from who he had been, but every day, she missed him.

On days like today, she missed him even more.

Picking up the business card, she sighed. "Okay, Maddie Cash, Realtor. Let's see what you can do."

As she texted the property and house information to the woman who said she could sell the property before the first flakes of snow hit the ground in the fall, a happy bark outside the house brought a smile to Jade's face, a much needed lift in her day.

Fred, the hound mix, always brought her joy, even in her most melancholy moments. After bringing him home six months ago, Jade quickly learned the dog loved to bark at everything from butterflies to the groundhogs that would pop their heads up just long enough to gain his interest. She watched him out the window, running aimlessly as his attention span sat between that of a gnat and a blink of an eye.

"He's going to be so bored living in town." The small yard of the rental house she'd moved everything to wouldn't be much room for him to run, but Jade didn't have a lot of residential choices right now. After trying to fulfill her father's dying request to repair the one-hundred-year-old farmhouse and keep the property in the family, she'd practically spent her last nickel. "If you'd paid your property taxes for the past three years, Dad, I might have had an easier time getting things in order. Ugh, I should have listened to Thomas and sold this place months ago."

Still, guilt ate at her. Her father had done so much for her and she couldn't complete his final wish.

A thumbs-up emoticon from Maddie flashed across Jade's screen, followed by "I'm on it" with a smiley face.

Maddie's enthusiasm made the weight of obligation lighter, but guilt still held on, especially as she flipped through the cookbook. "Fried chicken. We ate that every Sunday."

The mix of pepper, salt, flour, and powdered sugar he made to coat the chicken, always ended up all over this very counter. She'd help him soak the pieces with thick layers of farm fresh eggs before plunging it into the flour mix and handing it to him. He'd fry them to a perfect golden brown and Jade never thought she'd ever eat her fill.

Her stomach remembered as well. "I need some breakfast."

Fred ran in from the open front door and barked at her to join him.

"Having fun, buddy?" She absentmindedly placed the binder on the counter before scooping up the last box to take to her car. "Find any groundhogs?"

He cocked his head as a long string of drool hung from his floppy jowls.

"Oh, I bet you're thirsty. I'll get you some water here when we get into town. I'm almost done."

As soon as she hit the front steps, he ran out the door and took off around the large metal building. The Harlan and Sons Auto Repair sign still sat above the double entrance. A short-lived, but well-intentioned, business venture.

"Don't go far, Fred. I don't have time to chase you down today." But the longer she stayed, the more tired the dog would be and he'd sleep. She would be able to spend the day unpacking without interruption at her new place, right across the street from Bramble Park. "Too bad there's not a dog park over there."

Placing the box in her back seat, Jade's stomach uncomfortably twisted, knowing this would be the final walk through.

She double, triple-checked the four bedrooms and closets and closed the windows before leaving each space.

Sunlight highlighted the millions of dust particles lingering around as she moved from room to room, shutting the doors behind her.

The open living area floor plan had allowed them to easily walk from the family room to the kitchen. The broken, empty mantel over the blackened fireplace had been where her pictures and her father's shotgun were once displayed.

He insisted his weapon be in full view of whoever would be brave enough to ask her out.

A giggle escaped her, thinking of that first boy who walked in here, seeing the mountain of a man that was her father, standing there in front of the fireplace. His gun mounted on the wall behind him.

Amazing, that guy didn't run at the sight of it all.

Against that wall once sat the oversized couch where her brother James would pass out after working doubles at the local garage.

She'd position her favorite chair by the fireplace. One her father made with his bare hands in the workshop out back. She'd spent many winter nights curled up in the double rocker, reading about faraway lands, understanding good versus evil, and why a cat named Pete kept looking for a door into summer.

Straight across from her would be Harlan's gaudy brown La-Z-Boy chair he so loved. He'd positioned it the perfect distance between the TV, fireplace, and the kitchen.

Sweet moments tumbled in her brain of how the home had once been filled with love, comfort, and laughter. But the house held more than memories. It had been her second chance when she'd escaped her mother and stepfather.

Her third chance when she moved back from the incident with her husband.

Correction. Late husband.

It had been a place to refuel and reorganize when life had tumbled out of control. A home where things made sense and her father could give her solid advice and a strong hug.

She shivered as a cool wind drifted in through the open windows before she shut them tight.

Tears pricked the back of her eyelids knowing the house and the buildings out back would for sure be reduced to rubble whenever the new owners, whoever they might be, bought the place.

Now she'd have to start over on her own.

No safe haven.

No husband.

No father.

And, because her brothers were off either doing the most responsible or irresponsible thing, depending on which brother was being discussed, for all practical purposes, Jade

PATRICIA W. FISCHER

was completely alone.

At that moment, her reality finally penetrated the thick layer of strength she'd pulled from these last several months. Her heart slammed hard against her ribs and the bitter taste of sadness danced up and down her throat.

Bracing herself against the kitchen counter, Jade stared out the last open window at the Copper Mountain range and the cloudless azure sky. Taking a deep inhale of the crisp air didn't revive her today, but antagonized her angst of losing this place, this property.

Still, a nugget of excitement lodged deep in her gut. She could leave her past behind and write her own story. Only tell what she wanted people to know of her life outside Marietta.

Other than her best friend, Thomas, her brother, Junior, and her boss, Dr. Lucy Davidson, no one knew she'd shot and killed her husband in self-defense before returning to town last year.

And if anyone knew, I'd be the poster child for domestic abuse. No thanks.

Starting with a clean slate certainly sounded appealing and incredibly promising.

And exhausting.

For a few moments, she allowed herself the long overdue emotional purge until a voice, sounding remarkably like her father, whispered, "You can do this, baby girl. You've started over before. This is just another life challenge."

Closing her eyes, she listened to the silence, hoping to hear the voice whisper again, but instead of a voice, a quick chirp caught her attention.

A small golden bird sat on the windowsill.

"A yellow warbler. Daddy's favorite." Jade laughed through tears.

The bird chirped and hopped a couple of steps closer as if it wanted to engage her in conversation.

"What am I? Snow White, now?" She smirked, pointing to the binder. "Sorry, I only have this cookbook. No food today."

Another chirp.

Fred's faint barks signaled he'd ended up behind the metal warehouse, next to her father's woodshop.

"What did Daddy like to make? I'll tell you." She thumbed through the yellowed pages and the bird didn't move. Explaining recipes to an animal with no opposable thumbs was nothing but projection. Nonetheless, it felt good to talk about her father's perfect grilled cheese sandwich. "Sometimes he'd mix the cheeses like cheddar and Monterey Jack or American and swiss or pepper Jack and mozzarella."

The bird hopped closer as though totally interested in what she had to say.

Her mouth watered at the mix of cheeses the recipe suggested as combinations. "Sometimes he'd add grilled tomatoes between the cheese slices and always used sourdough bread soaked in butter. Mmmm, so good."

The bittersweet memory made her mouth water and her stomach growl. "Sorry, I didn't eat breakfast yet."

A couple more chirps before the quick feet of Fred came and went as the dog happily ran around the property, barking at random.

The noise startled the bird and it flew away.

"That's where I am now? Standing in an empty house, talking to animals?" She snorted in an attempt to lighten the mood. "Orphaned. Almost broke. History of an abusive stepparent. I have all the makings of a princess in distress and it's only eight thirty in the morning. My prince or knight in shining armor should be driving into town right now to sweep me off my feet to my happily ever after."

Chapter Two

"DAMN, EIGHT THIRTY already?" Dr. Edmund Davidson white-knuckled the steering wheel as the GPS indicated he had another five minutes of drive time.

He'd considered taking the short trip to Marietta from Bozeman after arriving late last night, but never having driven these roads and worried about hitting an animal in the dark, Edmund decided a good night's sleep would be a less reckless choice, especially since his body still sat on eastern standard time.

Although the rest helped revive him, it still hadn't kept him from getting a late start and not keeping to his schedule.

I should be there by now.

His frustration built with each passing mile, but he had to keep it together before confronting his younger sister, Lucy, about her impulsive move to the middle of nowhere.

She'd always been the one to face the world with bright-eyed wonder, but to move away and fall in love with the *magical land of Montana*, as she liked to tell them, had him and their other two siblings, Peter and Susan, stunned.

"That imagination of hers. This place can't be that great." Edmund took a long drag off his to-go coffee then reached for the half-eaten breakfast sandwich he'd picked up at the fast-food place next to the hotel. Looking at the hockey puck of a sausage patty, he cringed.

Wrapping it back up again, he tossed it on the passenger seat and went back to his java. "I'll stop at the diner Lucy talks about when I get there."

The phone rang. He set it to speaker before snapping, "What?"

"Good morning to you, sunshine." Peter, the oldest of the Davidson children, asked, "Are you there yet?"

"Get off my ass, Peter. GPS says a few more minutes."

"You said that half an hour ago. Are you doing what it's telling you to or did you pick a different route to be difficult?"

"Technology is only as good as the information we give it." Edmund purposely gave himself a time buffer to keep Peter from calling back in exactly five minutes and checking in. "The GPS I mapped out said ten more minutes. It's a straight shot from Bozeman or is it Billings?"

"Breathe, Ed. You're supposed to be positive when you check on Lucy. Don't go in there and be, you know, yourself."

Edmund could picture Peter's all-knowing smirk as he said those words. "Thanks. I'll do my best not to be *me*."

"Good."

"Would you boys knock it off? We're a family. We need to act like one, especially for Lucy." Always the voice of cautious optimism, second oldest, Susan piped in. "Edmund, I'm so glad you took this assignment. This is a very logical way to get back into the medical field."

"Logical? Should I begin to sing the Supertramp song?" Large trees lined the road. He passed another mile marker and he picked up his coffee again, draining the contents.

"Look, I'm sorry that woman screwed you over, but you could be sitting in jail about now. Maybe you should be happy you can drive around aimlessly, out of state. Or even locally *without* an ankle monitor on."

The honest comment only angered him more. How could he have been so blind? A woman as gorgeous and successful as Dr. Reyna Coldwell-Whyte having any interest in him in the first place, initially puzzled him. In retrospect, it looked obvious something had been very wrong, but he simply wasn't thinking.

At least not with my brain.

He counted his lucky stars every night that the evidence cleared him and he kept his freedom, even though it professionally ruined him. "Fair enough, Susan. I'll do my best to be cordial to the locals."

"But not too friendly," Peter added, his attempt to be funny.

Susan's exasperated sigh mimicked Edmund's annoyance. "Peter, please. I don't think we need to worry about Edmund's love life right now. The last thing he knows he needs is complications."

The corner of his mouth twitched as his older siblings subtly lectured him about his disastrous history with women. "I think I can control myself for three to six months. Besides, I doubt there's anyone here who I'd even be interested in."

13

Or who'd be interested in me.

"I think Edmund's great pickup lines will take care of that," Peter scoffed.

"I don't have any great pickup lines."

"Exactly."

"Seriously, Peter? You might be charming to many, but you aren't one to lecture about relationships." Susan jumped in as she always did, trying to smooth over the surfaces in the most practically honest way. "Edmund, I know you're amazing and just. The right person will love you exactly the way you are. Please don't settle for anyone less than that."

Her words were annoyingly trite, but true. For years, he'd held onto that idea too many times, only to be repeatedly let down and his heart broken. Despite his great ability to handle any situation academically or medically, Edmund had always found potential dating situations overwhelmingly stressful.

Multiple times he'd trip over his own tongue or say exactly what was on his mind without any sort of thought, dead-ending a conversation before it ever got started.

There's something to be said about arranged marriages.

But if this past year taught him anything, it was to listen to his better judgment when things didn't seem right and not be distracted by a pretty face.

Susan cleared her throat. "Please tell us, what does Montana look like? Is it as beautiful as Lucy says it is?"

"It's pretty. Quiet. In the middle of—"

"Nowhere. We get it." His siblings answered in unison, but they'd missed the point.

The comment wasn't a complaint, but a compliment. So far, Montana looked like a much-needed escape from the insanity of his life in Florida.

The road slowly wound like a lazy serpent before crossing over the Marietta River where, through the trees, a jaw-dropping silhouette of the mountain range came into view. He rolled down the windows and a wave of the subtle smell of freshly bloomed flowers filled the car. "Ho-ly shit. That's impressive."

"What? What's impressive?" Peter's voice, full of anxiety.

"This mountain range in front of me." The morning sun rose in a cloudless blue sky as the trees transitioned in to large fields of blue, purple, yellow, and red. He craned his neck to get a better view. "She wasn't kidding. These mountains are incredible."

"Mountains are nice, but to move away?" Susan's frustration laced her words. "I don't understand. What was so bad about her life here?"

"Maybe nothing, Susan. Lucy said she wanted to have her own life, her own place. Can't really blame her for that." After the last year, Edmund understood the want to get away all too well.

The green carpet full of flowers sat on either side of the two-lane highway. Brilliantly colored, the plants gently swayed with the tall grasses.

As he came around a bend, Edmund had to pull over on the roadside for a quick stop. He couldn't fully appreciate the view in front of him without potentially causing an accident. "I'll call you back as soon as I see her and her boyfriend."

"We'll talk to you then."

Getting out of the car and leaving the door open, he walked around the back, watching for oncoming traffic. Edmund removed his sunglasses and simply stared in awe. He'd always loved the mountains, but after the accident that killed their father and permanently injured their mother, anything with an incline proved difficult for their mom to navigate. The flat beaches of Florida were as challenging as she could handle which left hiking through the mountains out for any family gatherings.

To get his fix of the rugged outdoors as an adult, he'd driven to Georgia on several occasions, to explore multiple trails there. The highest, Brasstown Bald, had proved to be a good workout, but its elevation didn't reach five thousand.

But those, those rocks are definitely taller than five thousand.

Watching the sun reflect off the colorful peaks, he imagined what they looked like covered in the snow, the sun glistening off them and him walking the trails. "Maybe I could try cross-country skiing. How hard can it be?"

Not that he'd ever done that, but being here seemed like a good time to try it come winter, if he stayed that long. His heart sped up at the possibilities of sitting up there, where no one could find or judge him.

Seeing the magnificent view, Edmund understood why his younger sister had spoken so highly of this place. He took a deep cleansing breath as every knotted muscle in his exhausted body unraveled. It felt good to be away from the madness, the chaos that seemed to follow him these past several months.

The quiet seeped into every pore, wrapping around him like a warm blanket. Edmund relished the sense of peace and awareness until the faint bark of a dog, partially brought him back to reality.

"Nowhere, Montana looks pretty good right now." He took a long breath in, appreciating how it revived his tired body.

The flowers swayed with the gentle winds.

As he walked closer to the fence, he could see a large clump of trees on the other side of the property and imagined sitting there doing a whole lot of nothing.

A for sale sign caught his attention, but he scoffed at such an impulsive idea. "Maybe this assignment won't be so bad. Maybe it will be a new beginning, logically speaking."

The slam of a car door pulled Edmund out of his admiration of the scenery.

"You need any help there?"

Turning, Edmund watched a policeman approach. "Morning, Officer."

The man stood a good six feet and had obviously seen a set of free-weights. "You okay?"

Being unfamiliar with the law enforcement culture here, Edmund pulled out his wallet then rested his palms on the hood of his car, keeping them visible at all times. Being taller than average, Edmund tried to do everything in his power not to be seen as aggressive, especially against cops.

He'd learned a thing or two in the last few years when

talking to the local officers that visited the staff in the ER. "Nothing's wrong, sir. Wanted to take in the view."

"Guess you've never been here before." Extending his hand, the officer smiled. "Logan Tate."

Edmund responded in kind and handed his license over. "Edmund Davidson."

"Davidson? Any relation to Dr. Davidson?" Logan glanced at the ID then handed it back.

"She's my sister." A long, soulful howl erupted from out in the field. "Sounds like hound mix."

"We got a lot of them around here. Here to pay Lucy a visit?"

"Surprise visit. She's not expecting me until the end of the week."

Logan tucked his sunglasses in the *V* of his collar. His nametag read Deputy Tate. "Then I won't tell her. She's working the morning shift at the hospital today."

"How do you know that?"

"First responders always check who's working in the ER. Helps knowing who we're working with if we have to bring someone in."

The corner of Edmund's mouth twitched at the familiarity. "Sounds like something our paramedics and EMTs did all the time. They knew us in the ER so well they had our coffees and taco orders memorized when they'd make a run."

Giving a smirk, Logan nodded. "We've sure enjoyed having her here. She's a great doctor."

"Runs in the family." A few birds suddenly flew up from the tall grasses far from the fence, momentarily gaining

Edmund's attention.

"You mentioned working in the ER. You're a what, doctor? Nurse? PA?"

"Doctor."

"That's right. You're taking over Dr. McAvoy's job."

Annoyed, Edmund crossed his arms over his chest and leaned against his car, bringing him and Logan to an even eye level. "How do you know that?"

Logan's mouth stretched to a full smile. "You might as well know, not much happens in this town without everyone hearing about it."

Before Edmund could answer, a frantic voice came over his shoulder walkie-talkie. "You okay out there, Logan? Anything wrong? Do I need to send someone to help you?"

Logan motioned for Edmund to stay quiet. "It's nothing, Betty. Just a tourist couple needing directions."

"Thank goodness. You know, I always worry when you call from Harry's marker. That bend can be tricky if people don't know how to drive it."

For a few moments, the smile in Logan's eyes disappeared as his gaze betrayed him. His chin tilted toward the front of Edmund's car. "It's all good, Betty. Don't worry."

"Okay, we'll see you in town in a bit, Logan."

Walking around the front of the car, Edmund noticed a cross surrounded by flowers. The faded words *Harry* and *September 5, 2016* had been written across it.

Harry's marker. Damn.

"Betty's our dispatcher. Word of advice, anything you don't want the entire town to know within an hour, don't say in front of Betty or Carol Bingley. Carol's husband owns the pharmacy and she works the counter. Those two will repeat everything anyone says to anyone who'll listen."

"Good to know." Edmund pointed to the cross. "What happened there?"

A dark mask of anger replaced the officer's friendly demeanor. "Hit and run."

"Any idea—"

"None. No leads at all," Logan snapped.

The fury in his eyes told Edmund the case bothered him more than he cared to discuss and left someone he knew dead.

"Hope you find out who did this real soon."

"Won't be soon enough," Logan growled.

A loud howl followed by several happy barks echoed out of the tall grass.

Dog sounds like he's having a good time.

"Lost my dad to a drunk driver when he hit us head-on." Edmund grimaced remembering that day. "I was about twelve. Almost killed Lucy. Our mom had long-term disabilities from it. Never fully recovered."

"Then you know."

"What it's like to lose someone you care about in the blink of an eye? Yep. Yep I do."

Logan pushed a rock around with the toe of his boot. "Harry was a great guy. Best there ever was. Never met a stranger. Always there to help."

There were too many of these stories to count and, working in the ER, Edmund hated how so many of them ended.

How many of these *great guys* he'd pronounced dead.

Logan took a long breath. "Which is why he was here that night. Helping an older couple change a tire. They said a car came out of nowhere."

"What do you know about it?"

"The car. Not much. The couple couldn't tell us anything except the car went fast. Real fast." Picking up the rock, Logan threw it into the field. "We don't have much else to go on. No dash cams. Course, the couple gave us what they could."

Much else? Edmund had worked with officers enough to know they always held something back from the public. "Tire marks? Make, model, color of the car?"

"It's a standard high-speed rated tire for a sports car. Nothing that matches anything in *our* system. The couple said it was dark. Could be blue, black, or dark green. No one in this area has a car like that."

"Gives you something. Think it was a drunk driver?" The last words burned up Edmund's throat. How he hated people who thought so little of others' lives by getting behind the wheel when they knew they shouldn't.

"More than likely. It was Labor Day weekend." Logan straightened the cross when the wind blew it slightly to the right. "Seems if anyone in town knew anything, they would have talked by now. Or guilt would have gotten the better of them so when they got drunk enough, they'd confess their sins."

"You think it's an out-of-towner, then?"

"Probably. Surrounding counties know about it. Everyone's always listening." Logan's shoulders sank as if the weight of the world had rested on them. "But I have to keep believing one of us at the station, Brett, Rob, or I, we'll find who did this. Make sure they see jail time for it."

Edmund looked at the marker again. Come September, it would be two years.

Two years of not knowing who'd taken a life.

Two years of waiting for answers.

Edmund couldn't imagine the pain of it. It had been bad enough waiting six months for the trial of the man who'd slammed head-on into them that Sunday morning. Even with the defendant in jail the entire time prior to the trial and him immediately returning to prison after the final gavel slammed down, the time waiting for justice had been agonizing.

But justice didn't bring his father back or help his mother walk without pain ever again or speed up Lucy's agonizing recovery, cover her scars. "I'll keep my ears out. I hope you find who did this."

"I appreciate that, Doc."

Another covey of birds flew up out of the grass and the head of a large dog popped up for a moment.

"That dog okay?"

"Probably. If I see him, I can tell you whose he is." Logan craned his neck to look. "Where you staying?"

"The Croft? The Graft?"

"The Graff." He motioned for Edmund to get back in his car. "Come on. I'll drive you into town."

"I appreciate that, Deputy."

"It's Logan, Doc."

"Edmund." Taking a long look at the mountains again, Edmund tilted his chin toward them. "What's it like to hike those?"

"You gotta be prepared. The weather can sneak up on you if you don't watch out, but helluva lot of fun, especially if you go with someone who loves it as much as you do." The mischievous tone in Logan's voice hinted that he might have done more than hike in those mountains. "Plenty of secluded spots to enjoy and the view is second to none."

"Sounds like you know them pretty well."

"I do. A lot of us do. My girlfriend Charlie's a photographer. She's taken some incredible pictures up there and is learning the trails. But don't go up there without a local with you." Logan put his sunglasses back on. "It's easy to get lost, but I guess it works out from time to time."

"Why's that?"

"One of our rangers, Todd Harris, met his girlfriend when she got lost up there."

"A happily ever after then? I'll keep that in mind." Not that Edmund planned on taking anyone up into those trails with him. He'd had enough relationship drama to last a lifetime and, with his record, he didn't see his luck changing anytime soon.

Logan patted Edmund on the back. "Come on, Doc. Let's get you to the hotel."

Before Edmund could get back into his car, a loud bark came from the back seat. Then a dog poked his head out of the window as it happily wagged his tail.

"What the hell?" Edmund jumped back.

"Looks like you've met another resident of Marietta, Edmund." Logan scratched the dog behind his ears. "This here's Fred."

Approaching cautiously, Edmund stuck out his hand. The dog sniffed it, then licked the length of his fingers and palm, leaving a thick layer of slobber. "Great. Any idea who the owner is?"

A lusty chuckle escaped him. "Yep."

Edmund found the napkins from his take-out breakfast as Fred began sniffing around the car. As soon as the dog's nose hit the front passenger seat, he found the half-eaten sandwich and, wrapper included, ate it in two gulps.

Logan chuckled as he spoke into his radio. "Betty, can you call Jade and tell her Fred's out again?"

Immediately, Betty answered. "You got it, Logan. Still at Harry's marker?"

"Yep." He leaned against the car and scratched Fred's ears. "She'll get ahold of Jade in a minute."

"Jade? Why does that name sound familiar?"

"Nurse practitioner. Works in the ER."

And the bane of my sister's existence the first few months of her being here.

Edmund couldn't help but laugh at his luck.

My introduction to Marietta is starting off with a bang.

Chapter Three

"AS IF I don't have enough things to do than to worry about my dog running off and getting hit." Jade shook her head, overwhelmed with the list of things she needed to get done before heading back to work tomorrow. "At least I finished getting the house cleaned out. Ugh, Fred. You're making me nuts."

Even though adopting the dog had been an impulsive decision, Jade couldn't process the idea of living totally alone.

Again.

After last Christmas, she'd been inspired to adopt a local shelter animal because of the winning Christmas tree designed for the Mistletoe and Montana event. Every ornament on it had an animal in need of their forever home, but by the time Jade finally got around to getting over there, it was empty.

Because someone had paid the adoption fees for all the animals in the shelter, all the animals, including a very cute one-eyed dog, had been adopted.

Then on her way home, she saw Fred running on the side of the road after a truck that sped away. Poor thing was skinny, hungry, and had no collar. Her best guest was someone had just dumped him.

She happily took him back to her place, which had been wonderful because coming home to Fred's unconditional love and wagging-tail greetings had always brought a smile to her face when she entered the front door.

But man, the dog was work. He constantly needed to be entertained, drooled on her furniture, had some weird obsession with her keys, chewed on things when he was bored, and couldn't help but knock everything over he came within five feet of.

A new wave of tears stained her face at the possibility of losing Fred.

She white-knuckle gripped the steering wheel. "Ugh, get a grip, Jade. You're gonna have an accident. Fred is fine."

The upbeat guitar intro of Lynyrd Skynard's "Sweet Home Alabama" rang out from her purse. She let out an exasperated sigh. "Not now, Junior."

Immediately prior to Betty the dispatcher calling, Jade's brother, Junior, had screamed at her over the phone for a good ten minutes about selling their father's place because he'd heard a big treasure had been buried by the original owners.

Frustration got the better of her dealing with her brother's chaos and she yelled, "Sure there's a one-hundred-year-old treasure, Junior. That makes total sense because that's exactly what all desperately rich men do. They gamble away their entire fortunes to a nobody in a poker game and walk away without a word."

"You can't sell it," he barked. "I won't let you."

"I'm the executor, Junior. There's not a thing you can do about it. Now get your crap out of the garage or I'm calling the junkyard to come get it all." She paused. "Why don't you focus more on getting things straight with your probation instead of worrying about the house that you never cared about?"

He hung up on her, now to call her back, probably to scream at her again.

Lynyrd Skynyrd continued to play.

She gripped the wheel tightly, refusing to answer the phone and attempt to talk any sort of sense into her moron of a sibling. "What is it with him and this property now? He didn't take care of one thing while he lived there. Now he's so in love with the place he doesn't want me to sell?"

Thank goodness her father had the good sense to make her sole executor of his estate, otherwise she'd end up paying everything on the property and Junior would be living there free, contributing nothing except complaints, beer cans, and whatever he kept in that wannabe garage.

Ugh, why can't I effectively deal with his crap?

Large swatches of red and yellow flowers whipped by her as she neared where Logan said he'd be waiting. "A buried treasure. Humpf. That's the excuse you're going to use for not clearing out the building? Lame."

The story of their great-grandfather winning the land in a poker game wasn't new information. Jade had grown up hearing it, even had the poker chips to prove it, but to get her to not list the house because of a rumor of some new tall tale?

She didn't have time to play this game of chicken anymore when calling his bluff. She had to sell the place because shelling out rent *and* paying the taxes on the property for more than six months would set her even further back from retirement than she cared to think about.

Before driving, she'd texted him that she'd already told Maddie Cash to list it and he had one week to clear things out of the buildings behind the main house.

He'd responded with a middle finger emoticon.

"Great. Just great." With the weight of the world on her shoulders, she dried her face with the back of her hand as she neared the curve to Harry's marker. She repeated her mantra for a bit of a pep talk. "I can do this. I believe I can, so I will. I'm kickass. Change is good... Oh, my. Who is that?"

Standing there with her dog had to be one of the most handsome men she'd ever seen. At least he looked handsome from twenty feet away.

"Goodness," she mumbled as she put the car nose to nose with the stranger's. "And I thought this was gonna be a dull day."

Popping back one of the many mints she always kept in her cup holder, Jade subtly tried to run her fingers through her hair before exiting.

The man had to be well over six feet, beautifully tanned skin, wavy espresso-colored hair, and broad shoulders that had certainly seen the inside of a gym.

He stood in the grass between his car and the fence line. Fred's ears perked up when she exited the car, but he didn't move.

Exhaling a long breath, she began to approach, but noticed Logan's patrol car wasn't anywhere to be seen.

Good old-fashioned stranger danger kicked in.

She backed up a couple of steps and called out, "Officer Tate, Logan. He left?"

As the stranger replied, he stayed in place and scratched Fred behind the ears. "He got a call. Something about someone speeding south of town."

Please don't let it be Junior. She pushed her mental anguish away. She'd save that problem for later. "You've met my dog, I see."

Wagging his tail, Fred leaned against the man's long legs.

"He's one ferocious animal. Almost melted my arm off with all his slobber."

"He's a hound. They slobber." *Wow, Fred likes him? That says something about this guy.* She cautiously closed the gap between them.

He held his hand up. "I had napkins in the car. That reminds me. Fred ate half my breakfast *with* the wrapper. Good luck with that later."

"Ugh, thank you."

A split-second cringe before he chuckled, "Sorry. He'd eaten it before I saw it missing."

His beautifully deep voice made her want to giggle like a teenager. Jade got so lost listening to him; it took her a few moments to realize he'd asked her a question.

She blinked herself out of her stare. "What?"

Holding his hand out, he stepped toward her. "Lucy. Dr.

Davidson? Do you know her?"

Jade quickly took it in kind. "Yes, I know her. She works with me in the ER." *Please don't be an old boyfriend of hers.*

"I'm Edmund, her brother."

Oh, great. Her *brother.* That tidbit of important information gave Jade relief simply because her best friend, Thomas, and Lucy were one of the cutest couples in town. An old boyfriend showing up out of the blue would certainly throw a wrench into things as dictated by multiple romantic comedies, probably starring Reese Witherspoon or Renée Zellweger.

"You're Jade Phillips, aren't you?"

"Yes, I am, but my maiden name is Carter. Trying to transition back to that." When he said her name, Jade readied to hear less than stellar things about herself. It would have served her right since she'd given his sister such hell the first few months she lived in Marietta. "But don't believe everything you hear."

Giving her a wink, he smirked. "Of course not."

Interesting response. "What brings you to Montana?"

"I'm taking over Dr. McAvoy's job, but I hadn't planned to be here until Friday so Lucy's not expecting me yet." He adjusted his sunglasses.

With Lucy being barely five foot, Jade didn't expect any sibling of Dr. Davidson to be so tall. "Well, I won't tell her if I see her before you do."

"I appreciate that."

Fred leaned hard against Edmund's legs.

"Fred sure likes you. You must be a good guy."

"Um, yeah, I-I-I guess. Dogs have a good sense of, um, of who someone is. I-I-I'd appreciate you not saying anything to her before I get into town."

"To Lucy? Yes, you said that."

"Oh, right. I did. Sorry. Jet lag."

"Right." She bit her lip watching him fumble for words. *How charming.* "Where are you staying?"

"It's called Graff, I believe."

"You believe correctly. You're not staying with Lucy?"

Despite being covered by jeans and a dark button-down shirt, he had the body of a runner, long and lean and muscular. A quick wind blew a lock of his hair across his forehead. "Didn't want to crowd her like that for as long as I'm staying."

"What do you mean, crowd her? You planning on staying awhile longer than the standard three to four month temporary contracts?" Her fingers itched to move the stray lock of hair back into place, then wander across his broad shoulders and thick chest.

What are you thinking?

She tucked her thumbs in her belt loops as her sudden onset of libido intrigued and concerned her. She hadn't felt anything remotely sexual about anyone since her late husband, Brenden.

Honestly, months before he died, any inkling of blush-inducing tingles had long faded from her life.

Now they were suddenly back with a vengeance.

I'm not thinking straight. I must be tired.

Edmund shifted his weight as he loosely crossed his arms

across his chest. "I'll be here until they find a permanent replacement."

"While you're here…if you need a tour guide, I'm your girl. Woman." *Did I really just say that?*

A flash of crimson colored his cheeks, making him all the more appealing. "Thank you, Jade. I-I-I appreciate that."

Breathe, Jade. He's just a guy. "Of course."

Fred barked at a yellow warbler that landed on Harry's marker.

Annoyed, the bird fluttered its wings a few times and chirped angrily back at Fred while remaining perched on the top of the cross.

The dog's head cocked and his ears perked up as though he wasn't sure what to do with a creature that couldn't care less about what he said.

"I think you've met your match, Fred." Edmund laughed.

"Those are feisty little creatures. They were my dad's favorites and they sure are pretty."

"Yes, they are pretty." Even though he'd kept his sunglasses on, she could feel his gaze on her. When she stared back, his eyebrows hit his hairline and he tried to back away, but Fred sat on his foot. "I promise I'm not a creep, but those birds…and you…are, are, are nice to look at."

"Oh, thank you." She swallowed hard, trying not to let the nervous laugh that bubbled in her stomach get away from her.

"Sorry, it's that when my sister mentioned you, I expected a Nurse Ratched type. Severe bun. Scowl. Old…er. A battleax. Not, not…you." Another wave of red colored his cheeks and had now bled to his forehead.

How absolutely adorable. "Relax, Edmund. Consider me a modern-day Nurse Ratched, but without the unbending approach to patient care."

"Thanks. Glad you know who I mean. Not everyone has seen that movie."

"I'm kind of a movie freak. Love them."

"G-g-g-good to know." He smoothed out his jeans. "I, um…"

Before she could totally relish his geekish awkwardness, her stomach let out a large growl, ruining the moment.

Way to be classy, Jade. "Sorry, I skipped breakfast."

"Can I take you to get something to eat?" He sucked in a breath as if the invitation processed after he'd said it. "Damn, my mouth is working faster than my brain today."

As much as she appreciated his invite, she thought it curious. "You sure? Aren't you going to surprise, Lucy? Because a new guy sitting in the Main Street Diner talking to *me* is sure going to get tongues wagging."

"She's working this morning in the ER. I'll text her. Tell her where I am." He held his hands up in surrender, taking a step back. "Unless you're busy with other things. People."

Oh, my gosh, as if he couldn't be more stinkin' gallant right now. "No, no, not at all. I just gotta get Fred back to the house first. I can't take him to the diner."

"You're available, then?"

"Totally *available*." She heard herself and mentally cringed.

Did you say totally available? What are you? Fourteen in the 1980s. She checked her reflection in his sunglasses to verify she hadn't started curling her hair between her fingers and smacking invisible gum.

Edmund gave her a nod. "Great, I'll check in at the hotel. Meet you at the diner in about an hour."

"Perfect. Come on, Fred." Jade coaxed, but the dog looked up at Edmund and collapsed on both his feet. "I can't even with you today. Fred, come on."

Staring up at the newcomer, Fred's tail thumped against the grass.

"I think he likes me." Kneeling, Edmund rubbed the dog's belly and back playfully.

I think I like you too. "Appears so. Come on, Fred."

"If you're okay with it, he could ride with me." As if he understood it, the dog jumped to his feet and into Edmund's car by way of the open window.

"No, no, no!" Annoyed at the lack of control she had in pretty much anything in her life right now, Jade cringed at Fred's excited barking as he slobbered all over the back seat of Edmund's rental car. "I'm so sorry. He's usually less obstinate than this."

"Guess that means I'll have to follow you home." A crooked smirk indicated Edmund wasn't at all annoyed at her dog's decision. "Only if that will help."

That stopped her in her tracks, sending her heart rate skyrocketing. "You sure you want to? Follow me home? Won't it be out of your way?"

"Unless it makes you uncomfortable. If it does, I'll pick

Fred up and deposit him in your car right now."

Stop being so damned chivalrous. It's too intriguing. "No, it's fine. Might as well get to know each other since we'll be working together."

"Lead the way, Nurse Phillips, I mean Nurse Carter."

"Absolutely, Dr. Davidson." By the time Jade returned to her car, her hands trembled with excitement. She tilted her rearview mirror and talked to her reflection. "Calm down, he's just a guy."

An extraordinarily handsome guy who your dog likes and who you'll be working with.

She exhaled a long breath. *And the brother of the doctor you fought with for the first two months you were here.* "Finding him the tiniest bit attractive doesn't spell disastrous irony at all."

He waved at her as she backed up before making a U-turn into town. The simple gesture caused her stomach to flip-flop again.

Goodness. I need to get out more.

As they caravanned toward Marietta, Jade spoke out loud, listing every reason she shouldn't get to know the new arrival more than professionally as she cranked "The History of Wrong Guys" from the musical, *Kinky Boots.*

Like the character, Lauren, from the show, Jade listed the reasons she and Edmund would be a disaster in the making as she sang along to her own lyrics.

"One. We'll be working together. Two. He's not going to stay." She turned from Highway 89 into town. "Three. Your track record with men sucks. Four. He's Lucy's brother."

That last one made no sense. For the past couple of months, Jade worked with Edmund's sister and that alone should put him solidly in the "decent man" category. More than once, the good doctor had helped Jade not only keep her job, but treated her like an equal and proved to be an annoyingly great human being.

Plus, Lucy had fallen totally in love with Jade's childhood friend, Thomas McAvoy. The two were an amazingly fabulous couple. Honestly, Jade couldn't be happier for them. "Her brother would have to be just as good, right?"

Or he could be a total screw-up like hers.

A glance in the rearview mirror showed Edmund still behind her, which brought a smile to her face as she sang the chorus of "The History of Wrong Guys" once again, this time with the original words.

Fred's head stuck out of the back driver's window, his ears and jowls flapping in the wind. He barked intermittently from happiness.

As idealistic as the scene appeared, Jade knew the reality. "Ugh, no, Jade. The reasons you should be listing are why he shouldn't get involved with you. One. You're a financial mess. Two. You can't handle your felon brother. Three…"

Shaking off the self-sabotage, she convinced herself that she imagined more of the easy flirtation than she needed to be. He'd simply been kind, friendly, and respectful because of her dog.

Three. Because nice guys like him deserve a helluva lot better than me.

Within minutes, they arrived at a newly painted one-story bungalow house across from Bramble Park and two houses down from Bramble House Bed and Breakfast. The small yard wouldn't be much for Fred, but it would have to do until she could get her bank account built back up.

Thank goodness her job at the Marietta ER paid well and with the exception of the property taxes and failed repairs on her dad's place, she'd kept her own expenses low.

Even without much for Fred to run around in, she wanted this house because of its proximity to the park and the Marietta River. The previous owners had constructed a walking trail outside the backyard gate where anyone could reach the banks of the river without too much trouble. Between these two places, it gave her plenty of room to walk and get outside with Fred when she was home. On days off, she could take him up the mountain trails and tire him out.

Of course if Junior didn't move his stuff soon, she would have to deal with all his crap herself.

As if that would be anything new.

She'd been dealing with her younger brother's crap since he began getting in trouble with the local law enforcement when he was in high school.

She couldn't remember the amount of times he'd call her, instead of their dad, to bail him out. His timing had always been uncanny as he'd get into trouble when she had a big test to study for or a massive project to complete.

Her father kept telling her to leave him in jail overnight, but Jade simply couldn't do it and that's why Junior called her and not their brother, James, or their father.

Now, she regretted not leaving him a couple of times because today, she had to deal with a man-baby who demanded she "not touch his stuff."

Even though he was a complete mess, he was the only member of her core family she had left in Marietta. To her, that meant something, but to her brother, family ranked about as important as following through.

So almost nothing.

I hate being alone in the world.

Sadness weighed heavily on her heart at the many changes in the past couple of years, but she pushed it away. She couldn't go there now. "Get your brave face on, Jade. You've got a visitor."

Parking in her driveway, she quickly grabbed Fred's leash before exiting the car.

Edmund came to a stop in front of the house as Fred barked toward the park.

"Hold on, Edmund, let me get his leash on before he sees—"

But the back window wasn't up enough to keep Fred from escaping and heading for across the street.

"Good grief." Jade took off, yelling at Fred to stop. Thankfully, he headed straight for a large pine tree close to the sidewalk and jumped up and down around the trunk.

Three squirrels sat in the branches, chattering amongst themselves at Fred's protest of their presence.

"Damn, he's fast." Panting, Edmund reached him first, grabbing his collar before Jade could attach the leash.

"Come on, Fred." With the leash wrapped around her

hand, she yanked and dragged the dog back to her house as he told the squirrels exactly what he thought of them.

They responded by chattering and flipping their tails around.

Basically a rodent middle finger.

"Those squirrels talk some smack." Edmund pointed to the tree trio. "You sure I can't help you—"

"I'm fine." She struggled against the leash as Fred stretched it to its max, all while barking his rebuttal at the tree rodents. "I don't need your help."

"You sure? Because you look like you do."

"Thanks for your honesty." Giving a strong yank, she strained against Fred's strength as another squirrel appeared to the left and ran down the street before jumping into a yard.

Fred jerked the leash, causing it to scrape and pinch her fingers. Pain shot up her arm, making her eyes water. "Ouch, ouch. Stop it Fred."

She tried to pull back, but got nowhere.

Without a word, Edmund scooped up the dog and tilted his chin toward the house. "You want him inside?"

"Yes." Shaking out her arm and putting a mental Band-Aid on her pride, Jade quickly grabbed the keys from her purse and unlocked the door. "Usually, he spazzes out about groundhogs, but I guess rodents are rodents. Squirrels will do him just fine."

Edmund held on tight against the struggling dog until he kicked the door closed behind them and laid the happy pooch on the couch.

Immediately, Fred shook, his ears slapping against his head then he wasted no time pressing his wet nose against the front window.

Chapter Four

RESCUING A DOG and meeting a gorgeous woman hadn't been the way Edmund had planned to enter Marietta, but with the way his life had unraveled in the last several months, he'd take the small favors.

As soon as Logan said her name, Edmund knew exactly who Fred's owner was.

Lucy mentioned the headstrong colleague multiple times during her first months here, but as of late, those complaints had all but disappeared. Either the women had figured out a way to work together, Lucy had decided complaining wasn't getting the results she wanted, or Jade hadn't found Lucy as much of an adversary.

Jade hadn't been what Edmund expected as he'd blurted out earlier, but seeing the curvy, hazel-eyed goddess with hair the color of dark chocolate had thrown him sideways. Thank God she had a good sense of humor about her and he'd been able to hold a good discussion without too much stuttering. He hoped his nervous excitement would calm and he could simply have a nice conversation with her.

She shook out her hand. "Thank you. I should have realized he'd fight."

The small home had shiny hardwood floors. The manufacturer stickers still hung on the recently replaced windows.

Boxes after boxes were neatly stacked three to five high against the walls.

A standing lamp, a couch, a double rocker, and mounted TV over the fireplace were the only pieces of furniture in the living room. Well-worn dining room table and chairs sat in the open kitchen. The appliances out so far were a coffeemaker and microwave. The top freeze refrigerator sat next to the backdoor. A low hum echoed through the room.

"Sorry for the mess. I'm right in the middle of moving in." She tossed her keys on the couch.

Hearing the clinking noise of the keys against each other, Fred went over, sniffed them and pulled them to the floor and left them there before walking back to the window.

"I wasn't sure if you were moving in our out." A large stack of books sat next to the double rocker, just right of the fireplace. A large T-shirt patchwork blanket draped over the back of the rocker. He quickly scanned her to-be-read pile, recognizing some of the authors. "You have anything in the car you need help bringing in?"

"Aren't you chivalrous?"

"I try." He picked the keys up off the floor and placed them on the top box of a stack next to the couch.

Fred eyed the keys and Edmund crossed his arms across his chest, giving his head a quick shake, no.

The dog gave him a *well-played* glance and went back to looking out the window.

Noticing the amount of work she'd already done to get

things here, he had to wonder. "How did Fred get all the way out to the highway from here?"

"I live...lived out that way. Well, my father's place is out there, but Fred wasn't on our property. That's one that's about a few miles away from where I met you. He cut across the land next to my dad's." Jade gracefully navigated around multiple stacks of well-labeled boxes before she got to the kitchen. "I know why Fred likes it there. It's got a nice little creek, great trees. Perfect view of the Copper Mountains like at my place. I mean, my dad's place, well I guess it is mine. He left it to me."

Fred playfully followed after her, jumping over obstacles, the tags on his collar jingling. He almost cleared the last box, but half jumped on top of it, sending it tumbling to the floor and a few of the contents spilling out.

"Great." When she bent over to clean up the mess, Edmund instantaneously became fascinated with the ceiling fan to avoid staring at her perfectly curved backside.

Way to go, Ed. Known her an hour and already you're acting like a lecherous ass.

Since he'd been duped by Reyna and almost sent to prison, his libido and general sexual imagination died. Yet something about Jade had ignited his interest and that alone made her more intriguing.

It was that or he was in to modern-day Nurse Ratched types.

Fred barked, pulling him back to the present.

Motioning to the room Edmund cleared his throat. "Why the move into town?"

She gave him a sad smile. "My father passed away. The last couple years, before he died, he let his house fall apart. Junior, my idiot brother didn't follow through with helping Dad keep his place livable. I moved back in the fall, really winter, of 2016 and tried to catch things up, but the property ended up being more than I could handle so I asked Thomas for help."

"Lucy's Thomas?"

A cringe momentarily replaced her jovial mood. "I hadn't heard it quite that way, but yes. Lucy's Thomas."

"How do you know him?" Was that snark in his voice? *Settle down, Edmund. You've only met the woman.*

"Thomas? We've been friends since we were kids. When his parents were stationed at Robins AFB for a short time. I was there with my mom and stepfather." She tossed the spilled items back into the box. "He's my best friend. He's like a brother to me. Sometimes more than a brother than my actual ones."

Relief flooded him when she said brother, but the last line she mumbled and he more than noticed. "You met in Georgia, then?"

"You know your military bases. Thomas was, is, a great friend. We stayed in contact after I moved here to be with my dad."

Losing a parent was a hurt Edmund knew all too well. "Sorry to hear about that. Your father."

"He'd been in declining health for a while. It was time for him to go." Her shoulders sagged. "And it's time for me to give up the idea of living out there for the rest of my life.

Makes it easy that he made me sole executor so all the decisions are mine to make."

"He didn't leave it to your brother, then?"

"To neither of them. James is in the Coast Guard in Alaska. He doesn't want to move back here. Junior can't handle money. He burns through it. I'm shocked that any cash he touches doesn't spontaneously combust."

Despite her attempt to be amusing, Edmund heard the sadness in her voice. "Your mom won't come to help with anything?"

"I have nothing to do with her," Jade snapped, then her eyes went wide as she added, "Sorry, she's not my favorite subject."

The abruptness of her interruption surprised him. "She here?"

"Lord, no. She wouldn't be caught dead in a town like Marietta."

"Right. You said she was in Georgia." Edmund smiled, but she didn't meet his attempt to lighten the mood. "She's not a fan of small-town life?"

"She's not a fan of anything that doesn't benefit her and doesn't deal well with reality or any sort of confrontation."

"Sorry, I didn't mean to—"

She pinched the bridge of her nose before answering. "No, no, you didn't know any of this. It's an obvious question where parents are concerned, but to tell you the truth, I haven't seen my mother since I came to Marietta when I was fourteen. I honestly have no idea where she or my stepfather are."

Edmund leaned against the doorway, loving how the light reflected off her dark-colored hair. "That's a long time."

"Not long enough." She avoided looking at him for a few beats. "No worries. Life moves on, right?"

The soulful sorrow in her words hit Edmund square in the chest, bringing him to wonder what the events were that lead her to coming to Marietta. "Giving up what you know is hard."

Her eyes went wide with appreciation. "Yes. It really is."

When the corner of her mouth curled up, Edmund's heart sped up as heat warmed his cheeks. His reaction to her gaze unnerved him and he liked it. That alone concerned him because the last time he put his heart out there he almost ended up in a six-by-six cell.

Still, something about her made his first day in Marietta far more pleasant and significantly less stressful.

For a long moment, the only sound that registered was the quiet.

The only thing in that room of unpacked boxes was her and against his better judgment, the words began to tumble out of his mouth.

"Jade, would you be interested—" A warm, slime covered Edmund's hand. Glancing down, the adoring brown eyes of Fred stared up at him as he tried to take another lick of Edmund's fingers. A line of slobber hung from Fred's jowls. "That's disgusting."

"I'm so sorry." She snapped her fingers and turned in a circle. "Where is it?"

"What can I help you find?" *Does the dog have radar to*

keep anyone from talking seriously to his owner? When they were by the road and each time Edmund tried to walk closer to Jade, Fred kept sitting on his feet.

"His water bowl. Really, any bowl. He's probably parched."

"Right." Trying not to get dog slobber on any of her things, Edmund opened a box one handed to begin the search.

After he started on the second box, Jade found a bright blue bowl with FRED in green letters on the side. She filled it with water and placed it on the ground. "Here you go, big guy."

The dog stuck his entire face into the water, spilling half of the contents on the floor before lapping up what was left.

Jade rolled her eyes. "Dog, you're going to make me drink."

"Where are your paper towels?" The dog's exuberance and constantly wagging tail brought a smile to Edmund's face.

She threw her hands up in frustration. "No clue."

"A regular towel?"

"I think in the front bathroom. Just inside my bedroom." She pointed toward the hallway. "I think I might have put hand soap in there...for your dog drool-covered hand."

"Thanks." He inched around the lined-up boxes in the hallway. Within seconds, he found her bathroom and washed his hands. She had very few makeup items out on the counter, reflecting the natural look she'd so perfectly captured.

A well-used hand towel hung next to the sink. He grabbed it, but before heading out, the subtle smell of lavender and vanilla caught his attention.

He noticed the pillow spray next to her bed with *Rest* written on it before he joined her in the kitchen as she let Fred out the back door.

A large puddle of water slowly began to spread toward several boxes. He knelt to dry the floor and cut the water trails off.

"Please don't do that." She fell to her knees, reaching out for the towel.

Edmund saw the red marks on her palm. Dropping the towel, he took her hand in his as he inspected the injuries. "What happened?"

"The leash. Fred's a bit excited when he sees a squirrel."

Several places the skin had been peeled away had left her hand raw. Small petechial bruises had formed. "Looks like it hurts."

"I'll live." She didn't pull away, but scooted closer.

"Course you will." Her decreasing the space between them sent his heart pounding hard against his ribs. "You, you…um…need to get that cleaned up."

"What, you want to play doctor now?" Her eyes darted from his eyes to his mouth, before she bit her lip and sat back on her heels. Hanging her head, her shoulders trembled.

His body felt like he'd been Tasered and he leaned back a few inches before his shoulders touched the cabinets. With her sitting so close, every nerve ending signaled in rapid fire.

Don't do anything stupid. Say anything dumb.

When he realized he still held her hand, he let go as if he'd touched something hot. "Are you okay?"

Her giggle filled the room. "What a shameless way to welcome you to Marietta by asking to play doctor."

He let out a long breath, glad he hadn't been the only one to notice the double reference. "I thought it was sexy…um…funny."

Holy shit. Get ahold of yourself.

"You did?" Her eyes went wide with approval.

"I did." His heart thudded, echoing in his ears. His mind raced through the endless possibilities and multiple red flags. *Don't even go there, Edmund.*

"Dr. Davidson?" Jade rested her palm against his and turned their hands thumbs up. "Edmund?"

His mouth went dry as his brain frantically searched for the most neutral response. "Y-y-yes, Jade? Mrs. Phillips."

"It's *Miss* Carter."

"Right."

"Edmund, you really are the most gallant man I've ever met." She squeezed his hand to shake and sent fireworks through his veins. "I appreciate your help and concern today."

He gently shook her hand. "You're welcome, *Miss* Carter."

"Welcome to Marietta, Dr. Davidson."

Chapter Five

THANK GOODNESS JADE had the good sense to shake Edmund's hand and not give in to her desire to kiss him. Something about his awkward charm and his valiant help with her dog, Jade found absolutely appealing.

Plus Fred liked him and despite his playful personality, Fred only tolerated a few people. Whomever he didn't want around, Fred unapologetically peed on, which was probably why he kept running behind the metal building where her brother kept his stuff. Jade had no doubt her dog had peed all on every inch of the foundation.

As she parked her car on Main Street, she berated herself when it came to the newest resident in town. *What a ridiculous thing to consider, kiss a man I've known an hour.*

She glanced at her watch. It read ten thirty.

Almost two hours. Especially one I'll work with.

Still, after he'd taken his sunglasses off and she finally got a good look at those mocha-colored eyes of his, her heart beat a bit faster. Kind of like it was doing now as she watched him walk from his car to the front door of the Main Street Diner.

"Sorry to keep you waiting. I had to park down a block."

He had a charm about him, and a wonderful lopsided smirk that probably made her look at him a bit too long and her ovaries dance.

"We're here." She cleared her throat before fumbling with the door handle, pushing on the pull door.

"I think you have to pull it, Jade." Edmund rested his fingers on hers and gently opened the door.

Get a grip! He's just a guy. "Yes, sorry. A lot on my mind."

"No problem."

As always, the Main Street Diner smelled of delicious possibilities and they had to wait a few moments for a table. A front-window booth at the far end of the room had just opened up.

Jade pointed. "Let's sit over there."

"Looks great." He motioned for her to lead the way.

Behind the counter, the daily specials were perfectly drawn on a chalkboard and with the right amount of artwork to emphasize the latest dish.

Trinity, the owner's teen daughter, had designed the display. This summer, she'd make extra money by helping here at the diner.

"That's Gabby, she's the owner." Jade waved to the beautiful dark-haired woman behind the counter who waved back at them as they settled in. "She's been here about a year. Bought the diner from Paige Sheehan who had it for several years before that. Gabby's daughter, Trinity, is the one who's filling water and coffee."

"What brought them to Marietta? They from here origi-

PATRICIA W. FISCHER

nally?" Edmund tapped the unopened menu on the table.

"No, they're from Texas. San Antonio, I think. She met Paige and decided she wanted to buy the diner sight unseen."

"That's a big risk to take, moving to the middle of nowhere."

His last few words had her mentally counting to five before answering. "Middle of nowhere maybe, but that doesn't make it any less of a place to be."

Sitting back, he nodded. "You're right. Coming from outside of Orlando, this looks like…"

"Hicksville?" She'd heard all this before. From Brenden Phillips her ex-husband, who refused to consider moving to be closer to her father as her dad's health failed him. Of course, it was hard to keep the façade of his nice guy Realtor image up in a small town when his wife kept showing up for work with unexplainable bruises on her arms and finally, one huge black eye.

In San Diego, he could move freely between house listing jobs and she could get high-priced concealer and long-sleeved shirts in summer. "I know, but every town has its qualities. Marietta's quiet at night. When you're in town, the lights from the city won't drown out the sparkles in the night sky. When it's clear and warm enough, I can take my dad's old truck out to a part of the property, my favorite place, and simply stare upward until I pass out. It's like sleeping under a quilt of stars."

"I've always wanted to sleep under a quilt of stars." He fumbled with the menu as his gaze rested on her. "I've slept on the beach under the stars. Sunsets and sunrises are great, but sleeping or, um, whatever, on the beach, it's not as romantic as it sounds."

"Sand everywhere?"

"*Everywhere.*" A healthy shade of scarlet colored his cheeks.

She playfully grimaced. "That sounds uncomfortable."

"Parts of it are, but nothing beats a great sunset, no matter where you are."

"Amen." It had been too long since Jade sat across the table from someone and had a productive conversation that didn't involve work, her dad's property, or her brother's recent run-ins with the local law enforcement. The more they talked, the easier the conversation flowed, and the more she wanted to know about him.

Careful, Jade. Remember the last time you fell for a good-looking guy.

She pushed the doubt and fear aside as Edmund spoke about the beaches in Florida and the Caribbean.

It's a meal. Nothing more.

He patted the table in front of her. "But that's enough about Florida. Tell me about this favorite place of yours."

"It's on the far part of the property. It's great fun and so quiet. The only thing you can hear is the truck cooling off."

"Sounds like a perfect evening." His lopsided smirk sent a thrill through her. "Back when I began talking about Marietta, I wasn't going to say Hicksville."

"No?"

"I was going to say less discorded."

At that moment, she saw Junior's beat-up car take a slow

turn from Court Street to Main and cruise on by. "Oh, Dr. Davidson, I think you'd be surprised. Chaos is everywhere."

Damn, Junior's arrogant. I hope there isn't a warrant out for his arrest.

Edmund's eyes darted to her hand then the window. "You okay?"

"Yes, why?"

"You've balled up your napkin."

Clearing her throat, she glanced down to see her knuckles drained of color and the clean napkin wadded in her hand. She tried to smooth the napkin out as best as possible. "Sorry. Just thinking about something else. What are you going to have to eat?"

He gave her a guarded smile before opening his menu. "What do you suggest?"

Suggest? I suggest you run the other direction because I'm discord personified.

"Well, it's after ten thirty so you can go with breakfast or the lunch special. The grilled chicken with *pico de gallo* and sautéed vegetables served over cilantro lime rice with a side salad is what we're serving today. That's our house special today." Flo, the longtime waitress of the diner, pulled her pencil from her updo as her colorful giraffe earrings swayed gently.

"Water?" Trinity arrived and placed two filled glasses on the table before either of them had a chance to answer.

"Thank you for your help, Trinity."

Jade placed the menu back in the holder. "The special sounds great, Flo."

"I made the *pico*. Chopped everything up this morning." Trinity beamed. "Gabby finally shared *Abuela's* recipe."

"How exciting, Trinity. You're getting to work in the prep kitchen." Jade admired Gabby and Trinity's mother-daughter relationship. It was especially endearing since Gabby adopted Trinity, who'd been her best friend, Laurie's, daughter after Laurie died in a car accident. Gabby had been Trinity's legal guardian prior to Laurie's death. The way Gabby and Trinity acted when they were together, you'd think they were absolutely from the same gene pool.

The two shared the passions of making amazing, home-cooked food and designing an environment that made people feel welcome.

They both had compassionate hearts and would do any-thing to help someone in need.

Both had incredibly creative minds and beautiful smiles.

Those were only a few things Jade would never share, with her mother.

In fact, other than biology, Jade had nothing in common with the woman she hadn't seen since that day the police took her away.

Pointing to the display, Jade added, "I like the chalk-board, Trinity. How long did it take you to do that?"

"About fifteen minutes. It's easy when you know exactly what you want to put up there." She played with the pens in her apron pocket. "I'm also teaching art at the community center and at Harry's House this summer."

"How fun."

"We're having an art show at Harry's House later this

summer. Raise money for art supplies. Will you put some flyers up at work?"

The teen's genuine enthusiasm always brought a smile to Jade's face. "Absolutely, Trinity. I'm always glad to help with Harry's House."

"I can draw decent stick figures, but that's about it." Edmund chuckled. "But don't hold me to that."

Flo's eyebrow cocked and she tilted her chin towards Edmund. "And you are?"

Fine. Jade presented Edmund with her best *Price is Right* model hand flick. "Flo. Trinity. This is Edmund. Dr. Lucy Davidson's, brother."

Each of the women stuck out their hands and Edmund responded in kind.

"Welcome to Marietta, Dr. Davidson." Flo smiled.

"Nice to meet you, Dr. Davidson." Trinity shifted her weight.

A confused smirk appeared on his perfectly sculpted face. "I didn't say *I* was a doctor."

"Lucy's been in here plenty of times. Told us all about her family." Trinity counted the information off on her fingers. "Let's see there's you, Peter, who's the oldest, and Susan who's second to oldest. Susan's the only one who's not a doctor, but a midwife, right? Your stepfather, Charlie, is a local celebrity, is that right?"

The look of unease on his face perfectly illustrated what every new arrival to Marietta went through when they move here. "Don't worry, Edmund. It's an adjustment to know that everyone knows you first. Part of the charm of the town."

His shoulders relaxed as he gave them a nervous smile. "Yes, that's us. All in the medical field, except our stepfather. He's a local celebrity, a newscaster. Actually, an evening anchor. Until Lucy moved here, none of us had ever heard of Marietta."

Jade, Trinity, and Flo all looked at each other and gave knowing nods with Trinity replying, "Gabby and I didn't know anything about Marietta until she bought the diner."

"And I didn't until I moved here to be with my dad," Jade added.

"It's certainly a place you have to know is here, but we've got a pretty good reputation for people coming back after they've gone out in the world." Flo gave Jade a wink. "It's nice to be somewhere that people care about if you show up for dinner or not. Now, what can I get you, Dr. Davidson?"

"You don't have to call me that. Edmund is fine."

He had an easy way about him, a calmness that appeared to draw people in and encourage casual conversation.

Since she'd seen it in his sister, Jade wondered if all of the Davidson kids had such a remarkable quality.

Flo playfully tapped her pencil on the ticket book. "Okay, Edmund. I would love to talk to you some more, but I gotta get to work. What'll it be?"

"The special sounds great, Flo, and a glass of iced tea," he answered.

She pointed for him to place the menu back in the holder after giving the written order to Trinity. "Give us about ten minutes. Anything I can get you before?"

"We're good, Flo. Thanks."

"I'll get you some bread. I helped with that, too." Trinity turned a one eighty on the balls of her feet and walked to the pass-through window and handed it to Merlin, the cook.

Flo immediately seated a group of four that had just entered.

Gabby walked around, refilled coffees, and talked to regulars.

Casey, Brett Adams's sister, delivered food to tables and cleared away plates.

Like a well-oiled machine, the diner flowed with the happy customers and a steady flow of tourists. Rarely did anyone have a glass that was more than half empty and orders were filled with quick efficiency.

Within two minutes, Trinity brought a basket of sliced sourdough, whole grain, and what looked like orange cinnamon breads, on the table along with Edmund's drink. "Enjoy."

Several more people stopped at the table and introduced themselves, including Gabby, Gabby's boyfriend, paramedic Kyle Cavasos, along with paramedic Patrick Freeman, and flight and ER doctor, Tom Reynolds. Kyle, Patrick, and Tom had all recently returned from taking a heart patient to Billings.

After Dr. Gavin Clark introduced himself as he grabbed a to-go order on his way to his shift in the ER, Jade knew if Edmund hadn't called or texted Lucy, it wouldn't be ten minutes before his sister would call or walk through those doors. "Did you call Lucy?"

"I texted her when you were getting Fred situated before we got up here."

"Right. Smells good." Rich aroma of grilled chicken, the tart of lemon pie, and the crisp scents of fresh vegetables mixed in the air. "Thank you again for helping with Fred. I didn't think he drifted that far from the house."

"He was having a great time in the field. Chasing birds, I think." Edmund leaned back in the booth, casually laying his arm across the back of the bench seat. Even with him closer to the diner side of the bench, his fingertips almost reached the window.

Jade eyed the bread as her stomach encouraged her to take a piece. "How did Fred end up with you, anyway?"

"When I got out to look at the mountains, I guess he jumped in my car."

Now, that wasn't anything she expected to hear. "You got out to look at the mountains? Why?"

Letting out a long breath, he sat forward, resting his forearms on the table. "They looked like a great place to get away from the crazy of life. Get up there and simply breathe clear air and be above the noise. Where no one knows who you are. Where you, I, can just enjoy the world and not get caught up in it. Know what I mean?"

Oh, goodness. Do I ever. "Yes, yes I do."

"You hiked up in those mountains before?"

"Jade? Hike those mountains?" Nurse Shelly Westbrook stopped after walking in. "She's part mountain goat."

"Hey, Shelly." Jade stood and hugged her coworker and close friend.

After giving a quick hug back, Shelly flipped her long, dark ponytail over her shoulder. "This girl right here can navigate anywhere without a compass and knows those trails like the back of her hand."

"My dad taught me all that." Jade appreciated her father's lessons were so well respected.

"He was a good man, your father."

"Yes, he was. I appreciated talking to him the times I saw him in town."

Shelly rested her hand on Jade's shoulder, but right now, Jade didn't want to think of her father in past tense or the property or anything else that took her joy away. All she wanted to do was continue the great conversation she'd been having with Edmund without interruption, but it would be rude to cut her friend off. "What's going on with you, Shelly?"

"Oh, wedding plans. Getting the kids through the summer without being bored." Her eyes darted from Jade to Edmund. "What about you, Jade? Anything *interesting*?"

Jade clenched her teeth at her coworker's great enthusiasm to embarrass her. "Right. Edmund, this is Shelly. She's a nurse at the ER. Shelly, this is Edmund Davidson. He'll be working with us."

"Oh, you're Lucy's Edmund. Great to finally meet you. Lucy's told us so much about you."

"Nice to meet you, Ms. Westbrook." Edmund gave her a nod. "Looking forward to working with you, too."

"Me too?" Her eyes went wide with understanding as she looked back and forth at them. "Yes. Yes, of course. *You two* will work together as well."

Oh, lord. Shelly, please stop talking.

"And my aunt, Sue Westbrook, works the desk at the ER. She's my dad's sister." As if she could read Jade's mind message of "move along," Shelly pointed to a table behind them. "I'd stay and get to know you more, but I'm meeting my kids and fiancé for lunch so I've got to go. Great to meet you, Dr. Davidson. You have a great visit, now."

With that, Shelly gave Jade a wink and quickly walked away.

"Bye, Shelly." Turning, Jade waved to Freddie and Tia and Freddie's father, Gill. "Hey, guys."

The kids enthusiastically waved back as Gill stood, pointed to the bench and had Shelly take the inside seat next to him.

Not once did he even look up from his phone that he always kept tightly in his left hand.

"That's Shelly and her son, Freddie, her niece, Tia, and her ex-husband, Gill." Jade tried not to hiss out the man's name, but knowing what he'd put his family through, Jade had trouble not thinking poorly of him.

"I thought she said that was her fiancé." Edmund lowered his voice as he smiled at them.

"He's both. She divorced him when he wouldn't keep it at home, but supposedly, he's cleaned up his act and asked for a second chance."

Edmund raised an eyebrow. "I get the feeling you don't believe him."

"You know what they say, once a cheater…" She waved

her comment off. "Sorry, that's petty of me. I shouldn't be talking about Shelly without her here. She deserves to defend her choices."

"I get it. You want your friends, happy. Taken care of. Nothing wrong with looking out for them." He stirred his tea. "It's the sign of someone who has a strong character and moral compass."

His compliment caught her wonderfully off-center. "I don't think I've ever been told I have a strong moral compass before."

"Guess it must be that modernization of the Nurse Ratched types." He gave her a quick wink.

"Here's to modernization." She held up her glass and wondered what other delightful sayings Edmund had rolling around in that brain of his.

And she hoped he'd stick around long enough for her to find out.

Chapter Six

I LIKE HER.

As much as he told himself this meal couldn't be anything remotely romantic, Edmund couldn't help but look at Jade without hoping to socially see her again.

Observing her with the locals had been a treat. She obviously knew her way around town and, apparently, knew the mountains.

To see the way she clenched her jaw in worry for her friend indicated her devotion to those she held dear. A precious, undervalued quality.

Still, he wondered why that beat-up car cruising by had momentary stolen the joy from her eyes.

A former boyfriend? Didn't Lucy say something about Jade being married before? *Yes, Jade wanted to use her maiden name, Carter.*

He hadn't gotten a good look of the guy behind the wheel, but could that have been her ex-husband? Although he'd like to know, he'd tuck that question away for another time.

Provided there was another time. "Anyone else you know in here?"

She scanned the room before picking up a piece of the homemade bread and slathering a thick layer of butter on it. "Almost everyone who's local, I'd guess. I've probably treated or been friends with most everyone in here. It's a blessing and curse of small-town living, knowing each other's business, even when you don't want to."

"Professional hazard, I'd guess." He hoped his business stayed well out of the ears of gossip. Having the town know how he'd been duped, almost to the point of imprisonment, wouldn't instill a lot of confidence in his medical assessment skills.

"Tell me, Edmund. What made you want to come to Marietta?" She bit into the bread. "Oh, my gosh, this is so good. You've got to try this."

Her sudden blissful grin made it difficult to grab words that fit cohesively in a sentence. He wondered what else put such bliss on her face, then his brain went right into the gutter. Such wayward ideas had him instantly flustered. "Right. Okay."

"Sorry, I should know better than to try and talk when I've stuffing my face with Gabby's bread. It's always amazing." With a flick of her wrist, she pushed the basket closer to him. "The orange cinnamon is like eating dessert. You might want to eat something. You look flushed."

Glad you don't know why.

"Thank you." He picked up what he thought was his knife to layer on the butter, but ended up fumbling for it, sending it shooting across the table and onto the floor.

Thank goodness it was the teaspoon.

His nervous fingers attempted to pick up his water glass, but ended up spilling part of it on the table in front of him. "Shit."

Her face softened. "You okay?"

"Yes. Fine." *Damn.* He hated this. He hated how much easier it was for him to talk about myocardial infarctions, small bowel obstructions, or treat a code blue patient than attempting to sound smart to a gorgeous, intelligent woman.

He fiddled with his hands before awkwardly clasping them in his lap. He considered sitting on them like a child, but knew that would pretty much kill any chance she'd be interested in talking to him again.

A look of amused confusion crossed her face. "You sure? Did I say something?"

Shit. Shit. Shit. Why couldn't he have inherited the same smooth abilities to talk to women as their father or Peter had? Why couldn't his educational intelligence have all spilled over to relationship navigation?

Bite the bullet, Ed. Go with the honest approach.

Sitting up straight, he motioned back and forth between them as the young waitresses refilled drinks. "Look. I'm not great at this part of the, the, whatever this is."

"Okay?" Her forehead furrowed as Trinity walked away, a slight smirk on her face.

Snatching the napkin from the table, he rolled it between his fingers, hoping to calm his nervous hands. "It's always challenging for me to, to, talk to someone, um, interesting."

"Go on." She tilted her head as she bit her lip.

The rapid drum of his fingers on the table made him

cringe. He put his other hand in his lap, silently cursing his anxiety.

Could I look like any more of a spaz right now? "But, but, but once I'm comfortable with someone, um, interesting, the conversation is easy. I would like to get better talking with you if you'll give me the chance."

For a moment, he was certain she'd bolt for the door. Why wouldn't she? Who in their right mind would want to deal with a thirty-something-year-old man with social anxiety no matter what job title he had? Internally, he waited for the standard rejections. "Thanks but no thanks" or "You're adorable" as if he were a puppy.

"I would like that." Laying her hands on the table, palms up, she grinned. "I would like to get to know you, too."

"Really?" His voice squeaked like a pubescent boy. Clearing his throat, he tried again, making his voice sound as low as possible as he met her gesture. Simply touching her hand shot fireworks through his body. "Great. Good. Sounds good."

A throat clearing pulled him out of his full attention on Jade and he jerked his hands away.

"Here you go. Two specials." Flo laid the plates full of food in front of each of them and acted as though she hadn't seen anything interesting. "Y'all need anything else? Napkins, water refill, more bread?"

"Looks great." Jade smiled.

"I'm good." Edmund gave her a thumbs-up.

"Just let me know if you do. I'll be around." The waitress winked at him before leaving the table.

Waves of salt, citrus, and butter drifted up his nose, re-setting his brain and giving him a much needed momentary distraction to comprise a proper list of first date questions.

What's your favorite color?

What's your favorite season?

What's your favorite book?

He internally grimaced. *What kind of dull-assed questions are those? This is going to be the quickest, dullest lunch date on record.*

Before taking a bit of her chicken, she smiled. "Let's start slow, Edmund. Tell me your favorite movie."

Chapter Seven

WITHIN A FEW minutes, their conversation flowed and Jade watched Edmund's deer-in-headlights panic fade away.

It took no more than half a dozen neutral questions before his words were smooth and his anxiety appeared to lessen its hold on him, sending a thrill up her spine.

Edmund wasn't the first physician she'd met with social anxiety, but he had to be the best looking. Even in his bumbling almost Hugh Grant flustered moments, he couldn't be more adorable if he tried.

She would have hated it if he'd called their time short because she liked what she'd seen and she wanted to get to know him more.

For an hour, they discussed everything from books, movies, and travel adventures as they finished their delicious food and all the bread.

The world continued around them with few interruptions.

He confessed to being an avid reader, a movie watcher, and wanted to hike as many mountains as he could get to.

She shared that she liked only cream in her coffee, loved

to read in her double rocker next to the fireplace, and could never turn down a piece of fruit pie.

Apparently, Flo heard Jade's weakness and suggested they order dessert when she brought Jade a large cup of fresh-brewed java and a small pitcher of cream. "You're queen of the up sale, Flo."

"It's my job." She cleared the plates away. "Which pie can I get you?"

Jade ordered the peach. Edmund the lemon meringue and a cup of coffee.

When Flo left the table, Edmund continued to talk about his travels in the Bahamas and around the Caribbean. "The Cayman Islands have to be one of my favorites. The water is crystal clear. Looks like the boats are floating on air and the scuba diving is incredible."

"I've seen pictures, but I didn't know how much was photoshopped. I lived in San Diego before I came back to Marietta. I understand the Caribbean isn't as cold."

"No, it's not."

Resting her head in her hands, the corners of her mouth quirked up as she pictured him in a diving suit, the tank on his back, flippers on his feet. "Guess you know all about the ocean, growing up in Florida."

"You have to, the good and the bad but a lot more good."

"Your coffee, Dr. Davidson." Trinity rested the cup at the end of the table. "Sweetener is next to the salt and pepper."

"Thank you, Trinity." A healthy cloud of steam floated

over the coffee before he slid it in front of him.

Flo arrived with the pies, clean forks, and napkins, leaving with a wink and a smile.

"Tell me, what's the scariest thing you've ever seen while you were in the water." Jade could listen to Edmund's stories for hours. The soulful cadence of his voice danced lazily in her ears.

"I bet you think I'm going to say a shark, aren't you?" He scooped up a piece of pie on his fork.

She poured another bit of cream into her coffee. "Well, according to *Shark Week*, Florida is number one for shark attacks in the past several years."

"You watch *Shark Week*?" His voice went up an octave before he cleared his throat. His exuberance that of a geekish sixteen-year-old boy.

"Yes, every year. I record the entire week because I often work when some of them are on and sometimes I simply want to watch them again, but I watch every single one of them."

He appreciatively stared at her for a long moment, his fork frozen in the crust of his pie. "I had no idea there were women like you."

"I'm going to guess that's a compliment." She relished the sweet and tart of the peach and cinnamon pie blending on her tongue.

"Absolutely." A slow, upward curl to the corner of his mouth just about sent her across the table and crawling into his lap.

Goodness! That sexy smirk of his had her thinking of

things she shouldn't. Now, it was her turn to fumble for words. "So-so, you, um, were telling me about, the-the, um, ocean."

"Yes, yes. You asked the scariest thing. The right whales come have their babies off the coast there, just north of Cape Canaveral. We were out fishing and this huge whale surfaced next to us. No warning, nothing and then a huge, smelly, geyser of water came up from the ocean."

"Oh, my gosh!" She slapped her hand over her mouth. "What did you do?"

"I fell out of the boat on the opposite side from where she was." He tilted his head in an attempt to mimic his hasty departure from the vessel. "She came right up next to us, which is what they do."

"What do you mean?" Taking a long drink of her coffee, she nestled the cup in her hands as she rested her elbows on the table.

"These whales are too curious for their own good and would come up to the whaling boats to see what was going on. Of course, they were easy pickings for the whalers so they called them right whales because they were the right whales to hunt."

"That's terrible. Poor whales." *A doctor and lover of marine animals. If he reads sci-fi or has watched any* Dr. Who *episodes, I'm a goner.*

"Even if she were the kindest animal on the planet, she was big. If I'd fallen in the water between her and the boat, I would have been crushed. She wouldn't have meant to hurt anyone, but mass, acceleration, they don't lie." He cringed as though he'd meant to say something else.

Probably something less scientific.

"Mass times acceleration would be a lot of force, wouldn't it?" She knew she'd hit the bull's-eye when he shot her another appreciative look. "Just sayin'."

"I wondered if I'd gone too geekish with the physics reference."

I knew it! "Don't worry. Those references won't be lost on me. You like the ocean, but tell me, how tall were those mountains in Georgia? I never did hike them."

He pushed a piece of piecrust around his plate with his fork. "The tallest didn't even reach five thousand."

"Only five thousand? At the tallest peak, Copper Mountain is close to double that." She drummed her fingers next to her coffee mug. "My dad would take me up there, taught me what I needed to know about surviving if I ever got lost, though we never did."

Placing his fork by his plate, he leaned forward like an anxious child, yearning for a bedtime story. "What did he teach you?"

What an interesting reaction. "How to get around without a compass and not get lost. How to always be aware of your surroundings. How to pack, even for a day trip and even if no storms are in the forecast."

"Always be prepared, then? Was your dad a Boy Scout?"

"No, just a good man. Smart man, smarter than a lot of people who think they can hike up there and can't." She shook her head. "I can't tell you how many times Todd Harris has called us in the ER to let us know the first responders were bringing in someone who'd gotten lost up there."

"Todd Harris. Todd Harris. Why do I know that name?"

"He's one of the forest rangers. In fact, one of those people he saved last year was his fiancée, Molly."

"Sounds like something out of a fairy tale. Right! Logan mentioned that." Edmund smirked before stuffing a generous piece of pie in his mouth. "Good God, this is good pie. How does she make that crust?"

"Told you so." Flo winked as she walked by to deliver an order.

"Does she hear everything?" He chuckled as he finished the last piece.

Stirring another creamer into her coffee as Trinity topped it off, Jade agreed, "Flo's respectful of people's privacy. She's not a gossip, which is nice. I think that's one of the many reasons people like to come here. They feel safe."

"Tell me more about what your dad taught you."

His endearing reaction made her wonder why he appeared so intrigued by her father's teachings, but she remembered what Lucy told her about losing their father when she was ten. They were hit head-on by a drunk driver and in an instant, the four children lost their father and their mother was never the same.

No wonder he wants to hear stories about my father. How he must miss his own. "I loved to hike and my dad told me I needed to learn to shoot, in case I'd need to defend myself or find something to eat if I did get lost."

"Nothing wrong with knowing how to use a gun, learning to respect the weapon." He placed his coffee mug next to the end of the table to catch a refill.

"Exactly. I mean a handgun, not something ridiculous like a military grade gun."

"Right. You any good?"

Oh, man. This conversation was going so well. Her hands began to shake and she immediately shoved them in her lap. "At shooting? I fare pretty well. I can hit the bull's-eye most of the time."

"Guess I won't make you mad." He held his hands up in mock surrender. "Don't want you to shoot at me."

The entire joy of the hour they'd spoken instantly evaporated with that lighthearted, innocent comment. Unexpected tears stabbed at the back of Jade's eyelids. *Oh, my gosh, really?* "I'm sorry. I have to go to the bathroom."

He jumped to his feet before she cleared the table. "Jade, are you okay? What did I say?"

Waving him off, she headed straight for the ladies' room. "Nothing, Edmund. It's okay. I'll be right back."

Because the last thing I want to talk about how is how well I used a gun to kill my husband.

Chapter Eight

"I CAN'T BELIEVE it. You're here." Lucy threw her arms around her brother before he could get in the front door. "I missed you."

"Hey, Luce." The two-story house sat on the corner of Third and Bramble, just down the street from Jade's. He couldn't help but look toward her house as his sister hugged him.

The lunch date ended as soon as Jade returned from the bathroom. Her red eyes indicated he'd said something to horribly upset her, but he had no idea what.

He'd spent the rest of the afternoon in his room at the Graff trying to figure it out.

"I couldn't believe it when Gavin told me he'd met you and I got your text. You weren't supposed to arrive until Friday." Grabbing his hand, she led him inside and the immediate scents of lemon and grilled fish hit him. "Was the trip in too bad? Did you fly from Denver? What can I get you to drink?"

He chuckled, having missed her rapid-fire method of questioning. "No. Yes. Beer."

"Sorry, I couldn't get over to see you today. The unit

stayed pretty steady." Lucy smiled as bright as sunshine and hugged him again. "Oh, I'm so glad you're here. Come on, come in. We're in the kitchen."

We're?

The clank of pots got his attention as they entered. There, in front of the stove, stood a decent-sized guy wearing a blue T-shirt that had "Have you seen her?" and what looked like the Loch Ness monster on it, but the name Messie had been printed under the creature. He quickly stirred something in a pot and covered it back up.

"Honey. My brother is here." Lucy touched the man's elbow.

"Is that Nessie on your shirt?" Edmund asked as he sized the guy up. *Not quite as tall as me. I'd bet I could take him out.*

"Edmund!" The man wiped his hands on a towel. "Good to meet you. Thomas McAvoy."

"I figured." Shaking his hand, Edmund could see Lucy's hopeful look that the men would at least find each other tolerable. "Thomas. Good to meet you."

"Lucy's told me about all of you."

"Nice to know. She hasn't told us much about you."

"Edmund." Lucy gave him a side-eye as she slid a beer across to him on the counter. "You know very well I've talked about Thomas plenty."

"Humpf, that's all she talks about." Edmund opened the beer and tossed the cap in the trash. "Messie? What's with the shirt?"

Thomas leaned against the counter, his arms across his

chest. "Ah, Lucy had it made for me."

"There's a lake up in the mountains. It's called Miracle Lake. Perfect place for a story of a lake monster." Lucy pointed to the shirt. "So instead of Nessie, it's Messie. Get it?"

"It does have a good ring to it." Edmund liked seeing his sister this happy. She'd had her share of jerk boyfriends, but Thomas didn't look like a jerk.

At least not yet.

Thomas clapped his hands together. "Dinner will be ready in a few minutes. What can I get you?"

Edmund held up his beer. "I'm good."

"Great. Let's sit down and you can go ahead and give me the third degree."

"Fair enough." *Maybe this guy wouldn't be so bad after all.*

The three carried on easy conversations until the last plate had been cleared and they retired to the living room.

In their time at dinner, Edmund learned Thomas moved quite a bit as a kid, he had several locum tenens assignments, his last before here had been San Diego. He and Lucy hiked frequently and had moved in together only last week.

Lucy's wide-eyed look of caution at Edmund signaled she was ready for him to freak out at that last bit of news.

He bit his tongue, knowing full well his sister was a grown woman and could make her own choices, but that didn't mean he didn't worry about her.

Sitting on the couch, Edmund noticed a small dish next on the side table. In it lay one rescue inhaler. "Lu, the mountain air get to you?"

"Oh, that's not mine. It's Thomas's." She curled up next to her beau.

"Inhalers?" Edmund heard the snark in his voice after he'd said it.

Thomas's lips thinned as his cheeks pinked. "I've tried to go without them. Hopefully, getting out of clinical medicine will help."

"What do you mean?"

"The constant bombardment of respiratory illnesses is hard on my lungs. My pulmonologist back in San Diego said he thought a smaller unit and a cleaner town might help get the chronic inflammation down quicker." He cleared his throat and repositioned. "It's been over a year and I'm as well as I'm going to get. It's not possible to calm my lungs when I'm being hit with every cold and flu that comes in, no matter the volume."

"I understood you wanted to be behind a desk."

"Not at all, but being out of clinical might help improve me more, improve my life, help me live longer. I majored in statistics so I asked to be in charge of quality assessment and now you're here to take my place."

"Only temporarily." Edmund couldn't deny the toll working around acutely sick people took on a body, but inhalers? "Don't take this wrong, but you don't seem the type."

"What? Who likes breathing?" Thomas snapped, but relaxed when Lucy rested her hand on his arm. "I had bad asthma as a kid. Had a stint in the ICU when I decided I didn't need them anymore. Damn near died."

Edmund had seen his share of plenty of asthmatics over the years, but a poorly controlled asthmatic would lead to multiple issues down the road. "Look, maybe it was a jerk thing to say, but Lucy and I watched our mom struggle with chronic pain and illnesses after the accident. It took a toll on her health and it was hard to watch her slowly decline. I don't want Lucy saddled with someone like that again."

Lucy grabbed Thomas's hand. "What I get *saddled* with, dear brother, is my choice and none of your concern."

"I'm not going to apologize for looking out for you."

Thomas chuckled. "I wouldn't expect anything less. From what Lucy says, you four are fiercely protective of each other."

Before Edmund could reply, Lucy leaned forward, holding up her hand. "Let him finish. Then you'll realize that your apology *is* in order."

Biting his lip, Edmund tried not to laugh in surprise at his baby sister's ferocity. "This guy must really be something for you to be this protective."

"He is. Now, shhh."

Thomas repositioned, cringing like someone had pinched him. "My lungs were good after that ICU visit as a kid. Had a care plan and was able to get off my meds during high school. I was always able to run and exercise without too much need for them, but I always had them ready."

"Seems reasonable." Edmund finished his beer and held the bottle between his fingers.

"Coming up on two years ago, I got jumped by a patient in the parking lot in a San Diego hospital where I worked.

He messed up my lungs."

Sitting up, Edmund asked, "With what?"

"A knife."

Holy shit! "What? Why you?"

"Because I'd helped his wife, who was a good friend of mine, file domestic abuse charges against him."

"His wife, huh? And you were helping a friend." *Don't let Lucy have fallen for some scumbag.*

Lucy wagged a finger at him. "Before you get any weird ideas, Brother, hear him out."

Edmund motioned for Thomas to continue, then tried to take a swig of his empty beer bottle.

"His wife, my friend, would come to work with defensive bruises. First on her wrists, then arms. I asked her about it, but she said she'd fallen or tripped. Started wearing long-sleeved shirts in summer." His fist clenched and he softly pounded it on his knee. "I've known this woman a long time. Since we were kids and she's never been clumsy. If anything, she's surefooted. There isn't a trail she can't climb. She's always had the ground underneath her feet."

He wished this story didn't sound familiar, but sadly, he'd heard it enough times as an ER doctor and it always pissed him off. "What did you do?"

"Talked to her. Kept the lines of communication open, because she said she loved him, but when she came to work with a huge black eye and told everyone she'd been hit by a surfboard over the weekend, we had a come to Jesus meeting." He clenched his teeth. "Nobody really loves you if they hurt you like that. They only love the life they have with you beaten down."

"Agreed." Edmund's knee bounced in nervous tempo. There were few people he hated as much as drunk drivers and spousal abusers ranked high on that list. "What happened?"

"He'd threatened to kill her. I convinced her to file a police report and she got a restraining order. She moved out. He went to jail. We set it up where she didn't walk to or from her car without security when he made bail. She moved into a secured apartment. The night after the divorce was finalized I walked her to her car. He jumped us. Stabbed me." He stood and lifted his shirt. He had large raised scars across his upper chest with two puncture wounds below them.

"Holy shit. He got you good." Shaking his head, Edmund's eyes went wide. "No offence, but why stab you there? Seems he could have cut your throat and been done with it."

"I moved out of the way a few times. When he finally got hold of me, tried to slash my throat, she shot him."

"Dead." Lucy added as Thomas put his shirt down. "Thank goodness she always hits the bull's-eye."

It took a few moments for him to wrap his head around it since it hadn't been the story Edmund expected to hear. "Damn, Thomas. Why didn't you tell us?"

"Lucy said it would be better if you met me first before throwing that story at you. Learn to trust me without the drama, as she put it."

"That's intense." He motioned to the scars.

Lucy raised her eyebrow. "Soooooo?"

"I guess admitting I was wrong to pass judgment won't cover it?"

She crossed her arms over her chest, but a playful sparkle remained in her eyes. "Nope."

"Fine. I'm sorry, Thomas."

Thomas gave him a thumbs-up. "Thanks, Edmund. We're good."

"We're good. The woman, she's okay?"

An awkward pause filled the room before Thomas replied, "Yes, she seems to be."

That was weird. "You still stay in contact with her?"

"I do. She's doing great. Got some help afterward, has moved back closer to where she grew up. Has a great job. Just moved into a new place."

"Sounds like she's got it figured out. I hope it's a happy ending then." A hard yawn hit him when Edmund glanced at the clock. "I know it's only ten, but I need to get to bed. I'm still on eastern time."

"Thank you for coming over." Lucy hugged Edmund before he left. "When do you start?"

"In a couple of days, but I'll see you before then."

"Sounds great."

After their goodbyes, Edmund walked slowly to his car, appreciating the crisp night air.

Glancing down the street once again, he noticed only a few houses still had their front room lights on. If he counted right, the house two down from the big one on the end was Jade's.

The sudden end of their conversation this morning still bothered him.

"What did we say again? She said she almost always hits the bull's-eye and I said I don't want you shooting at me. What about that upset her?" Nothing made sense as he stuck his keys in the ignition, until what Lucy mentioned hit him out of nowhere.

Thank goodness she hit the bull's-eye that night.

"Bull's-eye?" Looking toward Jade's, bits of the day's conversations came at him from every direction.

There isn't a trail she can't climb.

He's like a brother to me.

She's like a mountain goat.

Known her since we were kids.

I hit the bull's-eye most of the time.

San Diego.

She's moved into a new place, closer to where she grew up.

"Oh, man." Edmund ran his fingers through his hair in frustration. "Shit. Did Jade...was that who Thomas meant? Did she kill her husband?"

Chapter Nine

A T FIRST, JADE thought she'd imagined it.

A knock on her door at ten at night. Dread stuck in her throat, hoping it wasn't her brother.

So far, he hadn't called her back since she gave him an ultimatum this afternoon.

Glancing at the couch, she made sure Fred was inside and hadn't escaped to terrorize some neighbor's cat.

He snored until the knock occurred again, but only his ear twitched.

"Great watch dog." She rolled her eyes and noticed something shiny under his face. "Are those my keys?"

Without opening his eyes, the dog's tail wagged, thumping against the fabric.

"What is your obsession with my keys?" She flipped on the porch light to see... "Edmund?"

"Jade, I know it's late, but can I talk to you for a second?" he asked through the door's glass window. "Please?"

"Sure, hold on." After letting him in, she excused herself and checked her reflection in the bathroom mirror. She grabbed a thick sweatshirt since putting on a bra would take too long, but swished and spit with some mouthwash.

Running back into the living room, she found him sitting in the double rocker next to where she'd left her wineglass, empty chocolate wrapper, and the latest romance novel on her too tall to-be-read stack. "Sorry to keep you waiting."

"You sure do have a lot of books to read."

"Some girls love shoes or clothes or sparkly things. I love books." *Well, if that doesn't chase him away, nothing will.*

He slid over and patted the chair next to him. "Sit with me for a minute."

The endearing gesture had her wishing she had put on a bra to certainly keep her physical reaction to his request hidden. Joining him, she pulled her knees to her chest.

The enticing combination of the mountain air and cologne spices lingered around her. "If we were dating, a late-night visit could be really good or really bad."

"I just had dinner with Lucy and Thomas down the street."

"O-kay. And? Everything good?"

"Yeah. Great." His forehead furrowed, like he debated on saying something. "I'm sorry for the gun joke."

"The gun joke?"

"Today, at the diner."

"Is this what this visit is about?"

His fingers drummed on his thigh. "Yes."

For most of the afternoon, she chastised herself for having such a ridiculous reaction to his playful comment. How would he know about her history? How she saved her own and Thomas's lives? "I overreacted. I'm sorry about that. It's nothing. You're fine."

"No, no. I, um, I mean, I didn't know." His cheeks puffed out as he let out a long breath and smoothed his jeans. "I, um, didn't know you'd had a rough time in San Diego."

"What do you mean?" It took a few seconds for reality to hit her. *He had dinner with Lucy and Thomas. Please don't say what I think you're saying.*

Sandwiching her hands between his, he stared. "I know you shot, killed your husband."

His confession knocked the confidence right out of her and she tried to yank her hands away. "What? What did they say?"

At first, he didn't let her loose. A sadness washed across his eyes, but after the second tug, he held his hands wide, surrendering his hold. "I made a jerk comment about Thomas's inhalers tonight and he told me why he was on them."

"Why would you make a comment about someone needing medicine?"

"I said it was a jerk move. Trying to be protective of Lucy."

"And how is mocking someone for needing help breathing being protective of your sister?" For a moment, he didn't look as cute as he did a second ago. The heat of embarrassment poured over her at him knowing what happened in her marriage. She had to make a conscious decision not to fan herself.

Resting his elbows on his knees, he rubbed his chin. "The car accident that killed our dad messed up our mom and Lucy. Mom needed a lot of help. Pain meds. Inhalers. Physical therapy. Antidepressants. Hospital stays. She'd be in bed for days at a time because she hurt so badly. Missed our father. We loved our mom, but we three were on our own a lot."

She touched his arm, her heart hurt at the pain in his voice. "But I thought there were four of you."

"Lucy was in rehab and the hospital for months after the accident. We relied on family friends and neighbors to get us there each day to visit her, to get to school, grocery store, and if no one was available, we figured out the city bus routes." His knee bounced in nervous tempo. "When Lucy was back to normal, the four of us raised ourselves and took care of Mom. When our stepfather came into the picture, he helped, but it had only been us kids for a long time."

"I'm so sorry. It sounds rough."

"It was."

She knew all too well the devastation of parental abandonment, when a parent wasn't able to care for their child. Or willing to.

Still, Edmund's parents wanted to, but couldn't. Her mother couldn't have been bothered with protecting Jade from her lecherous stepfather.

If it weren't for her own father's patience and compassion to help her heal, Jade would have been either in heavy duty therapy right now, imprisoned, or made far more bad choices regarding her personal life than she had already.

Dropping her feet to the floor, she scooted closer. "What does any of this have to do with Thomas?"

He clasped his hands. "If Thomas had something chronic, something that would make Lucy's life difficult, I had to say something. I didn't want her to be saddled with a guy who would be a drain."

"I think Lucy's a smart enough woman to make that decision for herself." His intoxicating scent drifted around her. She greedily breathed him in. "Thomas didn't want to get stabbed. He was there to help me out."

"He told me everything that happened to him. To you."

Focusing only on his concerns made her forget her own until he said "to you." Her stomach twisted uncomfortably and she began to move away.

The warmth of his hand on hers made her freeze. "I didn't want you to know about that. Any of that. If I had to tell you, I wanted it on my terms."

"Were you ever going to tell me?"

"Not the first day I met you. That's a lot to lay on someone." Her gut churned from the spontaneous stress of the reveal of her past. It was that or the bag of chocolate and third glass of wine she'd consumed as her dinner.

Turning toward her, he rested his arm on the back of the chair. "Fair, but that's not something you should want to keep from me, Jade. I can put up with a lot of things, but lying isn't one of them."

"I wasn't lying." *But I sure as hell wasn't planning to tell you anything.*

"You're telling me you never wanted me to know. Shouldn't that be something you'd want to share with me one day?"

Standing, she moved away. "And why in the world would I want to do that? Tell you about all the crap from my past?"

"Because I don't want to say something stupid again. Something that will upset you. Cause this friction between us."

Without even trying, he'd become adorable again. "You didn't say anything stupid, you just didn't know."

Fred lifted his head and barked once before laying back down again.

"Jade, look. I like you." His voice gently caressed the knots in her neck.

She tried to shake off the effect he had on her, but it stuck like honey. And she liked it. "You only met me today."

"I know, but you're great. Smart." He pointed to the stack of books, a slight smirk to his luscious mouth. "You like to read. You take care of people. Why wouldn't I like you?"

Over the years, Jade heard her share of lines from men. Too many weren't worth remembering, a few worked, and one helped her fall in love with the wrong guy.

Then there was Edmund, who sat in a class all by himself. His honestly calm and nerdishly compassionate approach cracked the armor around her heart. "You're serious."

"Yes."

"You. Like me? After hearing all that?"

"Yes."

Embarrassment spread like wildfire, across her face. "I

didn't want you to find out about it like this. I wanted to tell you myself on *my* terms. I can't believe they said—"

"They didn't say anything."

She threw her hands up in frustration. "Then how did you know?"

"Thomas explained why he was on the meds and his injuries from the attack, when and where they happened." His hands gently rested on her shoulders. "He told me about the coworker who shot her husband. Someone he'd known when he was a kid."

"It was how he told the story. Not that he said my name?"

"Yes. Not once did he or Lucy mention your name, but there were pieces of the conversation that sounded familiar." Stuffing his hands in his pockets, he shrugged. "But I figured it out. Like putting a puzzle together."

"You came here at ten at night to tell me you knew?"

"Yes."

"Why?"

"Because I didn't like that you were so upset this afternoon and talking about it at work wouldn't be respecting your privacy."

His answer knocked her gloriously off-center. She opened and closed her fists to keep her hands from grabbing him by the collar and kissing him. "Who said chivalry is dead? What did your mother say to you to raise a guy who actually gets how to connect with women? How to say things in a way that punches them right in the heart."

"Not all women." He stepped back, a grimace on his

face.

"I get the feeling there's a story behind that comment." A sudden fierceness hit her, knowing someone had hurt him. She shook it off, citing it as a ridiculous reaction to someone she'd known for less than twenty-four hours.

"I'm not sharing it right now."

"Okay. When or if you want to."

He ran his fingers through his hair. "Look, I can't promise I'll stay here in Marietta long term, but I like you. I'd like to get to know you, even if it's nothing other than a friendship."

She wanted to believe he could like her after what she'd done, what she'd been through. But as much as she'd convinced herself she could handle life on her own, and she could, bringing a *friendship* into her world brought an entirely new set of questions. None of them with answers she liked. "Friendship. With me? That's what you're saying?"

Swallowing hard, he tucked his thumbs in his belt loops. "Yes. That's what I'm saying."

The idea of starting all over with someone, anyone, should have Jade this side of frantic, but all she felt was calm staring into his eyes. With the exception of Thomas and Lucy, anyone who'd known her story, had looked at her with pity or the want to fix her, help her. Not a hint of any of that in Edmund's gaze. Nothing, but compassion. "You're serious?"

"Yeah, I am."

Until that moment, it didn't register he'd closed the gap between them. Now he only stood a foot away. Her fingers itched to run up his chest and clasp behind his neck. "I had no idea that men like you even existed."

"I'm sorry you had to go through that." Reaching, he traced the line of her jaw before carefully running his thumb around her left eye.

The one that had been so badly bruised.

"It's not right."

The tenderness of his touch triggered an unexpected sob.

Suppressed emotions of the turbulent time with her abusive late husband begged to spill out, but she forced herself to lock away anymore that might escape. Having a monumental meltdown less than a day of meeting someone would not bode well for future *friendly* conversations. "Edmund, I think you're amazing, but I do have a lot of baggage. Maybe you and I, we shouldn't even consider this. Just keep it simple. Friends. Coworkers."

She sighed and leaned into him as his finger gently traced her jawline. "Work related."

"Everyone has baggage, Jade. It's all about how we unpack it, but if this isn't anything you want—" He began to pull away and her hand shot up to keep his rested against her cheek.

"Please." The last thing she wanted him to do was to stop touching her.

He'd been nothing but kind. Gentle. A prince among men.

His eyes darted from her eyes to her mouth and that was all the encouragement she needed.

Grabbing his shirt with both hands, she gave him a slight

tug.

Cupping her face, their lips met in a soft, sweet moment with a slow lingering kiss that ignited her body like a match to dry tinder. She kissed him hungrily, probing his mouth with her tongue, and then nibbling his lower lip.

Edmund slightly swept his tongue in her mouth before his hand rested on her hip and slid to the small of her back, pulling her closer.

An ache settled low in her belly and the want for more grew exponentially. For too long, she'd been on her own, having to resort to battery operated machinery or getting lost in the stacks of books she poured through. She wanted, needed someone who looked at her like the lovers did in the pages she loved so much.

"Edmund." She sighed as her hands ran across his chest and down his arms. "Kiss me again."

Nibbling at the base of her neck, he smiled against her skin. "I should go."

At first, she thought she'd imagined it. "What?"

Pushing her hair out of her face, he brushed his lips against hers one more time before whispering, "I should go."

"You want to go?" Disappointment hit her hard as she held on to his shirt, hoping to keep him there, even if it were only for a few more seconds.

His eyes bore into her as though he had stripped her naked, body and soul. "I didn't say I *wanted* to, but I *should*, before this gets too, um, friendly."

"Always so honorable."

A blush colored his cheeks. He patted her back before

stepping away. "It sucks sometimes."

"I bet it does." As soon as he moved away, she immediately missed him. The tingle of peppermint lingered against her lips and the excitement of new possibilities tumbled through her mind.

Before he left, he leaned in and whispered, "After knowing how you kiss, I'd prefer to be a lot less chivalrous. Friend."

Standing on the front porch, watching him walk to his car and drive away, Jade shivered with delight at the unexpected and tender end to her evening.

And the possibility of new friendships.

Chapter Ten

"I DON'T WANT a nurse. I want a doctor in here."

"Sir, if you'll—"

"My daughter has strep. Either you write a prescription or get someone in here who can." The man tapped his gaudy jeweled watch. "We're burning daylight. Hurry it up."

Jade thought of Edmund's sweet kisses and plastered on her best fake smile. She checked the chart again. "Mr. Stevenson. Now, has Matilda had strep before?"

"No one calls me Matilda. I'm Phoebe." The girl rolled her eyes.

"Is Phoebe your middle name?"

"Duh."

This is going to be a fun day. "Has Phoebe ever had strep before?"

Mr. Stevenson waved his hands in front of his face. "No, no, I'm not doing this. Just write the prescription and we'll be out of your hair."

Biting her tongue, Jade mentally counted to ten. "That's not how this works, sir. Since we've never seen her here and you have no medical records with you, I need a medical history, a physical on your daughter, and to run a strep test—"

"I'm not doing that." The girl stuck her lip out and crossed her arms across her chest. "I'm not letting you test my throat. It hurts and I hate it."

"Then I'm not writing for any medication if I can't verify anything."

"Daddy, fix this." She dramatically crossed her arms across her chest, reminding Jade of Veruca Salt from the *Charlie and the Chocolate Factory* movies.

He oozed self-importance as he pulled out his wallet; his irregular-shaped platinum ring sparkled under the lighting. "I called her regular pediatrician and his partner was on call. She said she couldn't write anything for us because she's in Colorado and doesn't have a license here."

"That's correct, sir." Sort of. *If she'd really wanted to, she could have sent the prescription to a major pharmacy chain, they could transfer it, and this jerk could go pick it up at the closest location.*

"We can drive back to Colorado, which I won't do because I promised my daughter time in these mountains."

"And the last time we were here, it was a mess because Daddy's pretty blue Mercedes car got stolen." Phoebe stuck out her bottom lip. Her cheeks red. "And he lost his stupid ring."

Jade nodded as though she cared about the overpriced car. "I've been up in Copper Mountain many times. You're going hiking or camping, Mr. Stevenson?"

"Hiking." The father's nose stuck a little higher in the air.

His perfectly pressed button-down and brand-new Eddie Bauer hiking pants indicated he'd recently purchased them. The new hiking boots he wore screamed novice outdoorsman. *Those aren't even close to being broken in. Man, he's going to have so many blisters later.*

His daughter's sparkling new Kate Spade Minnie Mouse backpack and the Kate Spade bright pink fanny pack she wore cost about as much as Jade paid in rent this month. Both completely impractical for a hiking weekend. "Have you been up there before, Phoebe?"

"Not really, but it can't be that hard. It's walking."

Yep, absolutely novice. "Right. Okay. Let's tackle one thing at a time."

Mr. Stevenson rubbed two one hundred dollar bills between his fingers and held them out for Jade to take. "Come on. Just between us."

Who do you think I am, my brother? Backing away, Jade wagged her finger. "Sir, put your money away."

Rolling his eyes, he stuffed his money back in his wallet before tossing that on the counter. The familiar Michael Kors logo on it. "Why am I even talking to you? You're not even a doctor."

"I'm more than qualified to take care of your daughter."

"But you're not an MD." He sneered. "I want the doctor in here. Maybe *he'll* be reasonable about this."

If I had a dollar for every time I've heard this ignorant BS. "Fine. I'll go get *her*."

The man's jaw dropped to the floor. "Her? What, you don't have any men working here?"

What ridiculously misogynist thing to say in front of your daughter. "We do have men working here, but the *doctor* right now is a more than qualified *woman*."

Phoebe's defiance softened. "A lady doctor. Cool! Is she nice?"

"She's lovely." Jade patted the child on the foot.

"Fine. Get her in here. We've got things to do." Mr. Stevenson motioned for Jade to leave the room as though she were some servant to complete his requests. "Come on. Move your ass."

Breathe, Jade. Breathe. "Sir, if you talk to me like that again, I'll have a member of our local police department stop by and discuss manners with you."

Phoebe crinkled her nose. "Daddy. Ass is an ugly word."

"Fine, but make it fast." Clenching his jaw, he impatiently snapped his fingers.

Jade's blood boiled at his arrogance, his blatant sexism, but sadly, she'd experienced far too many times. It was one thing to be a snob, but it was entirely another to be a misogynist piece of crap in front of your daughter.

Plus, Jade would bet her next paycheck the man didn't know the difference between a virus and a bacteria and what treated each.

Before she could pivot on the balls of her feet to leave the room, a stern voice from behind her stopped her in her tracks.

"Is there a problem, here?"

When she turned, Lucy Davidson stood in the doorway. Behind her, Edmund.

Jade unconsciously touched her lip, still feeling Edmund's caress. *As if he couldn't have been more amazingly sexy last night.*

She blinked her way back to the present when Lucy cleared her throat.

"Good morning, I'm Dr. Lucy Davidson." She extended her hand so forcefully that the pompous man jumped and cautiously shook it as though he were afraid it might bite him if he moved too quickly. "What seems to be the problem here?"

Putting her head back in the game, Jade smirked. She had to hand it to Lucy. Despite the doctor's barely five-foot frame, she walked into a room like she was center stage at a WWE championship and going to win it all without question.

"Um, um, my daughter has strep." The man swallowed hard. "We need antibiotics."

"I see. Well, if that's what you think she has."

"Know she has." The father gave Jade an I-told-you-so look.

"Great. Then the exam and rapid strep test by Mrs. Phillips here should be an easy process."

The one thing Jade had come to appreciate about Lucy was her straightforward approach to just about anything, but hearing her say Mrs. Phillips reminded Jade she needed to get her name badge changed.

The corner of Mr. Stevenson's lip twitched. "Like I told your *nurse* here."

"Nurse practitioner," Lucy interjected and wagged a

stern finger at him. "Mrs. Phillips is a nurse practitioner."

The man paused, his determination far from where it had been a few seconds ago. "Yes, um…"

"Your hesitation tells me you don't understand what that means so I'll explain. A nurse practitioner has a master's degree and extensive training in their specialty. Mrs. Phillips obviously completed emergency medicine education and has worked extensively with pediatric patients. She's more than qualified to treat your daughter today."

Cocking an eyebrow, Mr. Stevenson stepped back as though he were deciding to come at Lucy full force or stand back and let the medical team actually do their jobs. "Fine, your staff is qualified, but we don't have time for that. Just write us up something and we'll go."

"Can you help me, Nurse Practic-tion-er, ma'am?" Phoebe scooted to the edge of the stretcher and slid until her feet touched the floor. Standing, she wobbled before Jade took her hand. Pointing in the direction of the bathroom, she croaked, "I have to go to the bathroom."

Ugh, her breath smells like infection. Yep, she's got strep. "You okay, Phoebe?"

"I got dizzy."

Her hands are cold, her face is flushed, her breathing slightly labored. She's at the least got strep and maybe pneumonia. "I'd guess so. You thirsty?"

"My throat hurts. I don't want anything."

"When was the last time she had anything for headache? Pain?" *With dried, cracked lips like that, you need something.*

Mr. Stevenson glared at Jade. "She wouldn't take anything. Said it hurts to swallow because she has strep!"

Dude, you don't get it, do you? It's not just strep. "Dr. Davidson, you want a UA?"

"Good call." Lucy nodded.

Phoebe made it to the doorway and waved Jade off. "I've got it."

The child took a few steps and stumbled sideways, but still refused assistance.

"Shelly, would you walk with her, please?" Jade called out to the nurse closest to the bathroom.

"Of course. This way, sweetheart." The nurse smiled so brightly, it lit up the room. She wrapped her arms around Phoebe's waist and stayed beside her until they reached the bathroom. Not once did the child refuse Shelly's help.

Shelly always had a way of making the day better, no matter how crazy it got in the ER. Her patients always felt well cared for and were genially appreciative.

I still worry about her remarrying that jerk. "Thank you, Shelly."

"Anytime."

"UA?" the father snapped.

"Urinary analysis." Lucy entered a short assessment into the bedside computer.

By now, Edmund had moved in and stood quietly near the door.

"Why the hell would anyone need to check my daughter's piss? She's in here for a sore throat." He grabbed his phone, his fingers sailing across the screen. "You people are quacks. I'm texting her primary."

Lucy nodded and slapped her hands together. "Great. While you've got your phone in hand, type in poststrepto-coccal glomerulonephritis."

His fingers froze. "Why?"

"It's when strep attacks the kidneys, shutting them down." She stood close and pointed to his phone. "Go on. It's post, like the mail, and then s-t-r-e-p-t-o-c-o-c-c-a-l—"

Taking a few steps away from Lucy, Mr. Stevenson snarled, "What in the hell are you talking about? It's strep throat. Not strep kidneys."

Edmund casually adjusted his stethoscope. "You've been to medical school, then?"

Mr. Stevenson narrowed his gaze at him. "No, I went to law school. Work at a high-profile practice in Denver. We cover corporate—"

"Not medical school, then."

The look on the man's face ranged from outrage to shock at everyone's indifference to his self-importance. "And who the hell are you? The orderly?"

"No, I'm *Dr.* Edmund Davidson."

"Finally, a guy in here." He held his hand up for a high five, but Edmund locked his arms over his chest. "Why aren't you running the show?"

"I don't need to run the show. Dr. Davidson and Miss Carter—"

"Who's Miss Carter?"

Edmund pointed to Jade. "Mrs. Phillips. These women have it well in hand. You'd do well to listen."

Oh my. As much as Jade hated to admit it, sometimes the

best defense against a jerk like this was a guy liked Edmund in your corner. "Thank you, Dr. Davidson."

He gave her a respectful nod as the father continued venting. "Why aren't you doing *something* here?"

"Sir, I'm orienting to the unit today. New to the town and the hospital," Edmund explained.

"Great. Another newbie. Aren't you too old to be starting out as a doctor?"

The vein in Edmund's neck pulsed faster, obviously affected by this asshole's commentary. "No, sir. I'm moving here from Florida. I can assure you, I've been out of residency for long enough to have plenty of clinical experience."

"Good. I don't want subpar care for my daughter." He gave Jade a sideways glance.

"I'm only going to ask you once to let us do our jobs, no matter if we're nurses, PNPs, or doctors and no matter what gender any of us are without sarcastic commentary or blatant sexism," Edmund added as he leaned forward. "Are we clear?"

Lucy confidently stood between the two men, staring at the patient's father. "You gonna look up poststreptococcal glomerulonephritis or are you going to trust us all to take care of your Phoebe?"

For a moment, Jade wondered if the father would bite back. His expensive clothing certainly implied he could be the type.

He scanned the room, his fingers suspended midway to his phone. "Look. I get it. We live in a litigious society, but we've been through this song and dance before. She's got strep."

After getting a good look at his daughter, Jade knew that and the dehydrated girl probably had an upper respiratory infection, most likely caused by strep.

Counting on his well-manicured fingers, the man replied, "Fever, hurts to swallow and talk. What else could it be?"

Tapping her chin with her finger, Lucy appeared to be thinking. "You work with the facts, right? Evidence is needed to prove or disprove your case?"

Mr. Stevenson squared his shoulders, tilting his chin up slightly. "Yes. Of course and I'm damned good at it."

"With the information I have so far with *no* medical exam, are you willing to bet your daughter's life that it's *only* strep?"

"I wondered the same thing, Dr. Davidson," Jade added. "The patient's cracked lips and increased work of breathing are concerning."

Mr. Stevenson's eyes went wide. "What? What are you talking about?"

"Fever, hurts to swallow and talk can also be signs of bronchitis, pneumonia." Lucy turned to Jade and Edmund. "What am I missing, Mrs. Phillips, I'm sorry, Miss Carter? Dr. Davidson?"

Biting the inside of her cheek to keep from laughing at Lucy's finesse, Jade nodded. "Well, there's cold with sinusitis and viral infections with post nasal irritation. Are her vaccines up to date? Otherwise, we'd need to consider epiglottitis, but we would regardless."

"Right, we want to rule out tonsillar abscess." Edmund nodded.

When Jade made momentary eye contact with him, he gave her a quick wink, making her nervously rearrange the pens in her lab coat pocket.

If the father ran his fingers through his hair any more forced, he'd be bald in the next few minutes. "Okay, okay, I get it. Fine. You know what you're doing. Do the test, but hurry up. I promised her I'd take her up to the lake."

In those brand-new hiking boots? You'll be limping in the first hour.

Phoebe returned and handed the urine cup to Jade before bracing herself against the doorframe and began to slide to the floor. "I don't feel so good."

Before her father could move, Lucy grabbed the urine sample as Edmund scooped the child and gently laid her on the stretcher. "Young lady, you look wiped out."

"The room is spinning, Daddy." The child whimpered as a single, tiny tear ran down her flushed face. "I feel so bad."

"What just happened?" He grabbed his daughter's hand in both of his. "Daddy's here, sweetie. Her hands are freezing."

"Her breathing is more labored than when she walked out of here. When was the last time she drank anything?" Jade placed a pulse oximeter on Phoebe's finger. "You're breathing hard, so I'm going to get your oxygen level here."

"Last night?" The father furrowed his forehead as he touched his daughter's face. "She said it hurt too much to swallow anything for breakfast. I even offered her a milkshake. How is she so hot and her hands cold?"

"When you're sick, your body decreases blood flow to nonessential parts of the body, focusing mostly on the core. Heart, lungs, brain." Lucy picked up the urine, holding it up to the light. "Her urine is really dark. She needs some fluids."

"Yep. Poppy, did you hear that?" Jade asked loudly.

"Yes, I did. Entering the orders now. What labs do you want?" nurse's aide Poppy Henderson called out.

Without pause in her assessment, Jade answered, "Chemistry series, CBC, UA, rapid strep, chest X-ray should be enough."

"Give me a sec. I'll bring in the orders and labels."

"The room still spinning?" Jade placed the blood pressure cuff on the child's arm and hit the machine's button. "Be still. This is going to take your blood pressure and the sticker on her finger measures your oxygen level, okay?"

Despite her earlier protests, the child weakly nodded. "Okay, ma'am."

Jade rapid-fired questions. "Does it hurt to pee? Back pain? Stomach pain?"

"No. No. No." Phoebe rested her forehead against her father's and cried. "Daddy, I don't feel good."

"Okay, baby. They are going to help you." Concern replaced his arrogance. "I'm right here. I'm not going anywhere."

It had always impressed Jade how parents could be the worst barrier to care for their children, but when the facts were laid out in front, most of the time, they could move aside and become a medical member's best ally.

The child held onto her father's hand.

Seeing the daughter-father interaction suddenly hurt Jade's heart. She remembered the times her dad sat at her bedside when she had food poisoning, the flu, and even bad menstrual cramps.

Good men are out there.

Glancing behind her, she saw one and hope nestled in her heart right before a nagging voice whispered, "After all you've done, you just don't deserve one."

Even after Edmund told her he didn't care about her past, Jade couldn't stop thinking about it all night and wondered if she should even give herself the chance to get to know him.

Standing near the door and out of the way, he gave her a thumbs-up and mouthed, "You got this."

Maybe I deserve to get to know him a little.

"Jade? Mrs. Phillips, I mean, Miss Carter?" Lucy leaned forward as she appeared to be assessing the child's legs and feet. "No rash, cap refill is less than three seconds. Not petechial bruising. Mr. Stevenson, does Phoebe have any history of chronic illness like asthma, diabetes? Allergies to any medications?"

He ran his thumb along his daughter's hairline. "Yes, she had some asthma when she was young, but hasn't had problems for years. Just the strep. No allergies to anything."

"You okay?" Lucy whispered.

Get your head in the game, Jade. "Yes, I'm fine. Just thinking. How many times has she had strep?"

"At least a dozen in the past few years." Mr. Stevenson

growled. "I can't get her mother to take her to the specialist to get her tonsils out. Said Phoebe only needs more vitamin C in her diet and she won't get sick like this. What a load."

The beep of the blood pressure cuff signaled.

Lucy pointed to the monitor. "Her blood pressure's low and heart rate one thirty. Her oxygen level is ninety-six. Like Mrs. Phillips said, we need blood work, urinalysis, a throat swab and to start some IV fluids. She'll also send it for a culture if needed."

"All her vaccines are up to date, right, Mr. Stevenson?" Jade stepped to the doorway. "Dave, I need your amazing pediatric IV skills."

Nurse Dave Fletcher, gave a thumbs-up. "On my way. What do I need to bring?"

"What do you want us to do, Dr. Davidson?" Jade knew exactly what the child needed, but with Lucy having to run interference with a difficult father, Jade wasn't sure how Lucy wanted to handle most of it.

"Your call, Miss Carter." Lucy pulled out her stethoscope and held up the bell as she looked at the child. "I need to listen to your chest and heart, okay?"

The patient's pale, cracked lips were a stark contrast against her flushed cheeks. "She needs fluids and probably a round of antibiotics."

"Agreed."

Internally, Jade gave herself a high five. Even though she and Lucy had gotten off on the wrong foot when Lucy first arrived, the doctor had always been respectful of Jade's capabilities. "Dave, I need a bag of normal saline, see if you can get a twenty gauge in her, but a twenty-two would at least get her hydrated and some labs. Her oxygen level's ninety-five and I've ordered a chest X-ray."

Stepping back and tucking her stethoscope in her pocket, Lucy nodded. "She's decreased in her upper lobes. She might get noisier with some fluids. Let's watch that, let RT know."

"Yes, she has all her vaccines. I fought with her mom about that too, but she's got all of them. I took her to the doctor myself. Why? What? What's going on?" The father stepped forward, still keeping hold of his daughter's hand. "You people are rattling off all this medical crap and I can't keep up."

"Mr. Stevenson, I'm so glad you had the presence of mind to bring your daughter to us today." Lucy patted the child's foot. "She's pretty dehydrated and she certainly has something going on."

"What is it?"

Giving a sideways nod to Jade, Lucy stepped back and motioned for Jade to step in.

Moving forward, she explained the situation as nurse Dave Fletcher arrived with his IV kit and Lucy stepped out.

Before following his sister from the room, Edmund gave Jade a lopsided smirk that had her momentarily distracted.

Focus. Focus! Jade pointed to the monitor. "Sir, fever and sore throat can absolutely be caused by strep, which you know, but it's made her dehydrated and that worsens her throat pain. It decreases her ability to tolerate that kind of discomfort, including swallowing anything, even her own spit. Let us get some IV fluids in her, get her hydrated and when we get the strep test results back, we can go ahead and give her a dose of antibiotics if strep is causing all this."

"Okay, okay. Whatever you have to do for my girl." He gave her hand a squeeze.

"Ouch, Daddy. Your ring." The girl pulled her hand out of her father's grasp.

"Sorry, baby." Giving Jade a defeated look, he slipped the ring off, placing it into his pocket. "Whatever you need to do."

"Thank you, sir." The flash of sparkle caught Jade's attention, but her mind quickly returned to the matters at hand.

Dave stood beside Jade and waved at the father and child.

"This is Nurse Dave."

"You're a nurse? I thought only girls were nurses." Phoebe cocked her head.

"Well, Dave is a super cool guy. We let him in the club."

"Wow, you must be really cool." Phoebe smirked.

Poppy entered, placed a label on the urine cup after verifying it was the patient's. She gave Phoebe a thumbs-up. "I promise you're in very good hands."

The child weakly waved.

Dave handed Phoebe a Peanuts and superhero sticker. "I went to nursing school because I got to take care of patients sooner than if I went to medical school."

"That's true," Poppy agreed. "I'll finish nursing school next year. Can't wait."

"What are you now?" Phoebe held the stickers between

her fingers.

"I'm a nurse aide so I help the nurses, but I also learn here so I do better in class there because I get to see everything I read about."

"Dave and Poppy are part of my team. We are all going to help take care of you. Make things better."

"A good guy team. Like the Avengers?" Phoebe gave a tired smile.

"Just like the Avengers."

"Dibs! I get to be Spiderman!" Dave raised his hand.

"I call Black Widow!" Poppy interjected before leaving with the urine sample.

"That makes you Captain Marvel." Phoebe watched Jade tuck her stethoscope back in her pocket.

Jade patted the child's hand. "Why do you say that, sweetheart?"

She held up the sticker that had Captain Marvel's symbol on it. "Because she's gonna fix everything."

Chapter Eleven

E DMUND TRAINED IN different facilities as a tech during pre-med then medical school and residency. He'd always appreciated a team that worked in sync and the staff at Marietta was no exception, but he didn't know what else he expected, especially with his sister in charge.

The tightness of working as a team spilled into the general community.

Around the unit and in each room, a flyer about the upcoming art show at Harry's House, a local boys and girls club, had been hung.

Any kid or parent who came in, the staff asked if they or their children were entering anything in the event and convinced a few to do so.

Like a choreographed show, each ER team member had timing down to an art when it came to knowing what patients and each other needed. Such environments always made for better shifts, medical harmony, and effective patient care.

Within ten minutes of him walking out of Phoebe's room, labs had been drawn, the IV established, and rehydration fluids hung.

Poppy helped label as Dave handed her the blood samples he drew before capping off the IV line. Jade quickly swabbed the child's throat and they sent everything off to the lab as they waited for the portable chest X-ray to be taken.

Always smiling, Shelly Westbrook roomed another patient after sweeping through the unit on her way to triage. Seeing how she brighten a room, Edmund had grown an instant liking to her. He could see why Jade was so fiercely protective of her friend.

Anyone who'd bring someone like Shelly down should be shot.

"I'm sorry, what are you doing again? With this?" Mr. Stevenson asked, his voice heavy with worry.

"Oh, yes, I'm happy to explain. We're going to give her a large volume of fluids to begin with called a bolus," Jade's words floated out of the room. "It's kind of like drinking a big glass of salty water in a short amount of time, but it's going through her IV. It's good she isn't vomiting so we can hydrate her both orally, I mean she can drink fluids, as well as getting some through her line."

"How do you know how much to give? How fast?"

"This is all based on weight…"

As much as he liked meeting Jade outside of the unit yesterday, seeing her work had been a beauty to behold. She had a rhythm, a system that was hard not to appreciate, plus she'd been remarkably professional when dealing with a borderline abusive patient. How many of those had she had to field in her career?

In her life?

The idea of her being on the wrong end of a fist angered him. *Good thing that guy is dead or I'd hunt him down myself.*

How he hated spousal abusers. They ranked far below pond scum and numerous past and present political figures.

"What do you think?" Lucy stood next to him as he glanced in the room where Jade talked to the father and child.

He pulled himself out of his introspection. "I think she's doing a great job."

"She?"

Out of the corner of his eye, he saw his sister lean toward him and then away. "Earth to Edmund. I was talking about the unit as a whole."

"I'm not spaced, Lucy. Just appreciate people who do a good job."

Lucy bit her lip and checked on another patient's labs per the computer. "Any questions so far about procedure or protocol? Need the codes for getting into the break room or doctor's lounge?"

"Nope. All pretty straightforward." He turned slightly toward his sister, but kept a watchful eye out for Jade.

"When do you start your computer training? Sugars are good. White count slightly elevated." She pursed her lips, something she did when evaluating information.

"Because I came early, Dr. Sinclair said I could be a late addition to the hospital orientation class tomorrow."

"Lucky us." Poppy tapped the counter. "Dr. Davidson. Mr. Nicolas, your asthmatic in room four said he's feeling tight again. You want me to call RT?"

"Let me assess him, he may need some fluids and I know he's anxious." She typed something in on the computer and mumbled, "Steroids were given two hours ago. He's had three treatments back-to-back when he first came in. Last one was about an hour ago…"

"Anything I can do to help?" He wanted to be on his own so badly. This two- to three-week hospital orientation, including learning the electronic medical records and billing system, would be torturous to get through, but his heart beat a lot faster being back in the unit.

There were times during the investigation he never thought he'd have the chance to practice again. Getting through the boring paperwork and process would simply be a blip in the grand scheme of things.

Lucy patted his arm. "Nope, just an older gentleman who has a history of respiratory issues. It took forever to convince him he had asthma."

Noticing the man's age, Edmund raised an eyebrow. "Eighty-nine? Not to play devil's advocate—"

"But you will. How do I know he's got asthma?"

Edmund smirked at his sister's ability to take as much as she could give. "Yep."

"He told me he had bronchitis multiple times as a child. Needed frequent hospitalizations for breathing problems and they called it reactive airway disease."

"Ah, the all-inclusive RAD."

"Reactive airway disease. What's that?" Poppy scooted forward. "They haven't mentioned that in my pulmonology unit."

Lucy shook her head. "They probably wouldn't. It's not used anymore because it was a diagnosis they used to give asthmatics since insurance would be more likely to cover it. Asthma was considered a pre-existing condition. It was a loophole."

"And it wouldn't keep people from serving in the military when they were older, even if they'd had no attacks for years," Edmund added.

Poppy cocked her head. "Why would asthma in childhood decide if you could serve as an adult?"

"Because the military used to have a zero acceptance for anyone with asthma. You couldn't have it at all. Now, it depends on how well your asthma is controlled, how long ago your last attack was, along with which branch you're serving, your role, and where you are stationed."

Reading over Lucy's shoulder, Edmund scanned Mr. Nicolas's medical history. "Pneumonia at least once a year for the past thirty years and he responds well to the Ventolin treatments. Sounds like asthma to me."

Thirty minutes later, Lucy wrote the orders to admit the asthmatic patient after talking to the primary physician.

Within ten minutes, Dave wheeled by with Mr. Nicolas as they left for the stepdown unit. The portly patient gave Edmund a wink and touched the side of his nose.

"What a jolly man," Lucy giggled as she waved him goodbye. "He's got quite a lovely personality."

Edmund chuckled. "Is it me, but does he have rosy cheeks, a nose like a cherry?"

"He really does!" Lucy agreed, smiling gleefully like a

child on Christmas morning.

Jade started a second bolus on Phoebe as a yelling filled the hallway from the ambulance doors.

Within seconds, Shelly quickly wheeled a woman upstairs who was in active labor with her third child and wanted to push. "Poppy, call the floor, I'm coming with a gravita four-para three, full-term. Water broke thirty minutes ago and they drove."

"Got it." Poppy gave a thumbs-up before dialing. "Where did they park? I don't want the car in the ambulance spot."

"They are in visitors' parking. I saw them when they pulled in."

"Perfect."

"Ahhhhhhhh!" The woman screamed as Shelly rounded the corner toward the elevators. "I always hate this part. This suuuuuuuuuuuucks."

Following, a disheveled man with three small children in tow who cheered her on. "You're doing great, honey. We love you."

"Shut up! Just shut up! I don't need that right now."

"I always hate this part," he mumbled as the held the kids' hands and they disappeared down the hallway. "It sucks."

Knowing just outside the ambulance entrance had always been a common place for employees who smoke to hang out, Edmund questioned why Shelly had been out there since she'd never smelled of cigarettes. "Why was Shelly out on the ambulance entrance?"

"She's always handling some family crisis with her ex," Lucy whispered. "That phone of hers is always exploding because he can't find his ass. If she re-marries him, it's only going to get worse."

Good to know life in and out of the ER was always in constant states of chaos. Just how much chaos depends on the day.

In room seven, Dave set up a suture tray for a teen who sliced his hand open when he jumped off his fence while holding a beer bottle and didn't stick the landing, but fell backward, breaking the glass bottle as he still held it.

His father stood at his son's bedside, a stone-faced glare at his son as the teen begged not to be grounded for the next two months because he'd been an underage drinker and caused his father to lose half a day of work.

No one asked him if he was entering anything in the art show.

Guess no matter where you practice emergency medicine, it's never dull. Always a challenge.

"I'm gonna sew up this kid's hand. You think you can hold down the fort for me until I'm done?" Lucy draped her lab coat over the back of the chair before clipping her hair back. "Tom Reynolds should be here in about half an hour."

"I think I can handle it." He could more than handle it.

Being back in the ER fed his soul, gave him a reason to get out of bed in the morning. When Lucy called at six to tell him to come in and start on his in-unit orientation today, he couldn't get ready fast enough.

Getting to work with Jade had been a bonus.

His eyes betrayed him when she walked by and returned to Phoebe's room when the IV machine beeped several times.

The corner of Lucy's mouth twitched. "Okay, Dr. Feelgood. I'll be in room seven if you need me."

"I'll be here. Gonna walk around, get familiar where things are."

"Uh-huh. Don't wander too far. Still have the exciting world of coding to cover."

"Great." Edmund soaked in every detail. The exam rooms, how to work the beds, where the linen cart and supply rooms were. The medication machine, how to work the bedside monitors. The smell of the disinfectant they used to clean the beds, body fluid spills, and rooms between patients.

For the first time in months, Edmund's anxiety dropped off the charts and the world looked new again. After the insanity of the pre-trial prep, the accusations, and finally the evidence to prove his innocence, he'd made it back to the emergency room.

Until he arrived this morning, he hadn't realized how much he missed it.

"Think of the kids with fever as a pot of water on the stove with no lid." Jade's calm voice floated out from Phoebe's room. "The hotter you run the heat, the quicker the water evaporates. If she's breathing faster, she burning off water quicker and if she's not taking any in, she gets dry. Make sense?"

"I'll remember this next time she has this crap. I've told her mother she needs her tonsils out, but her mother refuses to consider it. Says it can be cured with some natural herbal snake oil her boyfriend sells. Said kids her age don't do well with that kind of surgery."

"People have their tonsils out at all ages. The recovery time is faster with younger kids but you can say that about everything."

The high-pitched ting of something metal tapping echoed from the room. "You wouldn't believe the fights we had about vaccines."

"How frustrating for you." Jade's voice remained professional and confident as the father vented.

One thing Edmund appreciated about nurses was their ability to explain things to patients and family members in an easy to understand way. Plus, because nurses spent an incredible amount of time with patients, he always valued their ability to listen to people when they simply needed to emotionally unload.

He'd seen his share of physician colleagues talk so far above the patients' heads and spend so little time at the bedside that it caused frustration and confusion.

Not to say all doctors acted that way. There were plenty that had great bedside manners and their patients always understood them.

To be fair, not all nurses he worked with over the years had great rapport with patients and not all actually understood how the body worked or the method of action with medications.

That had always been the exciting and exhausting part of working in a high stress unit like an ER. Sometimes, there wasn't always time for good bedside manners, especially in critical situations, so Edmund always appreciated solid and hard-working staff members to help smooth the edges and cover all bases when it came to patient care.

"Dr. Davidson." Jade exited the room and stood at the computer as she pulled up her notes. "Thank you for your help in there."

"Of course. No one should put up with that." While her fingers flew across the keyboard, he replayed the kiss from last night. He gave himself a mental high five for having the good sense to leave when he did. The sting of her peppermint mouthwash lingered on his lips and tongue for a good half hour afterward. "All good in there?"

"Yes, much better. Poor kid was dehydrated and she probably has pneumonia. We'll know more after the X-ray, but she's diminished in her lower lobes and some fine crackles in the upper."

"Sounds like. Mind if I walk in, talk to him?"

"You gonna give him the what for?"

"No. Thought a guy-to-guy talk might help put him at ease." He stood closer than was probably professional, but after last night, he wanted to soak in as much of her as he could.

She didn't move away. "Go work your magic, Doctor."

As he approached, he noticed Mr. Stevenson gave him a respected nod as he tapped a ring on the armrest again. The raised, irregular edges reflected unevenly with the overhead lights. The sparkle of the metal illustrated he took incredible care of it. "Interesting ring."

"Custom made. My fraternity brothers and I all got them when we graduated college at the University of Colorado." He held up his hand as he pushed it around his finger with his thumb. "Made the mistake of leaving it in my car a couple of years ago and the damn thing got stolen."

"The ring?"

"The ring and my car."

"That sucks."

"Are you allowed to say sucks if you're a doctor?" Phoebe cocked her head.

"Yes, young lady. Doctors, nurses, and anyone in the medical field will use the word sucks, because sometimes things do." Edmund leaned against the doorframe and gave the child a smile.

"My dad's ring. It pinches me sometimes and that sucks," she added. "It's got a weird design."

Mr. Stevenson chuckled. "Sorry, sweetie. It made sense when my frat brothers and I came up with it. Supposed to look like the Rockies profile, but to be honest we were drunk when we thought of it."

After meeting Logan Tate, Edmund wondered who'd steal a car in the middle of Montana and risk having to deal with the local deputy. As friendly as he'd been, the man didn't look like anyone a person would want to mess with. "The car that was stolen? What did it look like?"

"Mercedes-Benz S-Class Coupe."

Damn, that's a quarter of a million dollar car. "I'd guess a Mercedes in Marietta would stick out."

"It was a cool custom color too. Obsidian blue."

"It sparkled like the ocean at sunset." Phoebe sighed. "Daddy has a black car now, but we rented a car to come up here this time in case anyone wanted to steal that one."

The dad kissed the back of his daughter's hand. "My insurance company wasn't pleased to get that call. You look less flushed."

"And it hasn't shown up anywhere?" *The ability to unload a car that expensive in Montana would certainly raise eyebrows and wag tongues.* Now, if they were in Florida, that car would have been taken apart within the first hour and sold for parts. Chop shops were plenty in Florida. "What about the GPS?"

"Whoever got it, knew how to disable that within minutes."

"Morning. Here to do the chest X-ray." Radiology Tech Isaiah Flynn arrived with the portable machine and the men stepped outside of the room.

Shelly approached and handed Mr. Stevenson some coffee before entering to help position the child higher in the bed and lay the lead apron over her belly. "We're going to take a picture of your lungs and this is a kind of apron that protects your tummy."

"Like a Wonder Woman shield?" Slightly winded, Phoebe's eyes sparkled. A sure sign of her improvement.

"Exactly, like a Wonder Woman shield." Isaiah laughed.

"I was an ass earlier." Mr. Stevenson's lips thinned as he slightly turned toward Edmund. "I want to apologize."

"I don't think it's only me you need to apologize to." Edmund thumbed behind him, hoping to encourage the man to say the same to Lucy and especially Jade. If they'd been anywhere other than here, Edmund would have laid the guy out treating those women the way he did. "You've got an entire unit of people here trying to help, men and *women*."

"I'm usually not such an ass out of court. My divorce… I don't have a great relationship with her mom. With women right now. Man, she really worked me over. I never saw it coming."

Rocking back on his heels, Edmund cringed hearing the very same words he'd repeated to himself after the handcuffs were around his wrists and he was led out of work. The humiliation, the twenty-twenty hindsight, damn, the entire situation blindsided Edmund because he didn't want to see the obvious. "Life can surprise you."

Taking a long drag of coffee, Mr. Stevenson slowly nod-ded. "It all makes sense when I think about it. Her changes in behavior, her not being reachable by phone at times, her spending habits. I should have known something was wrong, but I didn't want to believe it. Didn't want to believe she'd do that our Phoebe."

Yeah, I should have seen it too. Would Edmund ever stop kicking himself for being so lust blind?

He glanced back at Jade and hoped she wouldn't think him less if she knew how he'd been so easily tricked.

"Okay, breathe in and hold, hold, hold your breath." Isaiah pushed the button and a loud clunk sounded from the machine. "Good, Phoebe."

As Isaiah backed the portable X-ray machine out of the room, Shelly removed the plate out from behind the child and handed it to him.

"I'll have your films in about five to ten, Jade."

"Thank you Isaiah. Excuse me, gentlemen." Jade moved by the two men to reposition the child higher in the bed. She brought an extra blanket and partially frozen apple juice and a spoon. She tapped the bedside monitor and the low hum of the blood pressure cuff inflating added to the noise. "Need to check your vitals. Thank you so much, Shelly, for helping with radiology."

"Phoebe, you think you can drink some of this? It's kind of like an Icee right now." Jade held up the juice as Shelly excused herself, pulling her phone out of her pocket and frantically typing as she approached the unit desk.

Edmund hoped Shelly would be okay.

Phoebe stretched and rubbed her tummy. "Yes, I'm a little hungry."

"Oh, good. That tells me your body needs fuel. See what you can do with this, but don't drink it too fast, okay?"

"Yes, ma'am." Holding up her Captain Marvel sticker, the child asked, "Do you like superheroes?"

"Love them." Jade sat on the edge of the bed and asked what Marvel movies the patient had seen and the two started a lively conversation of the last Avengers film.

"She's really good with kids." Mr. Stevenson raised an eyebrow. "I need to apologize to her."

"Yes, yes, you do." Edmund patted the man on the shoulder before walking away. *Mission accomplished.*

Within an hour, Phoebe slept soundly. Her cheeks now a light pink instead of bright red, her heart rate held steady around one hundred and her breathing less labored. As his daughter slept, Mr. Stevenson offered a heartfelt apology to both Lucy and Jade.

Jade stood next to him at the ER desk before walking into another patient's room. "I don't know what you said to him, but you must work some magic with those words, Dr. Davidson."

Leaning closer, he whispered, "Glad to do it."

"What did you say?"

"A magician never reveals his secrets. You'll have to guess."

Her eyes went wide. "I have a pretty good imagination. Asking me to come up with something could be…interesting."

His body burned from her flirtatious banter. "Good to know, Miss Carter."

Chapter Twelve

THE FOLLOWING DAY, Edmund started the computer orientation and got an extensive hospital tour. He only caught a glimpse of Jade when they passed through the ER. Following that, Edmund filled out piles of paperwork for human resources, went back on the computer to perfect the billing process until the end of the day.

Cross-eyed and mentally exhausted, he then grabbed a bite to eat at the diner and returned to his hotel room. There, he took a long shower where exhaustion mixed with jet lag. By the time he toweled off, he barely had enough strength to walk to the bed. Letting gravity take over, he fell into the sheets and immediately drifted off to sleep before checking his phone.

The next morning, he woke revived and ready to face the day. Glancing at the darkness out his window, he frowned.

No hint of the sun arising.

"What time is it? Four?" He groaned at his internal body clock waking him at the usual time, which would have been great if he'd still been on the East Coast.

Staring at the ceiling, Edmund wondered if he should get up or try and sleep another few hours, but real sleep would elude him.

No matter. Considering he'd suffered insomnia during the investigation, waking up a couple of hours early from the best night's rest he'd had in months was a mere blip in his morning.

Reaching for his phone, he noticed a few missed calls from Peter and Susan and one text that had his heart racing double-time.

Fred says hi. A selfie of Jade and Fred smiling at him.

He could get very used to seeing her face on his phone all the time. Hell, he could get very used to seeing her and her gorgeous smile every day.

I'd like to be the reason she smiles.

And that possibility bothered him.

Edmund had never considered himself a *catch* when it came to dating. His awkwardness with women had been called everything from freakish to cute to endearing, but never sexy or desirable, which was why he fell so hard for Reyna last year. After working together for two years, suddenly, the gorgeous doctor started batting her long eyelashes at him and blanketing him with compliments.

Edmund instantly fell in love with her.

Too bad her attraction to him had all been a ruse, to keep him distracted as she embezzled hundreds of thousands of dollars from the ER doctor partnership they, and five other physicians, were a part of.

As soon as she was caught, she lied about his involvement. It took weeks before the evidence proved his innocence and she finally admitted he hadn't a clue to what she had been doing.

But the damage had been done. He lost his job, friends, and the respect of his peers.

Clenching his fists beside him, he mumbled, "How could I have been so stupid? If I hadn't been thinking with my cock, I'd have seen what she'd been doing."

Edmund had mentally beaten himself up more than once over his past months of insanity and, every time, he'd decompress with a hard workout and a long run.

"Only four thirty." Darkness still held and the quiet of the hotel calmed his nerves. The lingering scent of the sandalwood soap he used last night drifted around him and the soft sheets caressed his naked body, all encouraging him back to sleep.

He looked at the picture on his phone again after setting the alarm.

What was it about Jade that had his attention so quickly? Unlike Reyna, she had nothing to gain by being with him. If anything, being Lucy's brother should be relationship repellant and yet, he clicked with her the moment he gazed into her beautiful eyes.

His eyelids finally became heavy enough to let him rest. He dreamed of their kiss and imagined where else he could put his lips on her until she cried out his name.

The timing of the phone alarm beeping couldn't have been more inconvenient since it interrupted his erotic dream about he and Jade doing creative things under the stars of a clear night.

As annoying as it was waking up with an erection hard

enough to hammer nails, he appreciated the effect Jade had on him since he'd been certain he'd never feel like, much less lust for, another woman after Reyna.

Being threatened with jail time because of your lover's illegal activities can certainly kill a libido.

After a quick shower, he dressed and waited for the first rays of sunshine to peek over the horizon before heading downstairs to the hotel gym. A quick round of free weights and body weight exercises later, he asked the front desk staff the best routes to take for a run. They gave him some ideas and handed him a water bottle before he headed out into the cool, crisp morning.

He gasped when the air hit his face. Summertime in Florida would have held humid temperatures in the seventies or eighties at six thirty in the morning.

Here, the air held little moisture and had to be no higher than the sixties.

During his first lap he ran down Front Street, by the Palace Movie Theater, the Chinese restaurant and Big Z's hardware store. Then made a right after the fire house, continued on Fourth Street, past the public schools and rec center and a right on Bramble Lane. Running down the sidewalk, he became lost in thought of the quiet of the morning until the faint, familiar bark caught his attention.

Looking up, he saw Fred in the window of the small bungalow house. With his slobbery nose pressed against the glass, Fred's tail wagged furiously as he looked as though he expected Edmund to take him along.

The front porch light still glowed, but it didn't appear

anyone was up.

She probably will be after all that noise.

Giving the dog a wave, Edmund continued around Bramble Park to Court Street.

He gave a wave to Gabby, Trinity, and Flo as he passed the diner. Once this run was done, he had every intension of coming here for breakfast.

As soon as he hit Front Avenue, the Graff came into view and the sun had come out to say good morning. Taking a second lap, he increased his speed, but slowed when he came close to Jade's house. This time, Fred wasn't at the window and the porch light was off.

She must be up.

With a good burn to his muscles, he kicked in a notch to finish his run, get back to shower, and possibly invite Jade to breakfast before it got too late in the morning when he heard a familiar bark followed by a distressing yelp.

"Fred?" Running through the park, he found Fred cowering behind a bush and a disheveled man yanking on Fred's leash.

"Come on, you piece of shit."

"Hey." Edmund wiped the line of sweat off his forehead with the back of his hand. "What the hell are you doing?"

The guy turned around, a cigarette hung loosely from his lips. "What's it to you?"

Fred's ears perked up and he tentatively wagged his tail as Edmund approached.

Anger raced through Edmund's veins as he jerked the leash from the man's dirty hands. "I'm a friend of Jade's and this is her dog."

"Oh, yeah? Well, I'm her brother and—"

"Her brother?" Lucy's story about the unruly patient from a couple of months ago played through Edmund's head. "Junior."

"Yeah and who the hell are you?" He tried to grab the leash back, but Edmund kept it out of reach.

"Lucy's brother."

"Who?"

"Dr. Davidson. The one who treated you at the ER after your car accident."

A wicked grin spread across his face. "Oh, sugar tits."

"What did you say?" Edmund stepped nose to nose but backed away due to Junior's halitosis.

"She still smokin' hot?"

Edmund clenched his jaw so tightly, it hurt. "Didn't she kick your ass?"

His arrogance faded. "Fuckin' whatever. Keep the stupid dog. Pick up his shit. Woke me up anyway." The smell of stale alcohol and pot sat in the air between them. The hard lines on the man's face illustrated his destructive life choices. "I'm going back to bed."

Damn, Jade had to deal with this before dealing with her abusive husband? "Bed? You should be going to work."

The dingy clothes on his body hung loosely and he appeared not to have showered in a few days. "I don't work."

"Figures."

A few cars drove by, but the morning traffic remained light.

"Did you also figure that I don't give a shit, Paul Bunyan?" He flicked the still lit cigarette in a bush. His yellowed fingertips were a sign of his chronic smoking, another drain on the pocketbook.

Whose pocketbook could be anyone's guess.

Crushing the cigarette with the toe of his shoe, Edmund fumed. "Figured that too, but I do give a shit that you're staying at Jade's. Does she know you're there?"

"She's my sister."

"So?"

"That means I don't need an invitation. I can show up when I want."

"Did she give you a key, or did you break in?"

The confidence he held a moment ago, slightly waned. Junior looked around, panic flashed through his eyes. "You a cop?"

Edmund's grip on the leash increased as the foul taste of angst coated the back of his tongue. "I'm a friend of hers from work."

"Then, I don't have to tell you shit. Get the fuck out of my face, dog walker."

Something cold touched Edmund's fingers. He looked down to see Fred nudging his hand. Edmund immediately patted the dog's head.

Fred sighed as he leaned against Edmund's leg as though he were relieved to be in safe company. "Where's Jade?"

"She went into work early. Left me with that thing."

"If you broke in after she went to work, she didn't leave you with anything. You can slice it anyway you want, but you're still breaking and entering." He patted the dog's head. "And his name is Fred."

An evil smirk spread across his face as his eyes were soulless, void of compassion. "He'll be Dead Fred if he wakes me up again."

That, I don't doubt.

The steady thump of the dog's tail wagging against the grass pulled Edmund away from the disgusting man who walked back into Jade's house and yelled, "I hate dogs," before slamming the door.

The car that cruised by the front of the diner, causing Jade to ball up her napkin, had been parked in front of Jade's house.

So it's Junior's. No wonder she stressed seeing him in town.

As soon as Jade's brother was out of sight, Fred perked up and began pulling on the leash to look around for squirrels. "Wait Fred. We need to call, Jade."

Pulling out his phone, he quickly dialed. She answered on the second ring.

"Well, that's a nice name to see on my phone this early in the morning."

The purr in her voice had him mentally stumbling over his words for a moment before he could say anything. "Sorry I didn't call after you texted. I fell asleep when I got back to the hotel."

"I'm not surprised. You've had a lot going on since you arrived."

"Jade. It's about Fred."

"Oh, no, he got out. Did he get hit by a car?" She

paused. "Wait, why are you calling me about this?"

"Out on my run this morning I met your brother and Fred at the park."

A long sigh. "Good grief. Junior's at my house? Did he at least have Fred on a leash or was he just running wild?"

"Your brother or the dog?"

"Ha-ha. I wish I could keep my brother on a leash, but I mean, Fred."

At least she's not in denial about her brother being a piece of crap. "No, he was on a leash." *But I'm pretty sure your brother hurt him.*

Glancing up, Edmund noticed Junior standing in the front window. As soon as he saw Edmund, Junior flipped him the middle finger before disappearing into the home.

You need a good ass-kicking.

"Damn, and he doesn't even have a key," Jade muttered. "Please tell me the police didn't see him."

Why would she ask that? "Not that I saw, but he did ask me if I was a cop."

"I swear, my brother is the reason I need hair color."

"Your hair is beautiful, Jade. Like dark chocolate." He hadn't meant to say it, but when she thanked him, he made a mental note to say things like that more often.

"Thank you, Edmund, but did he hurt my dog? I'll kill him if he did."

"Fred's fine, but I don't think he likes your brother, much." A hard yank on the leash sent Edmund running sideways.

Fred strained against his collar to chase a squirrel at the

far side of the park.

"My brother's not really patient with Fred. He doesn't like dogs in general. I know he won't be nice about Fred's barking while he's trying to sleep."

Then you know your brother doesn't have a job. "What do you want me to do?"

"I have to finish this charting and I have a QA meeting until noon."

"I can't keep him at the hotel." Sweat dripped in his eyes as he walked the dog around the park. "And I don't trust your brother to keep him."

"Oh, gosh no. Wait, where are you right now?"

"At the park across the street from your house." Pulling Edmund along, Fred finally settled at the base of the same tree he ran to when he jumped out of Edmund's car a few days ago.

Looking up into the empty branches, the dog barked and wagged his tail.

"I don't think he's up there, Fred." Edmund scratched Fred behind the ears.

Without taking his eyes off the tree, the dog leaned into Edmund's hand.

"He's at that tree again, isn't he?" Jade asked.

"Yes." Edmund chuckled, watching the dog scan the branches.

"Can you give me a couple of minutes? I have a friend who might be able to come get him."

Sitting back on his haunches, Fred appeared to give up on finding a tree rodent today. Edmund gently pulled on the leash and the dog followed without discussion. "I'll see if I can run with him, get him tired while you figure this out."

"I really owe you, Edmund. *A lot.*"

His body tingled at what that could mean. "Glad to do it."

"I'm sure Fred appreciates it too."

"How could I refuse Fred?" The dog gazed at him with adoring eyes. Who wouldn't want to help the slobbery canine?

"I'm really glad you're here, Edmund. What would I do without you?"

"You can thank you me later."

"Oh, you can count on that, *Dr. Davidson.*"

Chapter Thirteen

A S THE THRILL of Jade's sexy tone ran up his spine, Edmund soaked in the invincibility her attention gave him. He'd always wanted that kind of relationship like his parents had before his father died. One that made him feel bulletproof, cared about. Loved.

Loved? What the hell, dude?

After being too casually thrown aside by Reyna, Edmund wondered if that would ever be possible for him. Could he ever open his heart to the possibility of trusting anyone?

If he'd been asked a few days ago, it would be an emphatic *no*, but something about the way Jade looked at him, kissed him, made Edmund think twice about refusing to believe in his potential for happily ever after.

Apparently, they do exist. But he knew he was getting ahead of himself.

I'm just helping with her dog. While jogging down Bramble Lane at a faster than average speed, Fred kept up step for step, intermittently barking his approval of the run.

When they reached Community Park near the high school, both he and Fred were panting, but Edmund felt revived.

Edmund loved the burn in his muscles and how sweat poured off his body after a hard workout. Fred pulled on his leash until they reached the grass and found a few trees worth marking.

After finishing off the water bottle, Edmund rested his hands on his thighs as he caught his breath. Edmund absorbed how much easier the morning run felt in the cooler, less humid summertime air. It only made the time here far more appealing and increased his interest of staying longer than his contract.

Come winter, he'd probably have to stay inside on the treadmill.

The idea of even considering staying here bothered him more than he wanted to admit. When he arrived, his long-term plans for Marietta were to get this assignment done as fast as possible, get some reliable work back on his resume, and move back to warmer climates.

But that was before Fred sat in his car.

Before he met the people who lived here.

Before he knew how mind-blowing Jade's kisses could be.

Even now, the anticipation of seeing her again had him feeling like a teenage boy before his first date.

Spotting a water fountain out of the corner of his eye, Edmund made a bee-line for it to refill the bottle and get Fred a bit to drink.

A few giggles and young voices caught Edmund's attention. Several kids walked over from the elementary and middle school's direction and headed toward the rec center.

Fred barked and wagged his tail at the approaching crowd.

A young girl and boy ran to meet them as Edmund grabbed a quick drink. Cupping his hand, Edmund filled it with water and offered it to the dog, who happily accepted and drooled all over his hand.

"Is this your dog? He's cool looking." One young man asked as he ran his hand down Fred's back. "He's really soft."

Wiping the slobbered covered hand on his shirt, Edmund shook his head before filling the water bottle to the top. "No, it's my friend's dog."

"That's nice that you would help a friend." A little, dark-haired girl smiled at him and tenderly rubbed Fred's ear between her fingers. "We all need good friends."

The dog moaned and leaned into the child.

"Looks like you made a new one." Edmund chuckled.

"You're tall. Are you a basketball player? You've got big muscles in your arms. Do you lift trees like Shaq?"

"No, he's an ER doctor." Trinity came out of the rec center and motioned for the kids to come inside. "That's Dr. Davidson."

The little girl furrowed her brow. "But we already have a Dr. Davidson. It's Dr. Lucy Davidson."

"I'm her brother, Dr. Edmund Davidson."

"Oh!" The child's eyes grew wide. "I like Dr. Lucy Davidson. She helped me when I stuck a bean up my nose and when my friend Louis stuck a rock up his nose."

The honesty and kindness of children were never with motive or agenda and it always warmed Edmund's heart.

Unlike the jerk that was probably sleeping on Jade's couch right now.

"My sister is great at getting beans and rocks out of noses." Edmund smirked.

"But how is she so short and you so tall?"

Edmund had heard this question more than once and gladly, he stood taller than all his siblings. "I think my mom ate a lot of broccoli when she had me in her stomach."

"Oh! That makes sense." The child nodded as a few around her agreed.

"Nice to meet you, Dr. Davidson." Giving Fred a final scratch, the young man gave him a high five as he entered the rec center. "I'm William. This is my sister, Pippa."

"Good to meet you, William. Pippa."

"Our sister, Poppy, is going to be a nurse," William added. "She works with Dr. Davidson."

The familiar smiles immediately reminded Edmund of the perky and smart nurse's aide. "I met Poppy, yesterday. She looks nice."

"She really is." Pippa leaned her forehead against Fred's. "She helps make my lunch when my mom can't. She's super smart because she can come up with all sorts of cool ways to make peanut butter and jelly sandwiches in all these cool shapes."

"That is important to know."

As all of the children introduced themselves and gave Edmund a high five, he could see why a town like Marietta would be so attractive to so many. The warm welcome from some of the youngest residents said a lot about the people here.

Pippa gave Fred a final hug. "See you later, Fred."

"Okay, kids. Go ahead and grab your seats." Trinity pointed inside.

Edmund held the door open for the last of the students. "I thought I saw you at the diner this morning."

"I was, but helped Gabby open then walked down here after Casey arrived. I'm teaching drawing today. Keep the kids busy twice a week during summer break. I'll be at Harry's House this afternoon."

Harry's House? Why did that sound so familiar? His brow furrowed as Fred sniffed around the doorway of the classroom.

Pointing out the large window, Trinity smiled. "It's around the corner from the Java Café on Church Avenue."

The image of the flyer flashed across his mind. "The art show."

"Exactly. Many of the kids here have artwork on display there for the fundraiser."

"I drew a shark eating a surfer." William gave a thumbs-up.

"I painted a sunset with a unicorn in a baseball and ballerina outfit," Pippa added. "It took me forever."

Edmund's eyebrows raised in mock surprise. "That sounds very complicated, Pippa."

Fred lay down on the cool tiled floor and sighed.

The sunshine poured in as each student found a seat and one inquired what medium they'd work with today.

Trinity held up her elegant, brightly stained hands. "This

lesson, we're working with grease pencils."

"Sounds like fun." Edmund peeked his head inside the room.

The walls had large, brightly painted murals with animals, famous figures, and inspiring quotes that were perfectly positioned around the room.

"She believed that she could, so she did," Edmund said out loud.

"That's my favorite quote. Describes a lot of situations. Potential." Trinity beamed. "Believing in yourself can be the hardest and most empowering thing."

"That is true. Believing in one's potential can be difficult." *More than I care to admit.*

"I like the Dr. Seuss ones," Pippa added and recited the quote about the places she would go.

Plenty of natural light flowed from the open windows as the cool air gently floated in and the kids found their chairs after putting on art aprons.

An unobstructed view of the mountain range sat outside the windows that faced Bramble Street. Edmund wished he could have sat in a room like this to learn when he was in elementary school. "Who painted the room?"

Trinity beamed. "I did. It took me all school year. I'd come here after school and on the weekends."

"Impressive."

"Thanks. You're welcome to join us."

"Yes, Dr. Davidson. Please stay." Pippa jumped, her ponytail bobbing up and down.

Before he could say yes, a beep to his phone distracted

him.

Brett Adams is coming by to get Fred. He'll meet you at the park in five.

"Sorry, kids, I've got to go." Fred barked in protest as Edmund typed back a response.

A collective groan of sadness filled the room.

Edmund waved before he stepped out of the doorway. "But I'll be back to take a class with you guys. When are you here again?"

Fred reluctantly jumped to his feet.

"We're here again this time next week, Dr. Davidson, but come when you can." Trinity held up a piece of paper. "Okay, guys, eyes on me…"

"Come on, Fred. Let's beat our last time." With the leash securely in his hand, Edmund and Fred jogged back toward Jade's house. Fred kept a steady pace and a happy demeanor.

Seeing the excitement in the dog's eyes when they ran full force down the sidewalk enforced Jade's concerns of Fred needing more than the yard at the house.

Edmund wondered if he could come by and get Fred on the mornings he wasn't working to help her out.

And won't that score brownie points? Laughing at his own humor, Edmund had to admit his offer wouldn't be completely altruistic. He did want to spend more time with her and if the dog liked him, that was more likely to happen.

No sooner had they passed First Street, when a truck pulled up next to them with Marietta PD K9 Unit written on the side.

Edmund and Fred stopped at Fred's favorite tree and the

dog looked up for the squirrels as if the rodents would be waiting for him.

A burly guy with K9 on his baseball cap rolled down his window. "You Edmund?"

"Yes." Edmund panted as he took a swig of his water bottle before pouring some in his cupped hand for Fred. The dog greedily lapped the water as his tail wagged.

The police officer exited the truck as a head popped up behind the passenger side window. A large German shepherd pressed his nose against the glass and happily barked.

Fred's ears piqued and he trotted over to the truck. Without pause, he stood on his hind legs, his face pressed against the opposite side of the window.

"Brett." The owner shook Edmund's non-slimed hand. "Friend of Jade's. She just called me; said Fred needed a place to hang out today."

"Thanks. I know Fred would rather stay with you than with her brother."

Brett's eyebrow cocked and he pointed toward Jade's house. "Junior? He's here?"

"He's the reason I have Fred. I was jogging by, heard Fred yelp and Junior yanking on his leash."

The muscles in Brett's jaw clenched. "Son of a bitch."

"Then you've met him?"

"More times than I care to." Pulling out his phone, Brett's fingers flew across the screen and he tucked it back into his pocket. "Thanks for helping. Junior's got a warrant out for his arrest for missing a court date."

Of course he does. "He do that kind of stuff often?"

"Enough to where he has to get an attorney to come in from Bozeman to bail him out every time because no one within a sixty mile radius will."

"Every time? This a regular thing?"

"He should have a punch card for every time he's been arrested."

No wonder she asked if the police had seen him. Having a felon for a family member had to be exhausting. "What about Jade? How does she handle it?"

"She's told him to get his head out of his ass, but it doesn't matter. Junior's gonna do what he's gonna do. He'd screw her over if it saved him." Brett let out a long breath. "Thankfully, he hasn't hurt anyone too bad so far. A lot of juvie stuff in high school. In the past few years, some bar fights. He punched Dr. McAvoy a couple of months ago. One DUI and the only reason he got caught was he hit a deer then a tree. The car wasn't drivable after impact."

"Lucy mentioned someone hitting Thomas." He thumbed toward Jade's house.

"Yep, that's the court date he missed. Assault."

A familiar police car pulled up in front of the house and Logan Tate and a second officer got out.

Logan yelled, "He inside, Doc?"

"Last I saw." *Great. I save her dog, but turn her brother in to the police.*

One step forward. Two steps back.

Brett slapped Edmund on the back. "You might want to wait out here."

Chapter Fourteen

IMPRESS THE CUTE doctor with my ER skills and then my brother gets arrested in front of him. How fab-frickin'-fantastic.

The list of why she shouldn't allow this relationship to advance any further rolled through her mind to the tune of "The History of Wrong Guys."

One. My brother's a felon.

Two. He's never going to be any different.

Three. Edmund doesn't deserve to be pulled into this.

Jade fought back tears as she sat on the floor of her living room while trying to convince herself that as much as her brother blustered and yelled, he wouldn't be violent.

But today, he hit a police officer. Sheriff Rob Shaw to be exact and then resisted arrest with Deputy Logan Tate.

He might as well have a reoccurring role on Cops!

The TV still played the pawnshop reality show series her brother had been watching when Logan knocked.

Must have been a TV marathon day.

Empty beer bottles laid or sat upright next to her couch. Multiple empty candy wrappers were wadded and tossed on the side table.

And he ate all my chocolate. Jerk.

Fred greedily ate the spilled popcorn that had probably been scattered when Junior realized who stood at the front door.

Snorting as he worked, her dog enjoyed a small break from chewing the flaps in the cardboard boxes that she'd opened, but hadn't completely unloaded.

She pointed to a few popped kernels near the TV. "Over there, Fred."

He happily obliged.

The best she could tell, Junior had been sitting on the couch with a bowl of popcorn and a belly full of beer and candy, when Logan knocked. As soon as the officer called out to him, he chunked the bowl across the floor and took off out the back and ran right into Rob Shaw, knocking him to the ground.

Then he punched the sheriff in the face for good measure.

Why do you keep dragging me into your shitty choices? She slammed her fists on the floor even thinking about it.

Pain shot up her arm and she cringed, cradling her fist in her lap thinking of Junior trying to haul ass down the street in bare feet.

Due to his three-pack-a-day smoking habit, Junior had a coughing fit within two blocks and sat down in the middle of the sidewalk at Bramble and Third Streets, right in front of Paramedic Kyle Cavasos's house.

After a brief scuffle with Logan, Junior gave up, not that it would have mattered if he had kept running. Duke, and probably Fred, would have happily chased her brother down and bitten him square in the ass, before pinning him to the sidewalk. It would have been poetic justice too since her brother hated dogs.

What a dumbass.

The biggest kicker? Edmund had seen all of it.

I'm sure that made a wonderful impression. He'll be begging to go out with me now.

And as much as she hoped whatever instant chemistry she had with Edmund could have continued, her mind and soul were too exhausted from her brother's stupidity to cry about it.

Pushing herself to her feet, she grabbed the trash can and began cleaning up his mess. "Just like I always do." She sniffled as tears flowed freely at the fallout of visiting him at the police station.

Her hands still shook from their confrontation when he demanded she bail him out. Because he was a flight risk, had skipped his court date, his previous run-ins with local law enforcement, and now assault on two police officers, Judge McCorkle set his bail so high, he might as well have denied offering any.

The only way Jade could come up with that kind of money was to quick sell their father's place as is. That meant all the items in the buildings would be handed over to the new owner and Junior would have to wait in jail until the ink was dry on the contracts, whenever that might happen.

The intense fury in Junior's eyes alarmed Jade so fiercely that she waited for him to shoot fire out of his nose. "What is wrong with you?"

He didn't explain, but leapt to his feet and began to come over the table at her. "You stay the hell away, do you hear me? That building is mine. Go get the money so I can get out of here."

Brett and Rob wrestled her brother back to his cell, but his voice carried all the way down the hall, right to the front door as he mocked her for pulling the trigger in San Diego.

As if that had been anything I wanted to do.

To make the entire situation worse, when Jade looked up, the local town gossip, Betty, stood there and gave her a pitying look.

God, how I hate the pity.

She'd gotten the same look when she'd been removed from her mother and stepfather's house all those years ago and when she returned to work after she shot her husband in an act of self-defense.

I didn't need their pity. I needed their help. Their compassion.

Only Thomas had come through for her. Jade would be forever thankful, but not even Thomas would be able to help shield her from the gossip that would have spread like wildfire by now.

Jade had no doubt, Betty bided her time until Jade was well out of hearing range before calling at least three people on her rumor-has-it tree and they'd be having a fine time at Jade's expense.

Junior's arrest will probably be on the front page of the paper.

Burying her face in her hands as she collapsed on the couch, Jade sobbed at the entire, stupid situation.

She'd planned to help her father by working sixty hours a week during her San Diego assignment. The nice nest egg she'd saved had been for the house she planned to build on her dad's property, but that got derailed when her husband treated her like a punching bag and tried to kill her and her best friend.

Then her father died, alone and uncared for because Junior bailed on his responsibilities.

Half of her nest egg had been spent on an attorney when she had to defend herself against her abusive husband then an unsympathetic district attorney.

Acquitted and widowed, she returned to town to read the will, only to discover her father hadn't paid taxes on the property for the last few years and left her as sole beneficiary, much to Junior's disgust.

She tried to appease her father's wishes by getting the house livable, but because Dad hadn't fixed anything either, that took money as well. Repairs and paying the back taxes drained what she had left.

Once again, she'd made a plan to her life goals of getting back to living in Marietta, but taken detour after detour on the worst, pothole filled paths.

Fred hopped on the couch and rested his head on her lap.

Someone on the TV ranted about how their grandmother's teapot set had to be worth more than twenty-five dollars.

Jade rubbed the bridge of her nose as she tried to coax

herself to stop crying, but the stressors were making it increasingly difficult to remain calm.

As of now, she was a mere four paychecks ahead and now her brother wanted her to give up everything to bail him out for being a complete and total dumbass.

Again.

"Fred, why is my life such a mess?"

A lone beer bottle sat on top of the fireplace mantel.

"Why do I keep letting my little brother back into my life?"

Fred's soulful eyes rested on her before he let out a quick exhale that sounded a lot like, "Really? You don't know?"

"I know, I know, but unless James plans to give up his life in Alaska and move back here, which he won't, it's just you and me." She patted his head. "And I love you, but you're not a person."

His head popped up and he cocked it as if to say, "I'm not?"

No father. No brothers. No husband.

No one.

Sadness lodged in her throat, almost strangling her. "I hate being alone, but I guess I have to be if I'm going to survive."

"What about Edmund?" a voice in the back of her mind whispered.

Beautiful, delightful, quirky, sexy Edmund.

A man who deserved a woman that wasn't a walking Jackie Collins novel heroine. Even after his reassuring and kind words, how could Edmund see past the disaster that always seemed to follow her around?

"Why on earth would he want me now?" The soul-crushing realization that her entire core family had left her slammed down on her body. She slid to the floor and pulled her knees to her chest.

Fred unapologetically stretched across the couch for a moment before hopping off the couch and lying beside her on the floor, resting his muzzle on her shoulder.

"Thanks, Fred." She whimpered.

As the pawnshop show continued, Jade allowed the heaviness of her problems to lay over her, pinning her in place, making it difficult to breathe. She fought it, but couldn't push it away, as she sobbed.

Grabbing for air, she tried to move, but nothing worked.

Fred whimpered and licked her hand, pulling her out of her self-imprisonment.

She gave the dog a scratch behind the ears before pushing herself off the floor, turning off the TV, and curling up on the couch where she cried herself to sleep.

Chapter Fifteen

SEEING JUNIOR BEING led away by the local authorities brought back embarrassing memories of being arrested in front of his colleagues. Edmund shook his head at how blindly he'd believed Reyna, his former lover, after she told him everything he wanted to hear.

You're so much smarter than Peter.

You're so much better than your sisters.

You've got a great financial portfolio.

She enchanted him with her sexual creativity and plied him with homemade sweet, chewy candies as a way to express her affections, all the while, stealing money from the practice using his login information that he'd so willingly told her.

"What a witch," he mumbled as he walked through the aisles of the pharmacy.

Yet, it had been his own ego that had been his downfall. Despite the warning from his siblings, he refused to remove blinders when it came to Reyna.

For too long, he'd wanted someone to see him for who he was and not anyone's younger sibling or business partner.

He wanted a gorgeous woman on his arm. The kind of

beauties his brother, Peter, so easily attracted.

To feel like a king when he walked in a room, not the court jester and not the spare. "Should have known it was too good to be true."

As soon as he realized what she'd done, the wolves had already begun to circle. He'd turned her in, but it had almost been too late. For months, he fought to prove his innocence and that ruined his professional reputation and credibility.

To their credit, his siblings stood united with him, even bailing him out when he'd been arrested. His stepfather had been a silent supporter and for all of them, Edmund would be forever grateful, but damn, if he didn't feel layers of shame that threatened to bury him.

Marietta had been the unexpected answer to his prayers, but the town had given him more than a professional second chance.

The possibility of learning to trust again.

Jade. What she had to be going through right now with her brother. Even though Junior was obviously guilty, the embarrassment of him being arrested in broad daylight had to have stung.

Taking his phone out, he checked for texts. His shoulders slumped when the screen came up empty.

He'd hoped she would have reached out to him by now, but he could understand her not wanting to. Gathering a few more items in the pharmacy, he tossed in a couple of chocolate bars, the same kind of chocolate he'd seen the empty wrappers of in her living room.

Double-checking his items, he began to head toward the

front, but stopped when a hushed voice mentioned Jade's name.

"It was so sad. How Junior Carter treated his sister."

Immediately his ears perked up. Moving silently, he made his way to the front as they spoke.

"Oh, Betty. I can't imagine."

Looking around the corner, two older women each with their elbows on the counters, faced each other.

Those had to be the town gossips Logan mentioned. They appeared to be having a serious talk about Junior's meltdown, his transfer to county lockup, and how Jade couldn't afford to pay for bail.

"Not that she should, Betty. That brother of hers is trouble with a cap-i-tal *T*," the woman behind the counter said.

Okay, if that's Betty, Carol must be the other one. Didn't Logan say she worked at the pharmacy?

"Carol, as if Jade hasn't had enough pain in her life with her moving here when she was a teenager. Her mother in jail and now her brother." Betty sighed and dramatically shook her head though. "Guess that bad apple didn't fall far from the tree. So sad."

Anger bubbled in his gut at their blatant and very public gossip session. He well remembered the whispered discussions that stopped when he walked into a room, before he'd been put on administrative leave. How some seemed to relish in his downfall. How he hated feeling so powerless, so unable to discuss anything or vent to anyone, including his siblings since his attorney advised him to keep them ignorant of the details of the case.

Betty added, "But it looks like thankfully, Jade and James inherited their father's good nature. Let's hope they've got enough of their father in them to keep them out of trouble."

Edmund began to come around the corner to confront them when he heard Carol say, "It's a shame too, because she really seems to have potential, but she just can't seem to pick a good man to save her life."

For a second, Edmund wanted to scream, "I'm a good man!" But would his past cloud her trust of him? He pushed the idea aside.

"Good afternoon, ladies." Edmund stepped forward before they continued their gossip.

Both women gasped, apparently unaware he had even been in the store.

"Oh, my Lord! You scared us." Carol rested her hand on her chest. "How in the world did you sneak up on us? You're too tall to hide behind anything."

"Don't do that!" Betty fanned herself. "I about passed out."

"Hard to pay attention when you're talking about people who aren't present to defend themselves. Can you ring me up, please?" He placed his purchases on the counter, which included mouthwash, dental floss, bars of chocolates, and a twelve-pack box of wishful thinking.

"We're not...I mean it's not as though it's not public knowledge." Betty nervously adjusted her necklace.

"Not after you two talking about it in such a public

place."

"You have condoms, I see." Carol attempted twice before she peeled the two dollars off coupon with a church lady glare. "Just peel that manufacturer's coupon for those pro-phy-lac-tics."

Ironic. "You having a fun discussion at the expense of others?"

Chagrin stained Betty's face as she cleared her throat. "Yes, well, you must be a tourist. It's not anything most of the town folk don't already know about Jade and her fami-ly."

"When you two talk about it where anyone can hear, I'd guess not." *Two can play that game, lady.* It was times like this, Edmund appreciated his natural ability to say what others were thinking and not feel one bit guilty about it.

His sister Susan always told him it was his honest soul shining through.

Narrowing her eyes at him, Carol's lips thinned, her finger tapped on the box. "Well, I don't see—"

"Mrs. Phillips, or should I say Miss Carter, takes care of people all day in the ER and helps the community. Her private life is neither of your concerns." He rested his hands on the counter. "Now, if you can ring up my purchases without judgment, I'll be out of your hair."

Both women stood there, their drawn-on eyebrows somewhere near their hairlines. With trembling hands, Carol rang Edmund up as she quickly threw things in a paper bag.

"Well, I never!" Betty stomped her foot as he turned to leave.

"Maybe if you had, you'd need those condoms." Edmund tossed the cash on the counter, grabbed his items, and left without waiting for change.

Walking out of the pharmacy, he exhaled a long breath and laughed nervously. "Lucy's gonna hear about that one."

Maybe the hospital directors, Denver Sinclair and Ethan Watson might disapprove of what he said to the two harpies, but Edmund remembered Logan's warning and decided not to give his worries a second thought.

As he walked down Main Street, the smells of grilled meats and salt coaxed him across the street to the newest restaurant in town, Rosita's.

"Tacos. Nice." With his stomach growling, he crossed the street and walked into the place.

Large archways allowed plenty of room for customers and waitstaff to move through. Colorful paintings and blankets hung about the room, as a few TVs sat in a couple of corners with one behind the bar.

The perfect combination of freshly cut vegetables and grilled meats made his mouth water.

"Doc! Come on over." Logan Tate waved as he sat with a pretty woman who had a camera in her lap.

Edmund scanned the room before he realized who spoke to him and joined them. "Logan, good to see you again."

"Edmund. This is Charlie, my girlfriend."

"Nice to meet you, Charlie." He pointed to her camera as he sat down. "Like photography?"

"She's one of the best in the country. The world in my opinion."

Pink colored her cheeks. "He's a bragger, but I am pretty good."

The melodious British accent hadn't been what Edmund expected to find in Marietta. "Guess you're not from here either."

"Correct." She pressed a few buttons on her camera before snapping a photo of him. "Lovely."

"Charlie. What are you doing?" Logan's eyes went wide.

"What? He's got an incredible jawline and look at his shoulders. Arms. He looks like a dark-haired Armie Hammer." She playfully fanned herself as her boyfriend gave her a sideways glance. "If there's another calendar, you should absolutely pose."

"Really, Charlie?" Logan raised an eyebrow as the waiter brought Edmund a glass of water, refilled Logan and Charlie's drinks and replenished the chips. "You just met the man and now you're gonna embarrass him? Ask him to take his clothes off?"

Giving him a doe-eyed look, she rested her hand on his arm. "It's for charity."

Edmund wouldn't deny it was nice to be appreciated for all the hours he'd exercised, but no guy wanted to hear about how great he was from a woman whose boyfriend sat right there. Especially when the boyfriend was a police officer.

Edmund decided to appreciate it silently. "Calendar?"

"They needed to raise money for Harry's House."

"Where the after-school program is?"

Charlie's eyes sparkled. "Yes! These guys needed to raise a lot of money for it and I suggested a calendar."

"How'd it do?" Edmund popped a few chips in his mouth after dipping them into the salsa.

"Sold out and raised more than enough to fix the foundation and have extra for a year of operating costs." Leaning over, she gave Logan a kiss on the cheek. "My lawman here posed."

"I wasn't excited about it." Logan shook his head, but a hint of pink stained his cheeks.

"But you're so incredible in it. His brother, a few guys from the fire station, and a couple of the ER doctors, Tom Reynolds, Gavin Clark, they were also in it. Honestly, if they do it again, I'm putting you down for a month. You look like a summer or fall month. How about September?"

"Charlie." Logan growled. "The man just sat down. He hasn't even said he would."

"Of course he will. I'm an artist and I know when I see something gorgeous and you, my friend, would help us sell many calendars...for a good cause of course." She snapped another photo of Edmund as he laughed nervously. Holding the camera away from her face, she smiled as she scrolled through the pictures. "Oh, this is lovely. I can't wait to get it on my computer at home. See it full screen."

Internally cringing, Edmund assumed the photos wouldn't be complementary. He'd always taken rotten pictures, mainly because he didn't know how to smile without looking like he'd been Tasered. "Thanks, Charlie."

Logan rested his hand on Charlie's arm as he smirked at Edmund. "If you're gonna order, I suggest the *enchiladas verdes*."

As nice as it was to receive the invite, Logan's protective gesture on Charlie had Edmund wanting his food for takeout. "Thanks, but I'm getting something to go."

Because three's a crowd.

Giving him a knowing nod, Logan winked. "Taking it to Jade, I'd guess. Nice of you. She needs someone looking out for her."

What a great idea. "Yes, that was the plan."

"You're *seeing*, Jade?" Charlie raised an eyebrow after snapping another picture.

The way Charlie stressed seeing, made Edmund's mouth go dry. What were they doing anyway? Should he even encourage this friendship if he didn't plan to stay? "I helped her with her dog."

"Oh, you're the one Logan mentioned. Fred was in your car, right?"

"Yep. That was me." Holding up the pharmacy bag, Edmund nodded. "Picked up some chocolate bars and now getting some food to take over."

"Nicely played, but next time, get some from Copper Mountain Chocolates. Their sea salt caramels are worth dying for." Charlie gave him a thumbs-up as she moved a dial around on her camera and pushed a few more buttons.

Logan agreed. "She's right about the chocolates, but I think Jade would probably like some good company. She's had a rough day."

"I wish she'd accept her brother is a lost cause and walk away. Let him deal with the consequences of his actions." Charlie mumbled something about finding the right light in the restaurant.

A sickening feeling twisted Edmund's gut. Although his siblings stood beside him through the chaos of the accusations, he'd put them through unnecessary stressors and he'd been innocent. He couldn't imagine how Jade felt about her brother's propensity to break the law and blow off responsibility so easily. "Jade doesn't deserve this."

"No, she doesn't. None of it."

None of it? *Did Logan know about San Diego?* "Logan, Betty and Carol were talking over at the pharmacy—"

"And I bet they were talking about Jade's bad fortune, weren't they?" With his jaw clenched, Logan drummed his fingers on the table. "I need to talk to Betty about being discreet and keeping her nose out of everyone's business."

"Do you think it will do any good?" The corner of Charlie's mouth curled up as she kept looking at the screen of her camera.

"No, but I can't let it go unnoticed. She can't blab everything that goes on at the police station. People do deserve some privacy when dealing with that kind of shit." Logan took a healthy scoop of *salsa verde* with his chip before eating it in two bites. "What's wrong, Doc? Did they say something that bothered you? Damn, that's spicy."

Picking up another chip, Edmund shrugged. "Didn't like the way they were talking about her. She doesn't deserve that."

"I'll see what I can do about that." He took a long drink of his water.

The click of the camera caught Edmund off guard.

Logan put his hand on the front of the lens. "Charlie, stop it."

"Okay, but one more." She aimed and pushed the button as soon as Logan moved away and before Edmund had a chance to respond. "Oh, my gosh. My camera loves you."

Her excitement gave him hope he'd finally taken a decent picture. "Looking forward to seeing them."

"I'll make sure you and Jade each get copies." Snapping her fingers, Charlie nodded. "If you're feeling *really* generous, Doc, you might want to stop at the gift shop just down the sidewalk and pick up a couple of bath bombs for her. After a day like this, let her soak with a nice glass of wine in her hand and feed her those chocolates."

The entire idea of seeing Jade soaking in a bath with him at her side had him adjusting in his seat. Not that they were anywhere close to that in their *friendship*, but still. "You think she'd like that?"

"I know she'd like that."

Logan's forehead furrowed. "Didn't I do that for you last week?"

"Yes, you did and I loved every second of it." Charlie gave Logan a wink and kissed his cheek. "And I showed you how much I loved it. Twice."

Chapter Sixteen

WITHIN A HALF an hour, Edmund ordered a healthy amount of Mexican food, bought a bottle of wine, grabbed a couple of bath bombs—whatever those were— found a treat for Fred, and purchased some chocolates from Sage's store.

He quickly returned to the Graff, showered, and brushed his teeth. He filled the ice bucket from his hotel room to chill the wine before driving back to Rosita's to grab his order, and drive the short distance to Jade's.

Nervous as a kid on his first date, Edmund convinced himself to remain calm as he waited for her to answer the door, but anything to do with Jade had proven to be a challenge when it came to trying to keep things in true perspective.

Never in his thirty-plus years, had he ever been this worked up over impressing anyone.

Not his prom date or his medical school girlfriend.

Not even Reyna.

What was it about Jade that had him running up and down Main Street, purchasing things to make her rotten day, better?

Glancing down at the items in his hands, it suddenly hit him how much he'd brought and he wondered if he'd overdone it.

Before he could go put a few things back in the car, the door flew open.

"Edmund?" Her hair hung in a loose, messy ponytail. Her wrinkled scrubs looked like she'd slept in them. Her makeup smeared under her eyes, a sure sign she'd been crying.

Dammit, she shouldn't feel responsible for him. "Hungry?"

"What are you doing here?" She sniffled.

He hadn't expected her eyes to be clouded with defeat. "I thought you might like some company."

Sucking her bottom lip, she cringed. "Um, okay but I want to apologize for my brother's behavior today."

Frustration brewed in his veins. "Why are *you* apologizing? Your brother made a choice. It's his problem, not yours."

"Yeah, well, he has a great way of dragging me into it." She leaned against the doorframe and locked her arms across her chest. "Maybe we should put things on ice, you know. Maybe we shouldn't get involved."

"You and me getting involved? What does that have to do with your brother?"

Her brow furrowed like she'd heard him wrong. "Because, Junior's a part of my life and always will be. Why would a great guy like you want to be involved with someone who has this kind of chaos?"

"A great guy like me?" He placed the bags down at his

feet. "You give me too much credit."

"You're this wonderful flavor of vanilla."

"Vanilla? You think I'm vanilla?" *Man, I thought I was doing so well. Now I'm the most boring ice cream flavor. This is worse than being called cute.*

She held her hands up in surrender. "No, no, you don't understand. I like vanilla because it's a great solid foundation to build so many things on. So many wonderfully, delicious possibilities."

His mouth went dry and his jeans suddenly fit more snugly. "What are we talking about again?"

A playful smirk spread across her face while she ran her fingers through her hair, removing the ponytail holder. "You have siblings you can rely on. A family that adores you. You don't embarrass each other. None of you have been to jail—"

"Yes, I have." Edmund blurted. *Way to break it to her gently.*

Jade rolled her eyes. "Yeah, okay. You've been to jail. I'm not talking Monopoly jail, Edmund, I'm talking actual prison."

With his heart in his throat, he struggled to find the right words. "Did you wonder why I'd leave a big practice in Florida to come here?"

"To Nowhere, Marietta?" Her eyebrow arched.

"Jade, please." His fists clenched before he reached out, held his hand palm up. "Please, I need you to listen to me. Did you ever wonder why I came here?"

Her eyes darted from his face to his hand as she cautiously rested her palm against his. "I guess, but I figured you were here to help Lucy."

He swallowed hard at the warmth of her touch. One he would desperately miss after he told her the ugly truth and she slammed the door in his face. "I…I…"

"Edmund." She coaxed, her fingertips calmly stroked the base of his hand. "You're thinking too hard. It can't be that bad."

His rational and emotional brains combatted for dominance as she touched him. Exhaling a deep breath, he tried to focus on the perfect way to explain how he'd been a complete idiot. "I went to prison for embezzlement."

Jade snorted, but didn't move away. "Did you say embezzlement?"

"Yes, well, I was arrested for embezzlement."

"Well, that is bad. How long were you in jail?"

"About eight hours." Upon hearing it, he realized how absurd it sounded.

She bit her lip as he began to step back, her fingers wrapped around his wrist, holding him in place. "Now, *you* talk to *me*."

"I was part of a practice of seven other physicians. One had been siphoning money out of the practice into an offshore account. Hundreds of thousands of dollars before it was discovered."

She stepped out of the doorway and onto the porch, still holding his hand. "Let me guess. You being as smart as you are, figured out what was going on."

"Again, you give me too much credit. Some papers I wasn't supposed to see got mixed up with my quarterly statement. When I asked the doctor about an irregularity I'd found in some of the numbers, the answer didn't make sense." He clenched his teeth, playing it all in his head. "I kept asking questions. Kept getting answers that didn't work for me."

"And that happened to be the doctor that was stealing, wasn't it?"

"Yes. It all seems obvious now, but I didn't listen to my gut and because of that, I dragged my family through a media circus." Hearing the words out loud hit Edmund square in the chest, bruising his ego once again. "I trusted the wrong person. I screwed up."

"Did he pin it on you?" Her voice came out through clenched teeth as her fingers never released their tender grip. "Did he say you'd stolen it?"

Her protective reaction made the corner of Edmund's mouth twitch. "Yes, *she* did."

"She, huh?" Jade's eyes went wide with understanding. "*She* the one who you didn't want to tell me about?"

"She said I colluded with her after I turned everything over. She didn't make it easy for me and insisted I knew everything until evidence proved her otherwise. Then she confessed I'd been nothing but a patsy." The humiliation still stung. His head pounded from his admission as he stuffed his free hand in his pocket. "I dragged my brother, sisters, and stepfather through hell while trying to prove my innocence. And I did, but I lost my job, the respect of my colleagues and the medical community."

"Oh, gosh. How awful for you. How scary."

"Peter, Susan, Lucy, they had to justify their jobs, their innocence even though they'd done nothing."

Jade swallowed hard and held their hands against her chest. "Must have been difficult for them. Guilt by association."

"I had to start over. To regain who I am. Rebuild. That's why I came here."

"To Nowhere, Marietta."

"Yes," he said. "After dealing with all that chaos, I never thought I'd meet someone like you."

"Here?"

Reaching out, he moved a lock of hair behind her ear. "No. Ever."

Tears welled in her eyes. "Why are you telling me this, Edmund? You were innocent. My brother isn't."

"True, but you're not your brother no more than Lucy or Peter or Susan are me. We all have our own choices to make, responsibilities to keep, lives to live. I know, despite my mistakes, I deserve a good life. So do you. So do *we*."

"We?" In a split second, the despair in her hazel tear-filled eyes turned to hope. "You still want to consider a we?"

"I never stopped." After a quick kiss to the back of her hand, he grabbed the bags he'd placed at his feet. "Now, can I please come in and serve you dinner before it gets cold?"

Without a word, she cupped his face and kissed him. Her tongue traced along the opening of his mouth before tentatively sliding inside.

Electricity shot through him and straight to his cock. He had to make a conscious effort not to drop everything in his hands so he could wrap his arms around her.

With each pass, her tongue would explore more of his mouth, coaxing him to join her and he willingly obliged. Her fingers threaded through his hair as she hungrily kissed him.

His body buzzed from her touch. An ache brewed deep in his gut.

"Yes, you absolutely can come inside." She nibbled his lower lip.

He captured her mouth as his mind raced of sexual possibilities when the tapping of nails on wood reluctantly pulled them out of their lip-lock. He pulled away, mentally cursing the dog's timing. "I think Fred's trying to escape."

The hound stood in the middle of the doorway, halfway inside, looking at them like a child who wondered if anyone would notice if he bolted for the park.

"Fred, get inside." Keeping a hand on Edmund's chest, Jade snapped her fingers.

After barking at something, the dog trotted back in and turned in the direction of the couch.

Jade stepped back and motioned like a *Price is Right* model. "Would you like to officially come in?"

"Yes." Once he'd cleared the door, Edmund kicked it closed with his foot and put the items on the table. "I got a few things I thought you'd like."

"Wine? Chocolate from Sage's?" Tears ran down her face as she wrapped her arm around his waist for a quick hug before unloading the contents of the bags. "Rosita's? Bath stuff? You spoil me!"

Concern tightened the muscles in his neck, worried he'd overdone it as she pulled each item out and placed it on the table. "I guessed on what you'd like."

The more she smiled, the more confident he was he'd done the right thing by coming by, but the table began to fill up.

Shit, I bought a lot of stuff.

He clenched his fists at his side.

Way to look like a stalker.

Squeezing his hand, she beamed. "Edmund, this is all so wonderful. I'm overwhelmed."

Or not. "I saw Logan and Charlie at Rosita's. She said all this would be a great way for you to relax. Chocolate. Wine. A bath. Good dinner."

"You met Charlie Foster? She's fun. Great photographer."

"She took some pictures of me." *And I'm sure they'll be terrible.*

"I can't wait to see those." Jade put the vanilla lavender bath bomb near her nose and inhaled. "Oh, that smells so good."

"I didn't know what you liked, but vanilla goes with everything."

A mischievous sparkle in her eyes. "Like I said, so many delicious possibilities."

Damn. If she looked at him like that for too much longer, he would have an embarrassing wardrobe situation.

He needed to think of something else. Scanning the room, he noticed several boxes had been partially unpacked or simply opened. Puncture marks were in multiple flaps of the boxes. "What happened there?"

"I guess Fred got bored after I put my keys out of reach. Been chewing the boxes." She shrugged. "I should be thankful he found something that I can toss and it's not the couch or the doors."

"Challenging to keep him busy." He placed his hand in the small of her back and she settled into him. *I could get used to this.*

But the idea of settling in Marietta made no sense. He hadn't been here a week and he's already thinking of lifelong plans?

What was wrong with him? This wasn't like him at all.

He always worked with a plan, a goal in mind. One he'd repeatedly reviewed, looked at every detail, every possible outcome so there'd be no surprises.

Yet, as soon as he met Jade, she'd opened a part of his brain that he didn't think he had. A side of him that simply let his heart guide him to places unknown. To emotions unexplored.

And he liked it. A lot.

That scared the hell out of him because the last time he stopped thinking, he almost ended up in jail for ten to twenty.

But then again, with Reyna, he wasn't thinking with anything north of his belly button.

"Charlie is the one who helped get the word out about Harry's House with her photography." Jade opened the box from Sage's and held it up after inhaling. "Oh, my gosh, these chocolates smell amazing."

The rich flavors of caramel and salt made his mouth water. "Right, her photography. She mentioned the calendar. She said I should pose if they have another one."

The box tumbled to the table as she faced him. She rested her hands on his chest and played with the buttons on his shirt. "I would buy one hundred copies of that calendar if you're in it."

Her lust-filled stare had him searching for words. "I...um...okay, but I don't think there's a plan for another calendar right now."

"Doesn't matter. I've got the real thing right here." Jade rested her chin on his chest.

"Yes, you do." What did he do to deserve her adoring look? He shook off the question. He didn't want to know in case the powers that be made a mistake. Placing his hands on her shoulders, he leaned down and kissed her forehead. "You get everything?"

"I'm pretty sure I did and I love all of it."

"Good."

A rustling of plastic had them both finding Fred with his face in one of the bags from Rosita's.

"Guess he's hungry." Edmund laughed. "I got something for you, pup. Now to find it."

They cleared up the bags and placed the food containers out on the table while each of them verified the sacks were empty. Finally, he found the dog bone, hoping it would keep Fred busy.

As soon as the treat was unwrapped, Fred snatched it

from Edmund's hand and wandered over to the corner by the back door.

"Oh, you even thought of Fred. You're so amazing."

Edmund's pride regained a few levels seeing her so happy. He couldn't have done enough to keep Reyna appeased, but then again, she had been stealing from his practice and trying to keep him off her trail.

Two entirely different women.

And I'm with the better one. Don't screw this up.

"Oh, I didn't see this bag." She opened the pharmacy bag, but her lips thinned. "Um…Edmund?"

"Yes?"

"Charlie suggested chocolates, a nice dinner, and a warm bath. Were those the *only* things she mentioned that might relax me?"

"Yes? Why?" The review of his pharmacy purchases slammed against his brain. *Oh no.*

She pulled out his wishful thinking twelve pack. "Because you also brought me condoms."

Way to screw it up, genius.

Chapter Seventeen

I F JADE HADN'T seen it for herself, she wouldn't have believed it. Upon producing the blue box from the pharmacy bag, Edmund's eyebrows shot somewhere past his hairline and his sexy awkwardness skyrocketed.

"Oh shit!" He lunged, snatching the box out of her hand and then appeared to try and figure out what to do with it. After a few moments of fumbling with it, he ended up holding it behind his back like a child playing a game of out of sight, out of mind. "That wasn't…I mean I don't want you to think…I'm not an asshole."

She bit her lip as laughter bubbled up from her toes. Even in deep embarrassment, he couldn't be more kissable if he wanted to be.

Jade braced her hands on the table. "Edmund, you might be a lot of things, but an asshole isn't one of them. Besides, it's really brave of you to buy these locally since Carol tells everyone who buys what."

His face turned scarlet and his jaw clenched. "Damn, I'm so sorry. I mean, I hoped we'd need them at some point, but I didn't mean today. Tonight. This year."

Oh, Dr. Davidson, this is going to happen this year. "It's fine. Honestly, it's fine. Believe me, it's nothing I haven't already considered."

"Yeah?" His eyes brightened like a kid on Christmas morning as the corner of his mouth curled up into a sexy smirk.

"Absolutely." Unwrapping a chocolate from Sage's, she bit it in two and held the other piece in front of his mouth. "Now, eat some chocolate. You'll feel better."

"Isn't that what they said in *Harry Potter and the Prisoner of Azkaban?*"

Oh, man, he reads books I love. I'm a goner.

With his eyes on her, he leaned forward and gently took the candy from her fingers, then wrapped his hand around her wrist and kissed her fingertips. "You're right. Chocolate does make things nicer."

Her body ached for him, to kiss him, to taste him, to have his hands all over her and forget about the outside world.

Forget the crazy of selling her father's place.

Dismiss her brother that couldn't stay out of trouble.

Push aside the stress of idiot patients at her job.

Draw a blank about her dog chewing on boxes and his endless barking at squirrels.

All of it, but the tiniest voice reminded her she'd made a stupid relationship choice before.

This wouldn't be another one, right?

Taking him in, she wrapped her arms around his waist, convincing herself it wasn't. "Edmund."

"Man, I want to kiss you right now."

"I'm not stopping you." Sliding her hands up his shirt, she tugged him close. Her tongue ran along the seam of his mouth, coaxing his lips open. The sweet taste of chocolate on him only excited her more.

"Jade." The slap of the blue box of condoms to tile brought a smile against their kiss as he pulled her flush.

"Kiss me again, Edmund." Even with the shirt between then, she marveled at the strength in his arms, his shoulders. How his body felt beneath her touch.

He nibbled her lip before placing a line of kisses down her neck and sucking gently on the tender pulse point.

A shiver ran up her spine at the delightful circles he made with his tongue on her skin. Her nipples peaked as an involuntary giggle escaped her. "Tickles."

He playfully furrowed his brow. "I was going for erotic."

"Well, I didn't say *where* it tickled."

"No, you didn't." He nuzzled her neck. "Should I stop?"

Jade traced the hard line of muscle along his jaw and loved how it felt beneath her fingers. What she wouldn't do to have him in her bed, but the list of reasons she shouldn't allow this to happen, played in her head.

One. You've known him less than two weeks.

His hand rested solidly against the small of her back.

Two…um… He deserves someone better?

His tongue swept inside her mouth, as his fingers threaded through her hair.

Three… Being in his arms, tasting him, feeling him, his spicy scent circled around them…nothing detoured her.

Jade couldn't rationalize turning him away. "Stop? Absolutely not."

"Good."

Her body longed for him as he pressed his mouth to hers. As if she'd never get her fill. She gave a slight moan as he deepened their kiss. "Edmund."

The realm of possible sexual scenarios raced through her mind as she wished she'd shaved her legs this morning.

A rip of paper broke the tension and she jerked her head back. "What was that?"

"I don't…oh, man." Edmund jumped to his right and leaned down to scoop something off the floor. "Fred. No."

The once intact box of condoms, now had multiple punctures in it with one of the sides torn open.

Her fists clenched beside her. "Well, there goes that idea."

When Edmund laughed, she knew she'd said it out loud, but at this point, she didn't care.

If they wanted to restock tonight, the pharmacy wasn't a five-minute walk from here and that would certainly get the town busybodies' tongues wagging.

She buzzed hard enough from his touch to deal with the fallout of Carol Bingley's judgmental look. "Ugh, Fred. Stop chewing on everything."

Opening the back door, she tried to shift her rational brain back to center. "At least he's not marking anything. Yet."

"Guess if I go buy more of those tonight, I'll either impress or upset the lady behind the counter." He pulled out the string of condoms. Every single one of them had a large hole. "That answers that."

I just missed out on twelve orgasms because of my dog. "Sorry. As if this day couldn't get any more frustrating. Let me get that."

Waving her off, he gave her a quick kiss. He grabbed a bath bomb, placing it in her hand. "Go do whatever it is this does. I'll get dinner set out and open the wine."

"You bring me chocolate and wine and dinner. Now, you're sending me off for a hot bath? Good grief, you're like a fairy tale Prince Charming come true."

"Is that a good thing?" he asked, his nose scrunched up in uncertainty.

"In this case, yes."

"Then you're welcome." He patted her backside before encouraging her to go soak. "I got this."

"Thank you." She raced down the hall, looking forward to having a chance to clean up and be far more presentable.

A warm bath in the claw-footed bathtub with a new vanilla lavender bath bomb would have been the perfect ending to her day. But having said bath bomb delivered by a modern-day knight who looked like he'd been pulled from the pages of a historical romance novel, had to be the sprinkles on the frosting on the cupcake of life.

As soon as she dropped the bath bomb in the running water, she turned to look at her reflection and gasped. "I look horrible!"

Mascara bled down her makeup-free face. Her wrinkled, dog hair-covered scrubs were an obvious indication that she'd slept in them.

At least she'd been in the office all day and not seen patients so she wasn't covered in germs.

And he kissed me anyway. Wow.

Before she took off her shirt, Edmund knocked and opened the door a few inches. His arm extended in to give her a glass of wine. "Your wine, Nurse Carter."

Gingerly, she took the drink and placed a slow, seductive kiss on his wrist. "Thank you, Dr. Davidson."

"You're welcome, my queen."

When the door closed, she leaned against it, her mind raced like a runner on a never-ending track.

After the betrayal by her stepfather, she never thought she would trust again until her father helped her repair the damage done on her tender soul.

During her high school and college years, even into her twenties, she always cautiously approached physical relationships, always guarding her heart until Brenden, her late husband.

Touching her eye, she cringed at the moment when he turned her entire life on its end, shattering her faith in love.

Beaten, but not defeated, she promised herself never to be that vulnerable again. Never would she willingly hand her heart over to another.

Then came Edmund.

The way he made her laugh.

The times he'd stumbled over words in his attempt to impress her.

How he defended her and his sister against a patient's sexist father.

His honesty.

His kisses.

His touch.

Thinking of him brought a smile to her face and ignited the belief in happily ever afters.

Not to mention how he made her feel when she was in his arms.

Desired. Empowered. Beautiful.

In the blink of an eye, he'd cracked the armor she'd worn so tightly around her heart and soul.

And she loved that about him.

She swallowed hard.

She…loved him.

Reality hit and her hands trembled as she finished half her wine in two gulps.

"Oh no. What have I done?" She drained the glass and stared at herself in the mirror again.

"You can't love him. You just met him." Yet, no matter how hard she'd try to convince her reflection otherwise, it wouldn't change the truth.

She loved Edmund.

Sitting on the edge of the bathtub, she turned off the water, inhaling the sweet scents of lavender and vanilla, alarmed by how easy the idea of loving the man presently in her kitchen came to her.

"How did he do that?" She wondered, but didn't truly care.

As wounded as she'd been in her lifetime, she'd always wondered if she'd be worthy of such a passionate emotion.

Love. True love.

Just like the storybooks promised.

And it had happened without her even thinking about it.

Standing, she stared at herself again. "So you love him. What's next?"

Her new razor caught her eye and the corner of her mouth curled up.

Despite a ruined box of barrier contraception, she could at least uncap that bad boy and get to business of being far more presentable.

You know, just in case.

Once she'd cleaned up, she brushed her teeth and put on her cutest underpants and bra, Jade threw on a green jersey-knit dress before rejoining Edmund.

When she entered she couldn't believe her eyes. In the short time she'd been out of the room, he'd unpacked several of the kitchen boxes, placed a few more appliances out, and unpacked the cookbooks.

Her father's was the one stacked on top.

The table had been set with as dinner waited.

Fred still lay in the corner, wagging his tail as he chewed on a large rawhide bone.

"Feel better?" His eyes scanned her from head to toes as he took her hand and kissed the back of it. "You look beautiful."

Why has no one snatched you up already? "Thank you. Goodness, you were busy."

His shirt was no longer tightly tucked into his jeans, probably from lifting and moving boxes around. "Trying to help."

"Yes, it does. Thank you."

Holding the chair out for her, she sat down and he took the seat beside her, but immediately stood, leaned over, and kissed her again. "You taste like mint."

"I brushed my teeth." Her hand rested against his cheek. "Thank you for doing all this for me."

"Glad to." As he sat back down, Fred looked up for ten seconds before going back to his bone.

"You didn't do all this *and* have a chance to go back to the pharmacy, did you?" Jade asked as she attempted to be more interested in the delicious possibilities on the table than in the chair next to her.

"Sorry. No. It's probably closed by now, anyway." He chuckled and started opening containers. "Didn't know what you liked. I got a bit of everything. *Fajitas, enchiladas verdes,* chicken *chalupas, queso* and chips, and an old reliable, bean and cheese tacos."

"This looks amazing. I haven't gotten a chance to visit Rosita's as of yet, but seeing all this, I will for sure do it very soon." The rich flavors of the chicken *fajitas* mixed with the bright red, green, and yellow grilled peppers had her practically salivating.

"I didn't know if you liked corn or flour tortillas. I brought both."

"Corn please."

Edmund passed her the plate and she picked two.

The warm, thick tortilla weighed heavily in her hand. Her mouth watered in anticipation of tasting it covered with the grilled meat and veggies.

The first nibble had her hooked. Layers of salt, pepper, and a unique blend of spices tickled her tongue making her crave the next bite. "This is amazing. Thank you."

For the next hour, they talked, ate, and drank wine as Fred never stopped chewing on his new bone.

By the end of the meal, she was properly full, a little bit tipsy, and a whole lot of turned on.

"Let me clear this really quick before we retire to the couch." Standing, she began to take the plates, but he pulled her to sit on his lap.

"I'll take care of those. Sit here with me first."

She nuzzled his neck, kissing a path to his ear. "What, you do dishes too? Where have you been my entire life?"

"In Florida." His arm wrapped around her waist, pulling her close.

"You're honestly too good to be true."

"I'm not perfect." He rolled his eyes. "Not by a long shot."

She hated he'd been so hurt before. "I don't want you to be perfect. I want you to be you."

"That's the first time anyone's ever said that to me." He stroked her hair. "And it's someone as incredible as you."

"Always honest."

"Always."

Her body simmered like a pot on a hot stove. She wanted him in the most carnal way. "Mind if I undo a few of these buttons?"

"Whatever you want," he replied, a look of angst flashed

in his eyes.

"Just relax, Edmund." Her nervous fingers made quick work of the buttons.

One. Two. Three.

"I know you're amazing under all this."

Four, five, six.

Just as she suspected, lines of sculpted muscle hid under that button down. Her hands slid under his shirt, fanning across his chest. "Mind if I open all of them?"

She wanted to see more. So much more.

"Go ahead." He licked his lips as his gaze focused on her mouth.

Pulling her dress up to mid-thigh, she straddled him, and pulled his shirt out of his jeans.

With great anticipation, she unfastened the last few, watching the shirt fall open. "I've been hoping to see you shirtless all day."

"Why didn't you tell me? I would have taken it off as soon as I got here."

"Really?"

"No." He chuckled, a light shade of red stained his face. "I don't see myself that way."

"Oh, my, you should." She pushed the shirt off his shoulders and let it fall to the floor. "You're amazing to witness."

"Yeah?" He squeaked then cleared his throat. "You think so?"

"Absolutely."

"Always honest."

"Always."

His finger traced along her jawline and down her neck. "You have the most beautiful skin."

"But I'm not wearing makeup." Her fingers danced along his exquisitely sculpted shoulders and arms.

"You don't need it."

The predatory way he held her gaze, she silently cursed Fred having destroyed the condoms. Hard cords of muscle twitched under her touch. She stood, still standing over his lap. "Gorgeous."

"No one has ever called me that before." He cupped her face, kissing her hungrily, probing her mouth with his tongue, and then nibbling her lips.

"You're gorgeous," she whispered again as his hand cupped her breast.

Her fingers itched to unbutton his jeans, but with no barriers they absolutely couldn't have sex. "I want you."

"We can't." He slid back and stood, his hands encircled her waist.

"I know." She panted. *But I really want to.*

"We can do other things though." He turned them in a one eighty and walked her backward until her butt touched the counter. He placed his hands on either side of her. "Now, grip the counter. Don't let go."

Chapter Eighteen

*O*H MY. "AND if I do?"

He kissed the end of her nose. "Then I'll stop."

"You're a tease."

"And you're impatient." His fingers ran along the tender curve of her neck, moving her hair out of the way. "Trust me."

Trust me. Those two little words put an immediate halt on her desire.

She'd heard them before and been crushed. *What if this was all in my head?*

"You okay?" His brow furrowed. "Did I do something?"

"No, no not at all. I want to, Edmund. I do, but…" *What if this is a disaster?*

Even as hard as she'd fallen for him, that didn't mean it was reciprocated.

He stopped, resting his forehead against hers, his arms wrapped around her in a protective embrace. "We can stop if it's too fast. Do this some other time…or not at all."

His chivalry set her body on fire.

"No, I don't want you to stop." It wouldn't be the first time she'd been with the man for the sake of it feeling good, but for the first time, she wished for more. She hoped for…what exactly?

"Jade, what do you want?" he whispered. "Tell me."

True love.

She mentally attempted to shake off her nonsense, but it stuck.

I want the happily ever after. With Edmund. "I want you."

His hands fell to her waist. "You're sure?"

"I'm sure." Resting her chin on his chest, she took him in as her hands ran up his arms and rested on his shoulders. She pulled him to her and hungrily kissed him before grabbing the counter as he instructed. "I promise, I won't move them."

Without a word, he brushed his lips against her temple, then her ear, the pulse point of her neck as his hands moved down her arms, resting on her waist. "You okay?"

"More than okay."

His index finger traced a line from the top of her décolletage down her cleavage. "I've been a gentleman all evening."

"Yes, you have." Jade smiled, anticipating what he would do next. She leaned into his hand, hoping to encourage him to go further. "Wonderfully chivalrous."

"Now I want to be…um…um…a…"

"Scoundrel?" Her eyebrow cocked, hoping he'd take the bait and appreciate movie lines as much as she did.

"You need a scoundrel in your life?"

Bingo! "Yes." Her breathing quickened as his hand moved up her body.

He cupped her breast enough for her to feel the exquisite

pressure of his touch, but he didn't linger. Slowly, his hand moved along the curve of her waist, her hip, to the hem of her dress, leaving his fingers to rest on the bare skin of her thigh.

Her heart thumped wildly. "I usually go for nice guys, but...I...um..."

"I'm a nice guy." A seductive grin spread across his face.

"Yes, yes you are." She swallowed hard as he scanned her like she'd been put on display. "I need to touch you."

"Only if you take off your bra...without taking off your dress."

To get her hands on him, she would have done just about anything at that moment. With a quick push and turn, the front clasp of her bra came undone. Pulling her arms through the straps, she wriggled it out from underneath her dress and it fell at her feet.

His jaw dropped to the floor. "That's not what I expected, but that's impressive."

"Now can I touch you?"

"Be my guest." He placed his hands on either side of her, allowing her full rein of his body.

She started with his shoulders, then arms, and up to his chest.

Great sculptors like Michelangelo, Rodin, Picasso would have been inspired by Edmund. They would have taken great joy in mimicking his sculpted lines of muscle, his broad shoulders, his chiseled jaw. "Wow. Just wow."

Capturing her mouth with his, he swept his tongue between her lips.

His hands moved up her dress and cupped her breasts. His thumbs grazed over her sensitive nipples as she moaned.

"Yes, touch me." She gasped as he circled each nipple with the tips of his fingers. Even with her dress still on, she could feel the heat of his touch through her clothes as if she were wearing nothing. "I want this off me."

He shook his head. "I can't see you naked."

"Why not?"

"I won't be able to keep my hands off you and Fred ate the condoms."

She threaded a finger through his belt loop and pulled him flush. "I know, but there are other things we can do."

His free hand cupped her butt as he dropped to his knees and kissed her down her belly. "Yes, there are."

Right then, she thanked her lucky stars she had a chance to properly groom earlier.

He nibbled the inside of her thigh and inhaled her. "You smell good. Like a vanilla Christmas cookie. I love to eat Christmas cookies."

"It's the bath bomb you bought me."

"I'll buy you one hundred of them."

"If you're going to do what I think you're going to do, I'll never run out of them."

His hand ran up her leg, in a torturously slow slide until his thumbs were tucked under each side of her panties. "Then you better never run out of them."

"You can count on that."

He pulled her underpants down at the same tempo his hands moved up her legs.

By the time she'd stepped out of them, Jade didn't know if she could control herself much longer.

"I've wanted to do this all day." He growled as he tucked his shoulder under her left leg, and then stood on his knees, opening her intimately.

Her dress still remained between them. The feather touch of his fingers danced up her inner thigh.

She braced herself against the kitchen counter. "Do you want me to take my dress off?"

She panted, hoping he'd say yes.

"No." He gave her a devilish smirk.

Running his thumb along the seam of her, her face flushed with anticipation of him giving her more. "But I might not be able to see what you're doing."

"I know." One of his hands cupped her butt.

"Oh, God. You're killing me."

"What do you want me to do?"

She swallowed hard, screaming her desires in her head, but not knowing if she could say it out loud. "You know what I want."

"I want to hear you say it. Tell me what you want me to do."

Jade bit her lip. The words sat on the tip of her tongue as his fingers brushed her intimately. She'd never been good at dirty talk, but as Edmund played with her, she wanted to confess every dirty fantasy.

"You can tell me, Jade. Tell me how I can make you feel good," he coaxed.

"I...um...oh that feels good."

"Just wait." With the dress still between them, Edmund leaned forward and pressed his mouth against her, his tongue rested on her sensitive nub as the soft fabric caressed her clit. "You want that?"

"Yes." Her breathing was heavy as her eyes bored into him. His touch tingled through her. "More."

With his hands hidden by her dress, she couldn't anticipate where they were and she relished the unknown possibilities.

His thumb stroked the crease where the leg and pelvis meet. "Feel good?"

Nodding, she ran her fingers through his hair, her hips leaning forward.

"Patience, my queen. Patience."

Her head fell back as he played her like a classically trained musician played an instrument. "No, I can't wait anymore. Eat me."

"Yes, ma'am." A wicked smile appeared as he pushed the dress up, his tongue tickled her swollen clit as his fingers moved inward. He nibbled, sucked, and licked her sensitive nub, then ran his tongue along the seam before starting again.

Because she couldn't completely see where his fingers or tongue would move next, she couldn't prepare for what he would do. The equivalent of wearing a blindfold. "Yes, Edmund, yes."

His fingers taunted her, inching toward her vaginal opening, then dancing down her inner thigh.

She gave a disappointed moan.

"Don't worry, sweetheart. I'm not even close to being done." His fingers moved again as he nibbled her outer folds, then let his tongue slide between them, finding her clit as his fingers moved inside her.

Jade gasped as she attempted to keep a grip on the counter. "Oh my...damn that feels good!"

His fingers moved in and out as he continued to suck her nub.

Jade's mind became a wash of nothing but Edmund. His smile. His body. His caress, his tongue... "Yes, please don't stop."

Her hips rocked with the rhythm he'd set with his fingers dancing inside her.

Kissing her thigh, he growled. "You're so close, I can feel it. You're so tight."

She nodded as she tried to watch him eat her, but he'd let the dress fall in the way so where he planned to touch her next was totally unexpect—"Oh, my gosh!"

His thumb grazed her clit and her vaginal walls clamped down on his fingers.

Her eyes went wide and her hips rocked to a rapid tempo. "Yes! Yes! Yes!"

She rode his hand as he slowly kissed up her belly, between her breasts, and to her neck, nuzzling her as the last waves of her orgasm settled in.

Her heart beat wildly as she gripped his shoulders to keep standing upright.

"That was...that was..." Jade panted. "Amazing."

"It was supposed to be." Kissing her temple, he pulled

her into his arms and inhaled. "I wanted to make you feel good."

"Yes, you certainly did." After a few moments, she leaned back, her hands fanned over his thick chest. Staring into his eyes, she could see her future. Happily ever after and it didn't scare her anymore.

"What are you thinking about?"

But it might scare him. Tucking her thoughts away, she decided to enjoy the moment. "Dr. Davidson, I need you to do something for me."

"What is it?"

Turning them a one eighty she popped the button on his pants. "Hold on to the counter."

Chapter Nineteen

"ARE YOU A new doctor?" The woman asked as she adjusted her glasses. "Because you don't look old enough to be a doctor."

Edmund chuckled as Thomas stood at the back of the room. "Yes, ma'am. I'm old enough."

"How old are you?"

"Thirty-five."

"Right, you're three years older than Lucy," Thomas mumbled.

"Oh, goodness, you sure look younger than that." She tapped her chin with her finger. "I'm only a few years older than you are and I'm a grandma. That's why I'm here. I think my grandkids gave me the pink eye."

"The yellow, gooey drainage from your eye makes me think that too." After a quick examination, Edmund gave her a prescription and follow-up instructions. "Another happy customer."

"You feel like you can fly on your own after today?" Thomas asked as he put one of the iPads back in the rack when they began to walk toward the break room.

"I hope so. Been doing all this orientation for almost two

weeks now."

"This is your last orientation shift, right?"

"Yes. I should be good. All signed in on the computer and jumped through all the hoops for the computer geeks. Got the protocols memorized, the coding, and know my shifts for the next month. Did a couple of ride-outs with the EMS guys for good measure."

"Good, good." Thomas stood there, a stressed smile on his face. "So you've been seeing Jade?"

"And you're seeing Lucy."

"Right." Thomas held his hands up in surrender. "It's not an attack, Edmund. It's an observation."

"Surprised it took you this long to say anything. Especially since you and I have talked a few times since I got here."

"Yeah, well, Lucy told me it wasn't any of my business."

"My sister's a smart woman." Even though Edmund and Jade had worked together a few times since their dinner here at the ER, they were both professional and focused. Still, that didn't mean he wasn't thinking about her naked the entire time when she was around. "Yes, I'm seeing Jade."

"Good, she needs a good man in her life."

"I'll take that as a compliment, not sarcasm."

Thomas rocked back on his heels. "And she talked to you about her ex-husband?"

"Late husband. Yep. She's told me about her history if that's what you're asking."

"Glad she feels like she can." Thomas loosely crossed his arms across his chest. "She's had some men in her life that have let her down. Her stepfather, her brother, her ex-husband."

"She told me about all of them." His heart clenched at the discussion he and Jade had a few nights ago about the events that led her to come to Marietta and live with her father. Her ability to recover from the betrayals she'd endured amazed him, but she also kept a part of herself protected, hidden from everyone's view.

As much as Edmund appreciated Thomas's big brother talk, he didn't need a lecture. "What? You're worried I'm going to be one of those guys?"

"No, those guys were pieces of shit."

"Junior keeps calling her. Seeing if she's sold the property yet." Opening and closing his fist, Edmund counted to five to bring down his fury. "He won't leave her alone about it."

"What does she say?"

"She hung up on him last time, but I know she has a sense of obligation for him."

"She's a healer. It's who she is, which is why she's good at her job." He leaned against the doorframe. "I'm not worried about you being a piece of shit, but you're not planning on staying long."

"Maybe she isn't either." *What the hell, man?* Edmund hadn't meant to say that, but what if Jade left with him? Wasn't her father's property the reason she stayed? If she sold it, would she leave? With him?

"I'd be surprised if she would leave. She hadn't said anything to me about that."

"That doesn't mean she hasn't considered it." Edmund

stepped closer to Thomas, almost challenging him. "Jade's told me you've been a good friend, like a brother to her. I appreciate that and I appreciate you stepping up for her back when you were kids."

"But—"

"But I care about her. A lot and I won't do anything to hurt her."

Thomas didn't flinch. "I want her happy. She deserves that."

"Yes, she does and I want to be that man who does that for her. Makes her *more* than happy. I don't need your advice on how to make that happen." Edmund glared. "Spend your time keeping my sister happy and we'll call it even."

"Fair enough."

But Edmund knew that look. Thomas wasn't totally convinced of Edmund's rebuttal. To be fair, Edmund knew winning the heart of a woman who'd been so betrayed would be difficult.

Was he up to the task?

Was he even capable?

"Recheck in room three." Shelly Westbrook peeked around the corner and held the chart out.

The two men slowly backed away from each other and Edmund headed for Shelly. "Recheck for what?"

Shelly walked in step with him. "Phoebe Stevenson was here a couple of weeks ago for a very bad case of strep, dehydration and pneumonia. Jade told her to follow up in ten to fourteen days with their primary."

"I remember them. Why are they here, then?"

"They extended their trip." She pulled her phone from her pocket as it buzzed. "Dad said they're staying another couple of weeks. Wanted to follow the instructions."

"Okay, I'll check them." Edmund noticed her fingers began to tremble and tears welled in her eyes. Remembering what Jade had told him about Shelly's husband had Edmund concerned. "You okay, Shelly?"

Waving him off, she dried her eyes with the back of her hand. "I'm okay. Just dealing with a couple of things at home. Ugh, Gil, why do you keep doing this?"

Gil? Wasn't that the name of her ex-husband and fiancé? "Anything we can do to help?" Thomas approached, his voice hushed.

She gave both a tear-stained smile. "No, nothing like a bit of family drama to get me through the day. Please, don't worry about it. Go do the follow up."

Edmund held up a hand, keeping Thomas from following him in the room. "I got this, Dr. McAvoy. Go do your paperwork."

"Nice try, Dr. Davidson. It's a *full* shift to finish orientation."

Without looking back to see if Thomas listened, Edmund entered the treatment room after a quick knock. "Good afternoon, I'm Dr. Davidson."

"Hi! Is your sister here?" Phoebe's forehead crinkled. "Isn't it amazing that she's so short and you're so tall?"

"Crazy, right? I told some other kids at the rec center that it was because my mom ate a lot of broccoli when she was pregnant with me. What do you think?"

"I think it has to do with randomness of genetics."

"Nice."

The father extended his hand to shake. "Good to see you again, Dr. Davidson."

Edmund responded in kind. "How's it been going?"

"Good. Better."

A small flash caught Edmund's attention. The ring on the father's finger had reflected against the overhead lights again. *That has got to be the shiniest damned ring I've ever seen.*

The father continued. "Phoebe's still winded from time to time, but we are walking more each day. Her cough is still there."

"The cough will be the last thing to resolve. The exercise will help keep your lungs strong and improving, but pace yourself. It's going to take time to build your strength back up."

"We have to stop before I want to because Daddy's feet hurt. He said the boots give him blisters." She tapped her Minnie Mouse backpack. "I keep Band-Aids in here for him."

"That's nice of you, Phoebe."

"Is Captain Marvel, here?"

"Who?" Edmund laid his stethoscope around his neck.

"The nurse that took care of me. I said she was Captain Marvel. You know, for your Avengers nurse team. The one Daddy was sucky to at first."

Her father's lips thinned. "Out of the mouths of babes."

Edmund nodded. "Miss Carter. No, she's not here to-day."

"Like Agent Peggy Carter?" Phoebe pulled out a letter from her backpack. "I like her. She's really cool."

"She is really cool."

Handing the note to Edmund, the child smiled. "Would you give her my thank you note when you see her again?"

"I would be glad to leave it at the desk for her, Phoebe."

The child cocked her head. "At the desk? Why would you do that when you'll see her again?"

"Why-why would you say that, young lady?"

"Because you love her," Phoebe answered as if it were the most obvious thing in the world. "I saw you talk to her and when she'd walk away, you smiled real big, like this."

She grinned as widely as the Joker.

Love? Did he love Jade?

Like. *Yes.*

Lust. *Damn straight.*

But love?

A stifled laugh caught his attention. He glanced at the father, who shrugged. "Out of the mouths of babes."

Treating children had always been one of Edmund's favorite parts of the job, but with taking care of them came brutal honesty from mindful observation.

Sweat instantly formed on his upper lip and his hands shook. He tried to busy himself with reading the chart on the bedside computer, but his mind tumbled with happily-ever-after promises.

"Dr. Davidson? You need help with anything?" Thomas obviously followed Edmund into the room, as he should have since Edmund had to finish this shift to be off orientation, but damn if Edmund didn't need a moment.

Get your head out of your ass. No one falls in love...shit. Stop it. "Okay, Phoebe. I appreciate your comments. It gives me something to think about, but I wanted to know how you're feeling today."

As the child explained her greatly improved symptoms and she'd finished the antibiotic yesterday, Edmund shoved anything nonmedical to the far reaches of his brain. He couldn't get distracted, especially not in front of his sister's boyfriend who watched Edmund's every move.

Love? Did he love Jade?

The answer slammed into his brain without question.

With every fiber of my being.

Focus! "She tolerated the steroids okay, Mr. Stevenson?"

The father nodded, an amused smirk on his face. "It messed with her stomach a bit, pissed her mom off that I'd even given them to her, but I won't go into that now."

"Her mother not a medicine fan?" How many times had Edmund heard this argument with parents? Far too many.

"No, her mother is a we-can-cure-everything-if-we-eat-plants-and-chant nut...eater." The father reassuringly squeezed his daughter's hand. "The steroids upset her stomach if she didn't have anything to eat. She wasn't as hungry at first, but after taking her to that café in the middle of town, Phoebe couldn't get enough. I'm pretty sure we were there two to three times a day these past couple of weeks. Especially since she didn't feel well enough to even try hiking until yesterday, but we did walk around town."

"The restaurant across from the courthouse?" The neutral conversation about food helped calm Edmund's recent self-realization of being in love with Jade for about five seconds.

"Yes. Main Street Diner."

The place where we had our first date. Dammit. Get your head in the game.

"It's a good place. Rosita's is good too."

"I like their bean and cheese tacos," Phoebe added as she handed a Band-Aid to her father.

Edmund pulled out his stethoscope. "Okay, Phoebe. I need to listen to your chest."

"I don't need a hospital gown on for this?" The girl nodded and cooperated by moving the strap of her purse out of the way.

"No, your T-shirt is thin enough, I can listen through it. What does that say?"

She stretched it straight and read. "It says 'I'm not strong for a girl. I'm just strong.'"

"Nice. Take some deep breaths for me." Resting the bell of the stethoscope against her chest, Edmund listened. "Lungs clear and without crackles or wheezes. Her heartbeat strong and regular. Cough for me Phoebe."

Mr. Stevenson chuckled as he appeared far more relaxed that he had been when they first came in two weeks ago. "That food. I don't know what that diner woman uses, but it's like crack. I put on three pounds eating those pies she makes."

"Did you have the peach pie with cinnamon ice cream?" Thomas asked as he leaned against the doorframe.

"Three times." Phoebe turned her head and coughed. "That good, Doctor?"

Nodding, Edmund smiled. "Perfect. You still need any of the inhalers?"

"Yes, I took it this morning. I don't need to take the blue one as much. I'm glad because it makes me shake."

"The Ventolin? That's if you need it. Get tight chested. I would recommend you take it before you exercise or go out hiking. Always keep it with you. The other one is for twice a day no matter how you're feeling." Edmund listened to the lower lobes and heard nothing but clear breath sounds. "Good job. Sounds like you've resolved, but know that pneumonia takes time to recover. Kids heal faster than adults, but don't beat yourself up on the trails. You have an inhaler. I'd suggest to keep it close for another couple of weeks. Be sure to keep taking the inhaled steroid until you follow up with her regular doctor back in Denver and together you can come up with a plan to wean her off it."

"Thank you." Phoebe hugged him before Edmund could move away.

He patted the child's back and soaked in the beauty of seeing patients again. This case had been a nothing follow-up, especially since Jade had given the child such precision care and the patient and father were compliant, but it felt good to be back in the thick of helping people again.

"The woman who owns the diner, Gabby, is a trained chef, uses her grandmother's recipes for a lot of the specials." Thomas shook Mr. Stevenson's hand as they approached the door, but his gaze narrowed. "That's an interesting ring, Mr.

Stevenson. Where did you get it?"

"This?" He slipped it off, handing it to Thomas. "I told Dr. Davidson last time I was here my frat buddies and I thought it would be a great idea to get rings that looked like the Rocky Mountains, but we were drunk when we made that decision."

"Then it's custom?" Turning it around between his fingers, Thomas appeared to be inspecting it with great interest.

"Yep. Second one I've had since I lost the other one last time I came to town."

"Lost? Here?"

Edmund snapped his fingers. "Yes, you mentioned about your car and your ring was in it, right?"

"We were here a couple of years ago. End of summer trip. I put it in my pocket after it poked her hand. Probably fell out on the trail when we walked around."

"Or got stolen out of your car," Phoebe added. "We had to talk to the park ranger for hours and hours when that happened."

"Sorry to hear about that. You got to talk to Officer Harris? He's a nice guy." Thomas had a smooth demeanor when talking to patients, one Edmund could see as a great bedside manner.

It reminded Edmund of his brother Peter. People would gather to listen to him talk about anything, a quality Edmund would never possess.

And yet, Jade wants me anyway.

That little nugget of information gave Edmund a bounce in his step.

"Officer Harris gave me a coloring book and made me a junior ranger. I still have my badge." She pulled her backpack from behind her and reached in to find a plastic badge pinned to a journal with the solar system on it.

"Is that a planet?" He tapped the book.

"Saturn." She held it up proudly. "There are eight planets. Saturn is the largest when you include its rings. It has fifty-three moons, one of which, Titan, has its own atmosphere."

"Very nice, Phoebe. You like astrophysics?" Edmund loved seeing kids who loved STEM subjects. He always had plenty to talk to them about.

"Phoebe's in the STEM middle school back home, but we love to come out here, take the telescope, and watch the stars."

"When we see Officer Harris, I'll let him know you still have it." After handing the ring back, Thomas tapped the scar on his lip with his finger. "Thank you, Mr. Stevenson. Please come back if you need anything. Sorry you had to visit us during your vacation. When did you lose that again?"

"My ring?" His brow furrowed and shrugged. "I guess coming up on two years now."

Edmund's curiosity piqued. *Why does he care about that stupid ring?*

The father gave them a salute. "I'll take visiting you guys instead of filing a stolen vehicle report and fighting with my insurance company any day."

Thomas's jaw clenched. "Stolen vehicle?"

"That same weekend I lost my ring, my car was stolen."

"I thought you said the ring was stolen out of your car."

"Either I lost the ring on the trail *and* my car got stolen or whoever stole my car, took the ring out of it. Either way, it was a sucky Labor Day weekend." He kissed his daughter's hand. "Can I get a copy of her records for us to take with us?"

When Thomas didn't answer, Edmund stepped in and guided them toward the desk where nurse's aide and unit secretary, Sue Westbrook worked. "Sue, can you print a copy of Phoebe's notes and give them the hospital information?"

"I'd be glad to, Dr. Davidson." She reached across the counter and handed Phoebe a sticker and the father a business card. "Here's one for you and, for your daddy, the ER's information. That way if your primary pediatrician wants to talk with us he or she would know how to reach us."

"Remember, take those inhalers until you see your doctor back in Denver. Okay, Phoebe?"

Phoebe clutched her new sticker to her chest. "I will."

"Please bring her back for any problems." Edmund scanned the charts and walked the ER to verify there weren't any patients waiting to be seen.

The unit had a typical midday lull and with them treating patients faster than were coming in, Edmund figured he'd get to have lunch in peace. At least as much peace as he could have with another doctor staring at him. "Anyone waiting to be seen, Mrs. Westbrook? Mr. Fletcher?"

"Give it a few minutes. I'm sure someone will show up." Dave put his finger to his lips in the international be quiet signal. "But don't mock a good thing. Go have lunch."

As Edmund entered the break room, he found Thomas pacing and his face beet red. "What is wrong with you?"

Pointing to a scar on his lip, Thomas growled, "That ring is why I have this scar."

"What ring?"

"That last patient. That ring."

Edmund remembered the story of how Lucy sewed up Thomas's lip because of an attack in the ER. "That guy hit you? He didn't look the type."

"No, Junior did." Thomas rubbed the bridge of his nose.

Dread fell like a rock into Edmund's gut. "Why would Junior have a ring like that? Mr. Stevenson said its custom."

"Yep and he also said that his car got stolen so either Junior found it on the trails or—"

"Junior stole that car." *Well shit.*

Chapter Twenty

EDMUND AND THOMAS decided not to share the news of the ring and the stolen car report with Lucy or Jade until they'd talked to Park Ranger Todd Harris and Sheriff Rob Shaw.

Both Edmund and Thomas would be off in two days and decided to go together to make sure all the details of their accounts of events were consistent.

"This is going to kill her." Edmund hung his head as the men talked at the end of the shift. "She's going to hate us both."

"I know, but Junior can't walk from this." Thomas shook his head. "The guy needs to be locked up until he gets some sense into him."

"I don't think he'll live that long."

"He's reckless and dangerous and he's going to kill someone."

Pacing in the break room, Edmund rubbed the stress that had formed in the back of his neck.

As much as Jade knew her brother was a lost cause, she still hoped to get him to see reason.

Turning him into the police would kill any chance she

and Edmund had. "You're right, but we owe it to her to tell her before we turn him in."

"What? No, she'll tell him what we're doing."

"Why does that matter? He's probably sold the car long ago." Edmund watched his colleague and, probably his future brother-in-law, think.

Thomas's eyebrows raised like an idea had just popped in his head. "Have you ever asked why won't he let her sell the place? Even though he has no legal say, why he fights her so hard when she says she has to get the place cleaned out?"

"The buildings out back." Fury stormed in his gut. It was one thing to choose to drag himself down with illegal activities. It was another to drag his family along for the ride. "Only an idiot would keep stolen merchandise for this long."

"We're talking about Junior, here," Thomas scoffed. "He thinks he's never going to get caught and she's always going to bail him out."

"Then we talk to Harris and Shaw as soon as we can." Edmund extended his hand. "Not a word until we do, then I want to get her as far away from him as I can when the shit hits the fan."

"Agreed. The sooner Junior's sent away, the sooner Jade can move on."

"He's in jail for now. Whatever is in those buildings isn't going anywhere."

They shook and Edmund left work that day respecting Thomas a little bit more.

Before he reached his room at the Graff, he received a text from Jade to meet him at her father's property in an hour.

How ironic she'd pick there.

She sent him an address and written directions. When he arrived, the sun had begun its evening descent, sending its orange, yellow, and red rays into the darkening blue sky.

He walked out and stared at the two buildings not fifty yards from the main residence. "What secrets are you hiding back there, Junior? What are you dragging Jade into?"

Shaking his head, Edmund promised himself he wouldn't let her be screwed over by another man in her life, even if it killed any chance they might have.

"I won't let him drag you down. You deserve so much more."

The low groan of metal against metal echoed through the evening, catching his attention. An old Chevy Stepside came from around the far side of the house and headed for him.

It took a second to realize who sat behind the wheel.

"I'd know that smile anywhere." Instantaneously, his jeans were far too snug.

She pulled up next to him and put the truck in park. Her hair gently danced about her face. She wore almost no makeup and looked more beautiful than he'd ever seen her. "Evenin' cowboy."

"Evenin'." A new rack had been placed over the truck bed. "You've got something special planned for us?"

"Yes, I do. Get in."

It had been three days since they'd seen each other. They'd worked opposite shifts and long hours, but the conversation he would eventually have with her, regarding her brother, sat heavy in his heart and squelched his libido. "Jade."

"Look at this." She handed him an envelope as she drove them to the other side of the storage buildings and beyond, until the fields gradually sloped up.

"What's this?" He opened the letter and immediately realized what it was. "You got an offer for the property?"

"Yes! Maddie Cash is an absolute genius."

"Who's Maddie Cash?" He read through the paperwork as best he could as they traversed the decently flat fields.

"A Realtor in town."

"This is an incredible offer." *Oh shit. What about the buildings?*

"It is. I won't have to live in that tiny house on Bramble much longer. Fred will have a better yard. I'll have a savings account again."

As long as you don't need to use it to help your brother when he's arrested for grand theft auto. He wanted to tell her what he and Thomas suspected, but he wouldn't ruin her excitement. The relief in her eyes spoke volumes and what she sorely needed. "This is great. She must be good to sell it this quick."

"Lucy and Thomas mentioned I needed to sell the place several weeks ago when they were at Sage's chocolate shop. Maddie's a regular customer and Sage mentioned it the next time Maddie came in so she reached out to me." She pointed to the contract as they continued. "The day you came into town, I told her I was ready to sell so she did some research, sent out some feelers and contacted me yesterday about a nibble."

"Looks like it's a family buying the property. The Mac-leods."

She grabbed the paper and held it up like an Olympic torch. "Today, they sent me an offer, twenty percent more than the place is worth. Can you believe it?"

And a reason to leave. "What are you planning to do after you sell?"

"It's a world of possibilities. I could go work anywhere. Take a break from the medical field for a little bit. Take a real vacation." They reached a tree-lined area near a creek before she turned the truck around and backed it up where the bed of the truck halfway stuck out from the cover of the branches. "I won't celebrate until it's a done deal, but it's great to know there are people out there who are interested."

Glancing up, Edmund saw nothing but sky and the perfect view of the Copper Mountains. The brilliant sunset shot off its colors as the sky began the change from cerulean to midnight blue.

"Come on." Grabbing the picnic basket between them and a small case, she got out. "Let's celebrate my good news."

"What's in the case?"

"My handgun, in case we see snakes."

He paused and looked out the window. "Snakes?"

"Come on. It's going to be fine."

Carefully opening the truck door, Edmund scanned the area around them. "How quick do you need to have the place cleaned out?"

"Ten days. It's going to be difficult, but I think I can do it, depending on what's in there."

"What about Junior?" *Careful Edmund. Careful.* Although he didn't know if he needed to be more careful of the words he should use when discussing this or of potential reptiles that might not be glad he's visiting their turf.

The joy in her eyes faded as she rested the case in the picnic basket. "I haven't told my brother. He can find out after the deal is done."

Even though her response gave him hope she wouldn't inform Junior of the impending sale, he worried what she'd find when she cleared out the buildings. "Need help with cleaning up? Glad to do it."

"Yes, but I'm not going to think about that tonight. Tonight is about us spending time in one of my favorite places." Like a light switch, the joy in her eyes came right back on.

"I won't turn down that offer." He quickly followed and noticed in the bed of the truck were a large box, sleeping bags, and blankets. "What's all this?"

"I thought we could have a picnic out here and then have a little fun."

"What kind of fun?"

"Do you remember when we were talking about being under a blanket of stars? When you mentioned how impractical sex on the beach was because of sand getting everywhere?"

He cautiously agreed. "Yes, but what does that have to do with this?"

"Well, I thought you should see how we do it in Montana. No beach, no sand, but I do have blankets, a pickup, and a beautiful view."

Edmund let out a nervous laugh. He couldn't see the road, the fence line, or another house anywhere. Still, to be literally caught with their pants down wouldn't sit well with making a great impression with the townsfolk or the Montana medical board. "We can do that out here?"

"Honey, we can do anything we want out here. It's the advantage of owning the property and one thing I'll miss about it."

The loud creak and thud of the tailgate dropping echoed through the silence of the evening.

Jade climbed in the back of the truck and opened a box. She pulled out a string of lights and hung them on the rack. "A little ambiance."

"Nice touch, you need to plug those in somewhere?"

"Nope, solar-powered battery. Charged it this afternoon." She flipped a switch and a faint light in the bulb came on and gained strength with each passing minute.

"What else you got back there?"

She began to unroll what looked like an inflatable mattress and an air pump. "You wanna help or did you just want to do this on a hard, metal bed?"

Do what exactly? He didn't want to guess, but he sure hoped it was something along the lines of them being naked. A bag from the pharmacy peeked out from the picnic basket. He hoped he wouldn't pop his zipper from his excitement as he stood on the tailgate and watched her work.

She wore a strappy, cotton sundress that fit her so perfectly, it should have been illegal. Her boots were worn and scuffed, the sign of a woman who didn't mind getting dirty.

Just how dirty was another question.

"That's going to fit in back here?"

"Of course. It's designed specifically for SUVs and pickup truck beds." From the box, she produced an air pump.

"Don't you need to plug that in somewhere?"

"Nope. Batteries."

He noticed the shipping date on the inflatable mattress box label. "You've been planning this for a bit, haven't you?"

Her cheeks turned a lovely shade of crimson. "I thought it would be nice for us to have some alone time. No siblings. No patients. Nobody else. Just you and me, alone doing whatever we want."

His mouth went dry as she bit her lower lip. "Whatever we want, huh? You sure no one will see us out here?"

"Yep, the only other place with this kind of privacy is the land next door. Where you found Fred. They've got this grove of trees that's perfect for all sorts of privacy."

And it's for sale. What if I…no, don't get ahead of yourself. "Well, if you're sure we won't be seen."

"What, you don't want to be seduced under the stars?"

"Yeah, I want to be seduced." His jeans were so uncomfortable right now he'd be all for taking the risk even if they were parked in the middle of town. "What can I do to help?"

"Now, if you would please get the quilts organized, I'll open the champagne after I get this inflated." She popped the nozzle out of the mattress, flipped the switch, and within two minutes, they had a bed in the back of the truck.

She started to climb out, but as Jade walked by him, he wrapped his arm around her waist and kissed her. His tongue greedily slid between her lips before sweeping through her mouth. She tasted of mint and her hair smelled of vanilla, a combination of scents he could never see living without.

Because you love her.

Her body relaxed and she moaned against him as the strap of her dress fell off her shoulder. How he wanted to make the rest of her clothes fall so easily off her body.

"You know, if you keep kissing me like that, we're never going to get this set up like I want to." She unwrapped herself and put the strap back up.

"Leave it down." He swallowed hard, hoping she'd like his request. "Please."

Resting her chin on his chest, she gazed up at him. "Since you asked so nicely, I will."

With a flick of her finger, the material in question moved back where he liked it. Then she flipped the other strap off her shoulder as well. "I'm going to get the rest of the stuff out of the cab. Please make the bed so we can mess it up."

As she walked away, the straps bounced loosely against her sculpted arm as her hips swayed seductively. The bodice of the dress kept it in place, but he hoped he'd release them of their duty soon enough.

Who would have thought that a tiny piece of material would stir up so many carnal ideas?

The tree branches over them formed a natural canopy. A slight breeze had the leaves dancing, allowing bits of the sunset's colors to be temporarily let in while he laid the blankets and pillows out for them to enjoy.

A pop from the cab signaled she'd opened the champagne. "Can you get the food ready?"

"Can I ask you a question?" He organized the quilts in layers and the pillows sat against the back of the cab like the headboard of a bed.

"Yep." She climbed back in the truck, her dress lifting dangerously high as the breeze blew through.

"Why eat first? Why not, you know…drink a bit. Talk." *Let me rip that dress off you.*

She handed him a plastic champagne flute and knelt next to him. "First, we drink to good fortune and new possibilities."

"Cheers." They clinked their glasses, each took a sip and cringed as a sickeningly sweet followed by a hard sour taste coated his tongue. "Man, this is—"

She tossed the remainder of her champagne into the grass. "Awful. You don't have to drink that."

He did the same and took her glass before resting them both in the basket and tapping the pharmacy bag. "What else you got in there?"

"Patience, my dear." Reaching over, she pulled out two travel-sized bottles of wine. "How about this?"

Edmund ran his hand up her leg as she opened each of the bottles, handing him one. "Let's try this again. To good fortune and new possibilities."

"Cheers." She smiled before taking a long drink and putting the cap back on.

The dryness of the wine made him cringle slightly, but it had been far better than the horrid sour taste of the champagne. "Better."

Leaning forward, she backed him up to the pillows. "First, we're going to have some wine."

"Done."

"And then a bit of food and, finally, have some fun." She nibbled his neck as her hand pressed against the buttons of his shirt. Her fingers opened one button as she spoke softly against his skin.

"We can't have fun, first and last?" His hands ran down her hips, lifting her dress slightly before allowing it to fall back in place. "Because I'm all for fun. Especially with you."

She playfully sucked on her bottom lip. "I don't know, I kind of had this entire evening planned my way."

"Anything I can do to convince you to change your plans?"

"Maybe." She cocked an eyebrow. "What are you willing to offer me to change things up?"

Without a hint of hesitation, he cupped her butt and pulled her flush to him. "I could offer you a lot."

"I bet you could." She popped a few of his buttons, her hands rested on his bare skin. "Since you asked so nicely, I'll think about changing my plans."

"Glad I could accommodate you."

"Foreplay aside, let me show you something." She curled beside him, his hand rested on her hip as she pointed in front of them. "What do you think?"

The unobstructed view of Copper Mountain displayed in

front of them like some high-definition seventy-inch TV screen. The trees not only offered a natural canopy, but the perfect frame of the moment.

"I'm going to miss this." She took another drink of her wine.

"I bet. Hard to give up something you love so much." The words slammed into his heart as reality jolted the obvious.

I love you.

When she didn't respond, he knew he'd keep the secret a bit longer.

"I can't keep lying to myself about what I can handle." She sighed.

He ran his hand up and down her hip in a gentle tempo. "What do you mean? The property?"

"No, my brother. I can't make excuses for him anymore."

Even though she said it with conviction, Edmund could hear the sadness in her voice. "You'll never be alone, you know that, right?"

Snuggling closer to him, she slid her hand into his shirt, her palm resting on his chest. "You always know what to say to me."

"That's because I...I...um...like you. A lot." *Chicken shit. Just tell her.*

"Your heart's beating fast." Jade propped herself on her elbow. "You okay?"

"Fine, just thinking about you and having to give up this place."

She shrugged. "It's what it is. Can't change it. Besides, Copper Mountain isn't going anywhere. I can see it from so many places in town."

A sly smirk spread across his face. "Yeah, but you can't be naked outside while getting this view in town."

"Not without being arrested." Straddling him, she finished the last drops of her wine and placed the bottle in the basket. "I guess we'd better make this naked time outside count. You've convinced me. Get ready to have some fun."

Chapter Twenty-One

H IS HEART WENT rapid tempo as she kissed his bare chest while unfastening his buttons. As soon as she got to the last one, she pulled his shirt out of from his jeans and spread the material wide. "Oh my. How delicious."

Delicious possibilities. "You think so?"

A greedy lust washed over her face.

He could almost hear her say "mine" as her eyes raked over him and her hands wandered.

Pressing against his fly, she smirked. "I know so."

"Do I get to take something off you when you take something off me?"

She scooted down his body, resting on his thighs. "Not yet. Lift your hips."

He hadn't realized it, but she'd popped the button on his jeans and unzipped his fly. She rested her hands on either side of his zipper and gently rubbed him over his clothes.

A moan escaped his lips as he raised his hips as she'd asked. At an agonizingly slow tempo, off she pushed his clothes down to his knees. He began to kick them off until she took him in one hand, slowly stroking him.

No matter how many times they'd done this, every time

she'd stroked his cock, it felt new and wildly erotic.

Her touch almost caused him to come unglued. The softness of her palm rubbing against him had him grabbing handfuls of the blanket to keep him from helping her to go faster. "Damn, that feels good."

"You like that?"

"Yes."

"Then say it louder."

"Louder?" His mouth went dry.

"Yes, you wanted privacy. You've got privacy out here."

"Yes!" He nodded, watching her stroke him in her elegant hand as the leaves of the trees fluttered in the evening breeze. "That's right. Up and down."

"You like being out here?"

"It's perfect. You're perfect."

"It's one of my favorite places in the world." She kissed up his inner thigh. "I wanted to bring you here because you're my favorite person."

His fingers threaded through her hair as she rubbed him. "I'm honored. Now take your dress off."

"Goodness, you're demanding." Moving closer, Jade gave him complete access to her body and held her arms over her head. "I love it."

Sitting up, he kissed her as he made quick work of her clothes, tossing them somewhere in the bed of the truck. The setting sun reflected off her hair as though she had gold weaved through her chocolate locks.

As soon as her dress had been stripped from her, she continued to touch him, stroke him as he unclasped her strapless bra and flipped it over his shoulder.

It landed in the grass.

"That's a new bra, you know." Her lip stuck out in a playful pout.

"I'll get you a new one."

"You better."

"You're naked."

She raised an eyebrow. "I still have my boots and panties on."

With her on her knees, his face was in the perfect place, to take her nipple in his mouth. He ran his tongue across it, loving the way she responded to his touch.

With her free hand, her fingers threaded through his hair as her head fell backward. "Edmund."

His thumb danced slowly across her other breast. The rhythm of her touching him slowed but continued.

"Stand up." She growled and moved away from him, finally freeing him from his jeans, shoes, and socks.

Awkwardly, he pushed himself to his feet and she backed him up until his bare butt touched the glass of the cab. His body, bare as the day he'd been born, totally exposed for the world to see.

The hungry look in her eyes made him feel like he'd been served up for dinner. And he liked it.

"I've been waiting too long today to get to do this to you."

"Do what?" He waited with great anticipation as her lips touched his shaft and when the soft skin moved around him, he willed himself not to lose it right then and there.

She took him into her mouth achingly slow. Her tongue circled the tip before she'd take him in and sucking gently and pulling back.

Standing in the truck bed under a cover of trees with an uninterrupted evening view of the Copper Mountains should have been enough to make this night perfect. The setting sun reflected off the brilliant peaks as the evening breeze tickled his bare chest. His nipples.

Add in Jade working her magic with her tongue on his cock and Edmund could die happily right now.

"Damn, Jade," he whispered as she swirled her tongue around the tip.

"You know, you don't have to whisper out here. No one will hear you." She brushed her lips against the bare skin of his thigh as her fingers wrapped around his erection, moving at an agonizingly torturous pace. "You wanna get loud?"

The idea of unapologetically screaming in ecstasy only excited him more. "Yes."

"Let me hear you then." She slid him back between her lips and increased her suction and rhythm. Her fingers fanned out on his thighs as her thumbs slid up and brushed against the underside of his balls.

At first, he couldn't move past his own censorship, but the more she touched him, the more emboldened he became. "Yes, yes, Jade. Don't stop."

"Louder," she coaxed before taking him in again and slid her hand up to graze his chest.

"Damn, that feels good." He growled as his hips began to rock with the rhythm she set. "Yes, yes."

Her hands worked in perfect sync with her mouth as she moaned against him. The vibration of her voice reverberated around his cock, rapidly encouraging him toward release far sooner than he wanted. "Jade, you're gonna have to stop."

Before she let go she cupped him, making his knees buckle.

"Damn, woman."

She giggled as her hands wandered over his chest. "I love making you squirm."

"Let me return the favor."

Chapter Twenty-Two

THE FADING SUN'S glow over Copper Mountain had always looked picture perfect to Jade, but with Edmund moving her panties and her bare breasts being caressed by the evening breeze, its vibrancy took on an entirely new color scheme.

"You smell so good, like vanilla." He playfully growled as his tongue teased her nipple. "Like a sundae."

"How much do you like sundaes, Edmund?" Her fingers ran though his thick hair.

"I could eat sundaes everyday…for a very long time." He paused. "The rest of my life."

"What?" She sat up and scooted backward.

He made no attempt to come toward her, but sat back on his heels and nodded, a resigned look on his face as though he'd accepted something he'd been fighting. "I could eat vanilla for the rest of my life."

Edmund had broken the mold when it came to men. Not once had he ever made her feel trapped or scared. He listened and understood her more than most. His compassion and empathy. His ability to get her aroused at the wink of an eye and he'd never lied to her, about anything.

With all of it wrapped up in a chiseled package, Jade couldn't believe that anyone like Edmund would have entered her life, much less professed his...what? Really strong like for her?

His devotion to vanilla?

Complete joy and utter terror fought in her brain as her body relished his touch and begged for more. "You...um...like vanilla that much that you'd want to have it every day?"

"Not like. Love." He placed his hands on her hips and pulled her closer before he brushed his lips along her stomach. "I love vanilla."

"Love?" she squeaked and eyed the small bottle of wine to her right.

"Yes, love."

"I see." She reached out, grabbing the bottle. Uncapping it, she swallowed a healthy gulp of wine and then a second. "Love?"

Crawling up her body, he took the bottle from her fingers, finished the wine and kissed her. "Love."

"I see, but don't you think you'd eventually get bored with vanilla every day? I mean, you did say it's a boring flavor." *Why are you trying to talk him out of this?*

"Remember, you said there are delicious possibilities with vanilla, because it's great with chocolate." He licked her nipple. "Strawberry."

"Yes." Her mouth went dry as his touch made her go boneless. "Oh yes. What else goes with vanilla?"

His thumb danced along the opposite breast before

brushing over the tender skin at the tip. "Carmel. Pineapple. Peach."

"Cinnamon."

"Yes. Vanilla's what it all starts with and if you love vanilla, it can work with anything."

The sun's darkened rays peaked through the canopy, dotting Edmund with drops of evening sunshine. Admiration filled his eyes as he kissed her belly button.

Her list popped up to derail her happiness, but like the character in the musical, *Kinky Boots*, she finally gave into her want and pushed the negative away.

He loves me. Those three words weren't anything new to Jade's life. She's heard them many times over the years. From her boyfriends, her ex-husband. All of them couldn't hold a candle to the way Edmund said it.

"Show me how much you love vanilla."

"I thought you'd never ask." His thumbs ran across her nipples, making them peak.

She gasped as he took one tender tip in his mouth and gently sucked as his fingers danced across the other. "Yes, Edmund. Yes."

Her fingers ran through his thick, wavy hair while his tongue ravaged her breasts.

He kissed her down her belly button to run his finger along the seam of her. The heat of anticipation surged through her as he laid tender kisses on her outer folds.

He settled between her legs, his hands slid under her butt. A light evening wind caressed her bare skin. "Do you know how much I love doing this to you?"

"How much?"

He slipped a finger inside her. "I'm going to show you."

She let out a small gasp. *I'm a dead woman, but, it's going to be so worth it.*

His tongue slid between her lips and brushed her clit.

She moaned and fully relaxed her legs. "Edmund."

"That's it," he coaxed as his hands ran over her thighs and cupped her bottom. He flicked her sensitive nub with his tongue before sucking it. His fingers kneaded her ass as he buried his face between her legs.

Jade panted, her face warmed with desire.

He kissed up her belly again as he slid a finger in her again, his thumb on her clit.

She ran her fingers through his hair as he worked his way to her breasts again. Taking a peaked nipple between his lips, Edmund licked it before he gently sucked.

She arched her back, pushing more of herself into his mouth. "Yes."

Rubbing the opposite nipple with his thumb, he caressed her soft folds with his fingers. "You're so wet. So beautiful."

Her breathing increased as she rocked her hips to the rhythm he'd started.

"Edmund, I want you in me. Please," she begged. "Please, I want you in me."

Grabbing for the pharmacy bag, he wrestled out a condom, ripped open the wrapper with his teeth and covered himself in record time.

As soon as he slid inside her she wrapped her legs around him.

Their eyes locked as he pulled out and re-entered her in a slow, torturous move.

Jade thought she'd unravel right there. His presence blissfully filled her.

He growled as the tempo increased. "You feel so good. So damned good."

"Yes." She nodded as he moved in and out of her. Her all-consuming want for him drove her crazy with desire. She tightened her legs around him, encouraging him on. "Yes."

Edmund moaned as his hips rocked quicker, harder.

She met him with each thrust, grabbing his ass, pushing him deeper. Electricity surged through her as she came unglued. She kissed him hard and passionately rode his cock, her climax encouraging him to the finish line. "Yes, yes. Yes!"

He arched his back, thrusting his hips and stiffening as the pulsation of his release filled her up.

They lay in a tangled mass of arms and legs as each caught their breath and the sun set.

After a few moments, he lifted his head and kissed her again. "I love you."

Tears immediately fell down her face. "You love me."

"Yes. And I want to spend the rest of our lives showing you just how much."

Cupping his face, she sniffled. "I love you, Edmund and—"

"And I will always protect you."

His blurting the words made her nervously laugh. "I know you will."

"Please don't ever forget that." Worry clouded his eyes,

but she didn't want to ask because tonight was about them. Only them.

"I won't."

They quickly cleaned up and then curled up in the back of the truck with a quilt as they watched the sun fade for the day and their blanket of stars come out.

Chapter Twenty-Three

THE OLD METAL building looked like it was a good, strong winter storm away from falling over, but remarkably it had held up for the past several years.

Staring where her brothers had fixed cars and her father spent countless hours repairing odds and ends and creating furniture for their home, Jade wondered what the walls would say if they could talk.

When she decided the nursing school route, their dad wanted to establish a family business so he opened an auto repair shop with her brothers.

Sadly, his dream of all three children settling back in Marietta and dividing up the twenty-five acres and raising their grandbabies would never come to fruition.

James wanted out and headed to Alaska to join the Coast Guard.

Jade preferred to leave for a few years before deciding to settle back here.

And Junior, well who knew what Junior did during all that time?

No matter how she ran it through her head, the sadness of her father's failed dream lodged in her throat. With the selling of the property, for certain those dreams were no more than a wishful thinking from a man, long gone. "Sorry it didn't work out, Daddy."

Glancing behind her, she hoped Edmund would arrive sooner than planned, but he wasn't due for another thirty minutes and her itch to get started began to take hold.

The brilliant, blue morning sky didn't have a cloud in it. She closed her eyes, turned her face to the sun, relishing in the warmth of its rays.

The color spectrum appeared more vivid, alive, and beautiful.

Amazing what happens when you open your heart and allow love in.

Two nights ago, the man of her dreams professed his love for her and showed her how much, twice.

Even now, her body ached for him, but not only physically.

Simply being with him gave her a calm and comfort she couldn't explain or understand.

He loves me.

For too long, she blocked the ideas of her happily ever after, but without trying, Edmund opened her eyes to a realm of possibilities here and outside Marietta.

Yet, uncertainty whispered as she faced the metal building again.

"What if...what if..." The idea that her brother would screw things up for her and her love with whatever he'd hidden in there twisted her stomach tight, but she couldn't hide from it forever.

Convincing herself she could get an idea of what they'd have to tackle regarding the contents of the building, she decided to get started without Edmund.

Or maybe you want to see what's in there before he gets here.

"Let's get this over with." She approached the door and cut off the lock with the bolt cutters. It landed with a hard thump against the dirt, signifying unavoidable change she'd fought against for too long.

Out of nowhere, the unbelievable offer for the property had arrived on Realtor Maddie Cash's computer. According to Maddie, the new owners were so anxious to quick sale, they waved any building inspections since their plans were to bulldoze everything and start over.

She could leave with Edmund if she so chose or she could travel. Take a break from nursing for a bit. Get away from the chaos her brother so easily stirred up.

Man, I hope he stays in jail until after the sale. Lord knows what he'll do if he hears about it.

As she reached for the door handle, she paused. Was she ready for whatever her brother had in here?

Glancing behind her, she listened again for the crunch of tires on the gravel driveway.

Nothing but the sounds of the morning.

Pulling the handgun out of her right front jeans pocket, she mentally prepared for any obstinate critters that might have set up shop.

More than once she'd encountered a western rattlesnake or two on the property. The building had several spots where serpents and rodents could duck in and it would be an extremely nice place to lay eggs and babies. A lot of them.

Hopefully, that will be the worst thing in here.

She swallowed hard and took a step back, sliding the safety off.

It could be nothing. Just junk.

But a voice whispered from the back of her brain.

You know better. You know Junior better.

She swallowed hard.

Then what will you do? Turning in anything in this building having to do with Junior's illegal activity would send him to prison for life.

Could she carry that burden?

"Maybe he won't be stupid enough to keep anything here," she scoffed. "Please don't have screwed me over, Brother."

Rolling her neck from side to side to loosen the knots of angst, she refused to allow the negativity.

Life had certainly turned her way. She had a solid job. She had good friends. She had routine and consistency. A potential buyer for the property.

Edmund.

Her body tingled at the thought of him.

I love the way he smiles at me, the way he makes me feel I can do anything.

Love. The word made her giggle with delight.

Love. For the first time, she realized what all those poets wrote about, those singers crooned over, the brokenhearted died for, and what all those heroes and heroines fought for in the pages of the books she so loved to read.

"I love Edmund." She sighed and repeated it louder. "I love Edmund."

Empowered with those simple words, with the flick of her wrist, she threw opened the door.

The musty air breathed in the crisp morning breeze, stirring up layers of dust. She coughed as she fumbled for the light, but only a single bulb next to the door turned on. Not enough for her to see much of anything clearly, but she breathed a sigh of relief when she didn't see long rows of grow lighting and pot plants. "Of course he wouldn't have pot plants. Those require constant maintenance and TLC. Plus the ventilation in here sucks."

Working in the ER in California, she'd learned multiple things from patients about growing marijuana including the necessary acidity of the soil, who sold the best grow lights, and that growing plants indoors would reap one a better quality plant.

"Okay, he's not growing weed. That's one off my worry list." Taking a deep inhale, she didn't notice any acidic scents such as ammonia, paint thinner, or vinegar. Feeling hopeful, Jade looked around. No packages of cold medicine anywhere. No stoves. No old pots. Just piles of tools thrown every which way. "Looks like I can cross meth lab off the list."

Again, her patients had been more forthcoming about multiple drugs they'd either taken, sold, or made. Amazing what people would say when they didn't think they'd get in trouble for it.

The ER was always a learning experience.

"Okay, no meth lab. That's two." A nervous giggle escaped her, but her brother providing illegal drugs for the southern part of Montana had certainly been near the top of her list of what-the-hell-was-Junior-hiding-out-here questions.

The morning sun peeked in through the frames around the double doors at the far end of the building. As her eyes adjusted, she could make the outlines of several cars. All appeared to be in different stages of repair.

Or being taken apart.

Jade's heart clenched, thinking of how she'd have to deal with her brother's mess once again. "It doesn't matter. Someone wants the place. I can get out of here."

She backed up and walked around to open the far double doors and found them chained, but not locked. The years of being in the weather had rusted the metal chains together. The bolt cutters made quick work of them and she had them out of the way within seconds.

Feeling revived and determined, she opened one of the sliding doors, sending dust everywhere. When she turned to push the other door open, she froze as she spotted the familiar three-pointed star symbol. A Mercedes.

"Oh, shit."

Despite sitting in the building for who knew how long, the deep blue paint sparkled under the sun's morning rays.

"Blue. A blue Mercedes." She walked around the side and kicked the tire when she saw it only had two doors. "Coupe."

Closing her eyes, Jade tried to grab hold of her skyrocketing anger, but the hope of getting her life back had been completely derailed. "Damn you, Junior. Why do you keep doing this to me?"

The driver's window sat open and the keys were on the dashboard. Next to it, a ring. "Where have I seen that?"

Reaching in, she picked it up and noticed the uneven grooves. Holding it sideways, it looked like a mountain range. An exact copy of the one that Mr. Stevenson wore. "The Rockies. Oh, no."

Immediately, she remembered the description of the ring her brother used to split open Thomas's lip a few months ago during a fight.

"Shit. Shit. Shit." With her heart in her throat, she tossed the ring back into the car, slid the safety back on before tucking the gun in her front pocket, and pushed the other door open.

For a moment, she didn't register what she saw.

The front grill crushed in. A long crack in the windshield indicated something slammed into it. Dark specks of black splattered all over the front of the grill. "Good Lord, what did he hit? A deer?"

Studying the windshield, she could see a long smear of blood that looked like… "Is that a handprint?"

Another similar blood pattern rested on the hood.

Bile coated the back of her throat and she quickly backed away. "Oh, my God! Oh, my God!"

Tears flooded her vision as she defiantly shook her head. "He wouldn't. He wouldn't."

"I knew you'd lose your shit if you saw this."

Sadness plummeted to her gut like a boulder off a cliff hearing his voice. "You really have no shame, do you?"

"Why should I?"

Without thought, she turned, letting her fist fly. The impact of landing against her brother's lip shot up her arm.

Screaming, he stumbled backward, holding his face.

"Why should you? Grand theft auto, murder might be a reason or even just dragging me into this mess or…" Trembling, she shook out her arm as she tried to rationalize the obvious away, but there could be no mistake. On the windshield, the bloody imprint of a left hand with long finger streaks. "Did-did you hit…a person?"

"Son of a bitch, Jade. What the hell was that for?" He dabbed at his bloodied mouth with the back of his hand.

"Did you hit somebody?" Before she tucked her gun back into her front pocket, she verified the safety was on.

"Probably."

"Probably? That's all you can say is probably?"

"What do you want me to say?" he scoffed as though she'd asked him if he'd eaten all the cookies from the jar.

"Your indifference to human existence astounds me."

"Quit using five-dollar words, Jade. You're not impressing anyone." He ran his finger along the hood of the car, removing a fine line of dust. "This thing needs a bath."

And would destroy the evidence. "You haven't done that before now because…why?"

"I didn't get around to it. The car was too hot to unload."

"This thing has GPS."

"I got a friend who has these cool gadgets. He turned it off." He mimicked a remote control.

"Did your friend ask you why you needed a cool gadget?" *Oh, my God. What am I going to do?*

"Nope, but I got it a long time ago." He shrugged.

"It always works?"

"Always."

Holding her stomach, her morning protein smoothie wanted to rebel against her. "How many cars have you stolen?"

"Enough."

"Not to condone this, but—"

He pulled out a wad of cash and threw a five-dollar bill at her. "That's for condone."

"How do you have any cash? You don't work." She raised her hands in the air. "Don't tell me. I don't what to hear any of your crap."

He sneered. "You can get a lot of things if you know where they are."

"Oh Lord, Junior. What, you knock over a convenience store? Why haven't you done anything about this huge piece of evidence before now?"

"I got busy."

"Yes, because sitting on your ass all day and getting high takes a tremendous amount of time." Her hands shook so hard she rubbed them on her jeans, hoping to calm herself. "I don't know what makes this more distressing. The fact that you hit someone or the fact you don't give a shit."

"I don't give a shit," he snarled as he lit up a cigarette. "I heard you sold the place so I'm here to get my stuff."

Scanning the car again, she moved away as if it would bite her. "When did this happen? And how the hell are you out of jail?"

"I called in a favor."

"How did you make bail?" It finally dawned on her he wore a bright orange jumpsuit. "Did you break out?"

"So, I have this friend—"

"Stop, stop right there." Burying her face in her hands, she shook her head. Despair threatened to choke the happy out of her. "Don't tell me. I don't want to know."

He scoffed, waving her away. "Wouldn't tell you anyway."

She pointed to the car. "Where did you get this?"

"Up at the lake."

Remembering Phoebe's casual comment about them being here a couple years ago, Jade had to know for certain. "When?"

"You want a date?" He wiped his hand off on his jumpsuit. "You've got a wicked punch."

"Unless you wanna chew on your nuts, I suggest you tell me what this is before I kick you. Hard." She ran her fingers through her hair, yanking several strands out. "I want answers, Junior. Now."

"Why do you have to go dig this up?"

His apathy toward anyone else on the planet had always astounded her, but now seeing that he truly lacked a conscience, bruised her heart. "Ironic you mention dig it up. You hit a person! A human being."

"Why is that my fault? The jerkoff wouldn't get out of the road." Taking a long drag from his cigarette, he leaned against the building.

"It doesn't matter if she was in the road—"

"I said he."

"No you said jerkoff. You remembered it was a man. What else do you remember?"

He clenched his jaw and shook his head.

"And you've hidden the car." She rubbed her temples to keep her fury at bay. "I'm guessing you fled the scene. Did they die?"

"I didn't stick around to find out."

"Obviously." Her gut roared with pain, making it raw. "What happened, Junior?"

He began to leave. "What difference does it make? It's done, right?"

"No. No, it's not done." She grabbed the shoulder of his jumpsuit and yanked him backward. "Don't you dare blow me off. Hitting an animal, it's done. Hit and run on a person, that's an entirely different situation. What. Happened?"

He shoved her hand away. "Get off my ass. I'm not sure."

"What do you mean, you're not sure?"

"I only remember parts of it."

"But you remember enough to know it was a man. What, were you stoned or drunk or whatever that night?"

"Why are you being such a bitch about this? It was Labor Day weekend. Time to party." He danced around her.

244

Dread settled in her throat, temporarily strangling her. "Which Labor Day weekend?"

"Dad's last."

"So 2016? When I was in San Diego?"

"I guess." He shrugged, before taking another drag and tilting his chin up, blowing the smoke over his head. "Guys were partying at the lake. I told Dad I'd be back. No big deal."

Clenching her fists at her sides, she remembered the calls from her father, begging her to come home and take care of him. "You were supposed to stay with him. He needed help, Junior. He couldn't get out of the chair on his own."

"What, I don't get a break? I'm supposed to sit around, while he pissed and shit on himself. Hang out and do nothing?" A tear escaped him. He defiantly wiped it away. "I couldn't watch it anymore."

She'd never seen her brother cry. His unrestrained emotions unnerved her, but Junior had the beautiful ability to shed crocodile tears without warning. After years of watching him refuse to take responsibility for anything, this was simply an act to derail her. A pathetic distraction from facing responsibility.

Again.

"Cut the crap, Junior. You don't feel an inkling of guilt about this. If you actually cared about Dad, you would have done more for him."

A wicked smirk immediately replaced his sadness. "You know me well, Sis."

"Besides, I paid for the home health nurses to come in.

They should have been here to help. Where were they?"

"I fired the home health nurses."

"What? I paid for those."

"Overpaid. I saw what you were sending them every week so I told Dad we didn't need them. I'd take care of it."

"How?" Jade pointed. "I never told you what James and I were spending."

He cupped himself. "*Sweet talked* one of them to send me a copy of the statements. Then told them your address changed."

"You're a piece of shit. Do you know how hard I worked to pay for good health care for Dad?"

"He didn't appreciate it or want it."

"That wasn't your choice to make! That money could have gone to the taxes owed on the house or repaired something."

"I put it to better use." He took a long drag and blew the smoke in her direction.

"Like on one of the fun gadgets that turn off *GPSe*s?"

"Maybe."

Fury replaced her desire to save him. "You know what? I almost felt bad about Dad having me as the sole executor, but after that little comment, it's dawned on me that you've already gotten your inheritance."

"Already gotten…what?"

"You've robbed me, your dad, everyone in your life." Kicking up a cloud of dirt, she growled. "I can't believe this. I honestly can't believe you've screwed over so many people and don't give a shit."

"Why was I the only one watching Dad? Where the hell were you?"

"Where the hell was I?" She stomped her foot. "You knew damned well where I was. I was in San Diego, trying to keep from being killed by my ex-husband and make enough money to come back here. What the hell were you doing, Junior? Because I know you weren't working."

"You think you're so much better than me. You and James think I'm the family fuck-up." He leaned against the car, but she pushed him off it, hoping he wouldn't ruin any evidence.

She caught a glimpse of her watch. *Edmund will be here any minute.*

The seconds ticked, bringing her closer to losing everything she'd worked so hard to regain.

He'll never want anything to do with me after this.

But she couldn't let her brother walk away. "After seeing all this, yeah, Junior, that's exactly what I think. You don't hold a job, you keep getting arrested, you have no concept of responsibility."

"Get off my ass, Jade. You're not my mom."

"And thank God for that." She motioned to the car. "You're not walking away from this one."

"Watch me." He flipped her off and turned around.

"Junior!"

No pause. He stormed away.

She rested her hands on her hips and the cold butt of the gun touched her right wrist. Blinded by anger, she fired two shots in the air, bringing him to a screeching halt. "Get.

Your ass. Back. Over. Here."

With a slow turn, the shocked look on his face almost made her snort from amusement.

His eyes as wide as an anime character. "What the fuck?"

She thumbed the safety back on and put her gun back in her front jeans pocket. "Explain this!"

Kicking a rock, he slouched, clenching his fists at his sides as he walked toward the building, keeping a safe distance from her. "You don't tell me what to do. I'm not a child."

"Then act like an adult for once!" She pointed to the car. "You hit a person, Junior, in a *stolen* car!"

"Who told you I stole the car?" He ducked into the building at the other door.

"I'm not an idiot. I think we've well established this car is stolen." Jade chased after him. "Don't you dare hide. That's a Mercedes. Nothing you could afford, even if you did work."

"Since when did you know so much about cars? That's cool." He held his hand up for a high five, but she crossed her arms over her chest. "Way to be a bitch, Jade."

"I'm furious, Junior! Do you have any idea what you've done? What you've dragged me into? You promised to stay with Dad until my assignment was complete at the end of the year and you bailed. You left him alone and then you left town."

"What the hell do you know? You off with your job and living good in California. James in that frozen hell. Me here with nothing."

"That's because you won't do anything, Junior. It's a choice and your choices suck." Her brain hurt from ducking his multiple attempts to avoid the obvious, but she wouldn't let him slide. Not this time. "Who did you hit?"

He shook his head, his lips thinned.

She choked on the words. "You didn't even stop. See if the person was okay."

For the first time, Junior's arrogance disappeared only to be replaced by what appeared to be a hint of regret. "I didn't see him until he was pinned between my car and the other one. When I backed up, he reached out and crawled up the hood, slapped on the windshield. Probably telling me to stop, I guess. Blood coming out of his mouth, got it all over the glass. Disgusting."

Jade choked back a sob, thinking of the poor soul who made the attempt for his own life. Trying to get her brother to help. "Tell me. Who did you hit, Junior?"

With trembling fingers, he attempted to hold the cigarette still, but only got a short drag off it. "I didn't know for sure who it was until I read the paper the next day."

"In the paper? Oh, God." *Please. Please don't be who I think it is.* "Junior, who did you hit?"

"It's not my fault!"

She stepped closer, dreading his confession, but needing to hear it. "You know exactly who it was, don't you?"

"I don't have to answer—"

"Junior. Say who you hit."

"Get off my—"

Reaching out, Jade grabbed her brother by the collar and

pulled him nose to nose. "Who did you fucking hit, Junior!"

The arrogance in his eyes faded as he swallowed hard. "Harry Monroe."

Chapter Twenty-Four

H ARRY MONROE HAD only been twenty-seven years old. One of the nicest guys on the planet.

He never met a stranger and had always been there to help, which was why he'd been there that night. Simply helping an elderly couple change their flat tire.

And my brother ran him over and left him to die.

Even when living in San Diego, she checked the newspaper almost daily and it knocked the wind out of her to see the headline—*Harry Monroe Struck Dead.*

He'd been a few grades behind her in school, but she remembered him well. The guy always had a smile on his face. Always had a good day.

His sudden death placed a layer of sadness over the town that she could still feel when his birthday came around or the anniversary of his unsolved case hit each year.

Or when any event was held at Harry's House.

After reading his obituary, she wondered what kind of monster would hit someone and drive away.

Now she knew exactly who would do this…and she shared DNA with him.

Her knees buckled and she fell to the ground. Facing the

midmorning sun, Jade's soul collapsed under the weight of the world that would certainly come crashing down when she called Sheriff Rob Shaw and Deputy Logan Tate.

Nothing would be the same ever again.

Her job. Her dignity. Her brother.

Her father's property.

Edmund.

One. I shouldn't have given in to wanting him.

Two. I should have turned him away the first moment he smiled at me.

Three. I shouldn't have dragged him into my chaos.

The foul taste of disappointment coated the back of her throat and rebelled. She lunged forward and emptied her stomach in the grass.

The gun in her pocket fell on the ground next to her.

"How could you? How could you do this? To Harry. To his family." Jade wept when her stomach quit arguing with her. "To me."

The grass didn't feel soft under her hands anymore, but prickly and irritating.

The sun didn't warm her body, but made her uncomfortably hot as a line of sweat beaded along her hairline.

The uninterrupted view of Copper Mountain was now an eyesore.

As sad as she'd been about selling the land, she couldn't wait to get away from it now. Her brother had ruined it.

Tainted it.

Destroyed every happy moment, every memory she'd experienced here by hiding his atrocity.

Even ruining those amazing moments with Edmund not forty-eight hours ago because how could he stay with her now?

My stepfather abused me as my mother turned the other way.

I picked an abusive husband only to have to shoot him in self-defense.

My brother brazenly ran someone over without a hint of compassion or guilt.

She slapped the ground, sending a chunk of dirt across the grass.

Could I be any more damaged? Could my life be any more ridiculous? I'm a train wreck. That's what I am.

Sorrow crawled up from her soul and erupted from her lungs. She screamed without apologizes. "Damn you, Junior. Damn you for screwing up my life!"

A few moments passed before the slam of the house door echoed in the air. "What did you say?"

She didn't want to face him as she stomped toward the metal building. "Get the hell away from me, Junior."

"Come on, Jade. We'll dump the car—"

"Don't you dare touch anything. Not anything." Determined to get the keys before he could drive the car anywhere, she cut him off. "You're a walking nightmare, you know it? A complete waste of oxygen."

"What are you doing?" A look of panic on his face.

She grabbed a screwdriver off the table, reached in, and gently took the keys that sat on the dashboard. Making a pouch with her shirt, she dropped them in, holding them close. "Don't say anything to me. I don't want to hear anything other than I'm turning myself in, do you hear me?"

"Why would I do that?" He followed behind her as she headed for her car. "Jade, give me those keys."

"Get the hell away from me, Junior." Blinded by tears, she focused on making it to her car, locking herself inside, and calling 911. "Wait, how did you even get the keys?"

"They aren't for *that* car." He chuckled.

She held them up, noticing the Honda emblem on the keys. "What do you mean this car? Where are the Mercedes's keys?"

"In that car." He pointed to her hand.

"Oh good, Lord. I don't want to know."

His footsteps quickly approached. "Jade, you can't do that. You can't."

"I can and I will."

His history spoke for itself and he would never accept responsibility for his destruction. Ever.

Just like their mother.

And just like last time, she'd have to make a hard choice to save herself and lose everything.

Except this time, she'd do it all on her own.

Because that's what strong women do, right? They survive.

He grabbed her arm, jerking her around. "Look, I don't want to hurt you, but I'm not going to prison."

A sharp pain shot up into her shoulder, but the keys remained protected. She wrestled out of his grip, holding on to her rational brain by a thread. "I've worked my ass off to get where I am. I finally find happiness, real happiness and here you come along and strip it away from me. What is it about our family that we can't let each other have our happily ever after?"

He pulled another cigarette out of his pocket. "Happiness? You dating someone?"

"Yes. Edmund." She tilted her chin up. "And he's wonderful."

"Edmund? What the hell kind of name is Edmund?" His eyes went wide with understanding. "What? With that nerd at the park? Come on, Jade, you can do better than Paul Bunyan."

"Really? Better? No, Junior, I'm lucky to have Edmund. I'm lucky that he still wants me at all after meeting you and now…" She turned toward the building, the horror of what sat inside uncomfortably twisted her heart. "There's no way he'll stay. Not after this."

"Then don't say anything. He'll never know. I won't tell him." Each of Junior's sinister words hit like a dart. "Then you get what you want. I get what I want."

"What about Harry? Did he get what he wanted?" A new round of angry tears pricked at the backs of her eyelids, but she defiantly wiped them away. "What about Harry, Junior? Didn't he always talk about having a family? A lot of kids?"

"Yeah, he probably did." The confidence he held not moments ago immediately weakened.

Narrowing her gaze, she walked toward him. "Didn't he talk about how much he wanted to go a good job every day? His coworkers were like family to him."

"I guess." He scurried backward, like a rat on the run.

"Harry never wanted for a kind word. He always helped those in need."

"Stop it, Jade. Just stop it." He'd reached the side of the building then slid along it as she berated him until he reached the stolen car and sat inside.

"And didn't Harry love his family and want to stay in Marietta so his mom and dad could bounce those grand-babies on their knees?"

True tears ran down his face, causing her to pause not a few feet from him. "You ripped that from him, Junior. In one selfish, stupid, brutal act, you robbed him of everything he held dear. So I ask you, Brother, why in the hell should *you* get what *you* want?"

For the first time in their lives together, her brother had no rebuttal. No comical response. No sarcastic comeback. For a split second, the realization of taking another man's life seeped into that black soul of his appeared to hit its mark.

A sobbed escaped him as he cowered against the car. "I didn't mean to. I swear I didn't, but—"

"But you did, didn't you? You drove intoxicated. You endangered the lives of everyone else on the road because you don't care about anyone else's life, Junior." Leaning over him, she snarled. "And after I talk to Sheriff Shaw, it'll be official."

"What will be official?"

"You've stolen my life too." She turned on her heels and began to walk back to her car, but he knocked her over and ran for the fields, but suddenly stopped short.

The crunch of gravel echoed in the morning air as she

pushed herself to her feet. Her hands and knees were scraped and bloodied.

"Jade?"

"Edmund." She gasped.

A knock on the front door of the house. "Jade are you out here?"

She began to answer, but the click of the gun sent her heart falling to her feet. "Oh, no."

Turning, her brother held her gun at her, his eyes full of panic. "I'm not going back. It was a mistake. I didn't mean it, but I'm not going back to jail."

"Jade?" Edmund's voice called out as the slam of car doors caught her attention.

Who's here with him?

She called out, hoping to keep Edmund out of firing range. "Junior, listen. Please, put the gun down."

Rapid footsteps signaled his approach. "Jade?"

"I know you're upset, but please put the gun down." She released her shirt, allowing the keys to fall to the ground. "Come on, please, put it down before you hurt someone."

Edmund came around the corner and stopped. "Jade, get the hell out of there."

With shaking hands, Junior asked, "You still gonna turn me in?"

Her feet stopped moving forward as her lips thinned. "Junior, please."

"If you are going to take my life away, I swear I'll take yours."

As calm, cool, and collected as she attempted to be, she

didn't trust a gun in her brother's hand. He'd always been a sucky shot, but that didn't mean he couldn't do a lot of damage without much effort.

She held her hands up, a white flag gesture. "The keys are there. Give me my gun back or better yet, just put it down."

His eyes darted from her to Edmund's direction.

Her heart leapt to her throat. "Don't you dare."

Instead of handing it over, he moved his arm to point at Edmund. "I swear Jade, I'll do it."

Her heart slammed into her ribs as she pointed behind her. "Junior. Please, come get the keys, hand over my gun, and we'll call it even. Okay?"

"Jade, honey, get out of there." Edmund began to walk toward her, but she put her hand up.

"Please, Edmund, don't get too close." *Because I couldn't bear it if my brother was responsible for the deaths of two good men.*

"I don't want to go back to jail, Jade." Junior nervously shifted his weight. "I hate it there."

"That I believe, but shooting someone isn't going to solve anything."

A flash of movement behind her brother caught her eye. *The other doors slamming. Who did Edmund bring?*

"You gonna turn me in, Jade?" His hand shook, the gun still aimed in Edmund's direction.

She let out a long exhale, slowly closing the gap between her and her brother. "You killed someone."

His brow furrowed, the sting of betrayal on his face.

"How could you do that to me? I'm your brother."

"Give me the gun, Junior." She inched closer, her heart beat furiously.

"Jade, come on. Get out of there," Edmund shouted.

A look of defeat replaced her brother's panic. He fumbled with the gun, finally pointing the barrel at his own chest. "I'll do it, Jade."

The morning sun beat down on them. A line of sweat beaded on her lip as she tried to decide if she could get the gun out of his hand before he pulled the trigger. "Junior."

"I can't do it, Jade, but I can't go back to jail."

At that moment, a flash of movement came from the far side of the house.

Duke, the K9 cop, bolted out and ran right for her brother with Fred right behind him.

"Not the dogs!" Junior screamed and turned to run as Edmund ran for her.

Before she could process what had happened, the sickening sound of a bullet leaving the chamber echoed into the morning and Edmund collapsed on top of her.

Chapter Twenty-Five

EDMUND'S HEART LUNGED to his throat when he heard the gunshot.

In an instant, he thought she'd been hit, but when Junior fell to the ground, Edmund pulled her into his arms and joyfully listened to the sound of her rapid breathing. "I've got you. I've got you."

"Did he shoot you? Are you okay?" She cupped his face and kissed him. "Please tell me he didn't hurt you."

Junior screamed as Logan handcuffed him. "You shot me in the foot, you piece of shit!"

"No one had a gun out but you, Junior," Logan growled. "Get up. Let's go."

"Thank, God. I couldn't handle it if—" Her lip trembled and she buried her face in his chest, sobbing.

"I got you." He stroked her hair. The perfect scent of vanilla tickled his nose.

"I'm not walking. You can't make me." Junior went flaccid on the ground like a boneless chicken.

"That wouldn't be a smart decision." Brett called the dogs over before they ventured out in the fields. Both dogs reluctantly returned and stood by Brett, waiting for his next command. "I can always get Duke or Fred to help you make a better one."

Sitting up like a jack-in-the-box, Junior snarled, "Keep your dog far the hell away from me, Adams."

"Can you stand?" Edmund asked Jade and she nodded.

"Get a room." Thomas jogged by. "I'll look at this dumbass's foot before you take him in, Logan."

Jade's head popped up from Edmund's embrace. "Thomas is here?"

Her clothes were covered in grass and she flinched when he helped her to her feet. When he pulled his hands away, they were bloody. "What the hell happened?"

"Junior tackled me when—" Her forehead furrowed when she did a double take to see all the others present. "Logan? Brett? What's going on?"

With his heart rate returning to normal, Edmund inspected her palms. "We figured out that Junior was probably the one who stole Mr. Stevenson's car."

"We? How?" She looked around.

Junior still lay on the grass, complaining about how the dogs spooked him and the cops changed the rules.

Thomas removed Junior's shoe and quickly examined the foot. "Looks like you shot straight through. You should be fine, but you're going to need an X-ray and antibiotics."

"I don't understand. How did you—" Jade blinked several times, her bottom lip quivered.

He pulled a few pieces of grass from her hair. "Phoebe came in for a recheck a couple of mornings ago. Thomas saw her father's ring and heard the story about the car being stolen. We just put the pieces together."

"Like a puzzle." She looked at him adoringly.

He inspected her wounded hands. "Looks like it hurts."

"I'll live." She rested her chin on his chest.

"Course you will. You need to get that cleaned up."

"What, you want to play doctor now?"

He kissed her forehead and pulled her into his arms. How good it felt to have her there, to feel her heartbeat against his chest, to breathe her in. "I thought I'd lost you. That Junior took you away from me."

She wrapped her arms around him for a moment before she pulled away. "I'm sorry."

"What?" When he met her gaze, the anguish in her eyes returned.

"Edmund, I'm so sorry. This is such a mess."

He cringed at the pain in her voice. "Jade, please. It's going to be okay. It's his choice. Not yours."

Logan walked up and rested his hand on Jade's arm. "You okay, Jade?"

"No, not really." She wiped her face with her shirt before holding up her hands.

Large bloody scrapes ran across her palms. "He tackled me as I tried to get away to come call you guys."

Edmund's blood boiled and it took all the restraint he had not to walk over and beat Junior to a pulp. "Why didn't you wait for me?"

"Because I—" She pulled away from him as her face flushed. "Because I wanted to see what he had in there before you got here."

Logan crossed his arms over his chest. "Why? What did you think was in there?"

"Logan, it's my brother. Honestly, the top two were pot plants and a meth lab."

"Junior? Nah, he can't handle that kind of detail." The deputy pointed. "Should we take a look?"

All the color drained from her face.

"Jade, you okay?" Edmund slid his arm around her waist.

"No, Edmund, I'm not okay." Her words dripped with anguish. The woman who looked at him with love in her eyes moments ago, faded. "I just found out my brother committed grand theft auto and—"

"And?"

Her eyes went wide, as though she'd said something she hadn't anticipated. Standing, she waved Edmund off. "Logan, I-I have to show you something."

"Okay." Furrowing his forehead, the deputy nodded.

"It's the car."

"Which car? The one your brother stole?" Edmund kissed her forehead. "That's why we're here."

"No. Yes." Another wave of tears arrived as she motioned for them to follow her. "It's so much worse."

Junior's eyes went wide and he sprang to his feet with his hands cuffed behind his back. Limping, he tried to cut her off, but couldn't get five steps without falling to the ground again. "Jade! Jade! Come on, Sis, don't do this."

She didn't stop, but walked silently to the far end of the building. When she got to the corner, Edmund could see her shoulders shaking.

"Jade, come on. There's other cars. Logan! Logan. I got other shit. Go, go check out the north side. I've got a sweet Honda Pilot stashed behind some trees. I've got parts stashed over there." Junior's words came out in frantic bursts.

"Thanks, Junior. Nice of you to make our jobs easier today." Logan gave a respectful nod. "We'll get on that after I look in the building."

Edmund watched in fascination as Junior's eyes got wider and wider as they drew closer to the far end of the building. He could only imagine the toll this had taken on Jade. He caught up with her, resting his arm around her waist. "Jade, baby. It's going to be okay."

"No, Edmund. It's not." Weakly, she pointed at the Mercedes and Logan and Edmund stared.

"Is that blood?" Logan narrowed his gaze.

"It's a deer. It's just a deer," Junior pleaded as he attempted to limp over. Brett turned Junior toward the police car as Thomas helped and Fred and Duke wandered around, marking trees.

Edmund remembered seeing expensive cars like this all around Florida. The repairs would cost a fortune. "Damn, shame a deer crushed the grill like that…"

"A deer didn't crush…the grill." Jade let out a ragged breath. "Harry Monroe did."

A cold chill ran up Edmund's spine when he saw it. "Is that a handprint?"

Jade buried her face in her hands. "Yes. Yes."

"Holy shit." Logan stepped closer. "Did he say that's who he hit?"

She nodded as tears ran down her face like a waterfall.

"When did you find this?"

Jade sniffled. "Today, Logan. I found it right before you got here. That's why he tackled me. I grabbed the keys."

The muscle in Logan's jaw twitched as he appeared to be absorbing the scene.

Anger bubbled to the surface as Edmund's eyes darted from the front crushed grill to the man still yelling at Brett and Thomas. *Son of a bitch. How could you Jade? To Harry? To his family?*

Her shoulders shook as she silently cried.

Edmund momentarily pushed his fury aside. He could be mad later. Right now, she needed him. Wrapping his arms around her, Edmund expected Jade to collapse into him, but she didn't.

Instead, she gently moved his arms away and turned, cupping his face, giving him a slow, tender kiss. "I love you. I'm sorry."

"Why are you apologizing?" He hated the grief in her words. Hated that she'd felt a duty for those in her life that had let her down. "You aren't responsible for him."

The ambulance arrived to transport Junior to the hospital.

He screamed as they loaded him up on the stretcher.

"I'm so sorry." She walked silently toward the house, leaving Logan and Edmund behind.

He caught up with her, trying to cut off her escape. "Jade, wait."

Before Edmund could ask her anything, Logan cupped

her elbow. "Come on, Jade. Let's get your preliminary statement."

For the next fifteen minutes, Logan talked to Jade outside of Edmund's hearing range as paramedics Amanda Carter and Patrick Freeman treated Junior and then headed out as Sheriff Rob Shaw arrived.

Brett pulled out the crime scene tape and began measuring off the area.

Edmund offered to help, but Brett kindly refused.

"We need to take her down to the station to get her statement in writing," Logan explained to Edmund. "She's pretty shaken up about this."

"Can I go with her?"

Logan shook his head. "She said she didn't want anyone there."

"Come on, Logan, you can't believe that's what she wants right now. She's in shock. We all are."

A heavy hand on his shoulder kept Edmund from arguing further.

"Edmund, give her some space," Thomas replied. "She might be in shock, but trust me. Jade knows exactly what she wants right now."

"Fine." Looking in her direction, Edmund hoped she'd give him a glimpse, but she kept her back to him as she sat in the back of Logan's patrol car.

"Come on, Ed. Let's see if they need any help in the ER." Thomas pulled out his keys. "Working will pass the time and if they don't need our help, we can always go get drunk."

"Getting drunk sounds like a great idea." His eyes couldn't help but look toward the metal building once again. "Damn, I had no idea Junior had it in him."

"None of us did," Logan replied, fury burned in his eyes. "But I'm gonna make damn sure he never hurts anyone again."

When they arrived at the ER, it sat to capacity.

Reactions to insect bites in room six.

Stomach virus in room three.

Foot laceration in room seven.

Swallowed a quarter in room two.

Thomas and Edmund jumped in to thin the patient load and give the doctors in attendance, Tom Reynolds and Lucy, a break.

For a couple of hours, they treated patients and kept a watchful eye on Junior, especially when Nurse Shelly Westbrook walked into the room.

Per protocol, a police officer stayed at the bedside as Junior's wrist was handcuffed to the bed. Everyone was on high alert since the last time he'd been in the ER, he split Thomas's lip wide open.

With Betty as dispatcher, it took almost no time for the news to travel about who killed Harry Monroe.

Despite that, Edmund remained impressed at how little the staff discussed it.

At least when he was around.

Once the patient volume leveled off near shift change, Edmund decided to head back to the Graff as Thomas went home with Lucy.

For the rest of the evening, Edmund waited for Jade to call but his phone remained silent.

Not even a text.

The next morning, the front page of the Marietta paper printed a write-up about the crash, Harry's death, and even a picture of them towing the car from Jade's property.

At the very end, they mentioned how Jade had turned her brother in and how he was apprehended by the police department and K9 unit.

And Fred. Edmund mentally added as he read the article while waiting for a patient's CBC to come back.

For the entire twelve hours, each time he walked up to the desk, into a room, or even in the hospital hallways, the only topic of discussion seemed to be Harry Monroe and the man who killed him.

He glanced at his phone again and again, but not a word from Jade.

It wasn't that long ago he didn't want to see anyone in his family after his arrest. He sat in his house for days, shades drawn, lights out, soaked in guilt for bringing that kind of insanity to his family's lives.

After a couple of days, his siblings arrived and rescued him from his own grief.

Jade had to be going through the same thing and he'd be damned if he'd let her go through it alone.

At the end of the day, he made one quick stop, then went back to the Graff to shower and landed on her doorstep before the sun set. As he waited for her to answer, he decided no matter what Thomas said, Edmund would verify Jade was okay.

When the door opened, she didn't have to say a word for him to know what she'd been doing since he'd seen her last.

Her swollen face and red eyes, horribly wrinkled sweatshirt and yoga pants told him everything.

"Can I come in?" He held up a bag of chocolates from Sage's.

Her eyes darted from his face to the candies. "I don't know why you'd want to."

"Please."

Weakly, she nodded and stepped back.

Several Hershey's candy bar wrappers and an empty bottle of wine sat next to the couch. "Glad to see you're eating."

A stress laugh escaped her and sent her into another wave of sobs. "Edmund, you should go. I can't do this right now. Or ever."

"Come here." He attempted to hug her but she pulled back.

"Please, Edmund. Don't."

"Why?" Edmund reached for her, but she backed away. "What are you doing?"

"You deserve someone with far less drama." Moving around the kitchen table, she repositioned chairs in the same place. "I mean seriously. I've got baggage."

"Everyone has baggage, Jade." He dropped the bag of chocolates in the middle of the table, hoping to get her to quit avoiding his touch.

"I've got baggage inside of baggage."

"What you did yesterday, I'd say you're unpacking some

of it, even giving it away."

She shook her head and threw her hands up in frustration. "You know I'm going to have to testify against him."

"I figured. How long did you know?"

"That he'd stolen the car or hit Harry?" She played with the seam of her shirt.

"Both."

She slumped in the chair. "Only when I'd cut the locks off the building and looked inside."

"Why didn't you wait for me?" He sat next to her, but she leaned away. "I told you I would help clean up."

"Because, I wanted to make sure if he did have something ridiculous going on in there, I could prepare for you leaving. That I could tell you on my terms the mess he was in."

Her answered shocked him. "Leaving? Why would I leave?"

"Why would you stay? I can handle the disasters that happen in *my* life, but I can't deal with bringing you into it." She reached over and touched the bag of chocolates, but didn't pull them closer. A laugh escaped her. "You know, when I saw he wasn't growing pot or cooking meth, I thought, 'great, it's not going to be anything.' That, for once, he didn't throw a wrench in my world."

"And then you found the car."

"I found Mr. Stevenson's car and saw the blood on the windshield and hood."

Edmund shook his head in disbelief. "Why would he keep it?"

"He's never cleaned his room so why would he clean up this mess? He probably figured he'd deal with it only when he had to."

"He hit, killed someone."

Tears rolled down her face. "According to the police, my brother couldn't unload the car to anyone with it being so damaged, especially it being so high-end. Guess he doesn't know the right people. And none of my brother's *friends*—" she used air quotes "—would help him."

"Why not?"

"No one wanted to deal with his problems anymore." Pulling her knees to her chest, she wrapped her arms around her legs, holding them tight to her body. "I guess after he woke up the next day and saw the car, Junior decided he'd deal with it later and hid it in the garage. Dad was too sick to go out there. Figured I wouldn't go in there because he told me not to. Figured I wouldn't sell the house so his secret was safe. Figured I wouldn't tell anyone even if I did find it."

Anger pumped through his veins seeing her so wounded. "Jade—"

Her bottom lip trembled as her feet touched the floor. "And then went on his merry way, doing whatever it was he did to fill the hours of the day, not thinking about how he'd murdered someone."

It didn't go unnoticed that she wouldn't look at him. "I don't understand it."

"He killed someone, Edmund. He ran over a man and drove away. Just drove off and didn't think about it again." She grabbed the box of candies, tore it open, and shoved three in her mouth.

Cautiously, he rested his hand on her arm. "What happened when you found the car?"

"It was bad enough to find it but then to realize he'd hit someone."

"Did he tell you who he hit?" Edmund handed one square of chocolate to her when she finished the three she'd already taken.

"No, not immediately. I wouldn't let him walk away until he answered me, but when he told me how long the car had been there and about when it happened, I knew."

"But he told you."

"Yes and that…that was gut wrenching. How can someone walk away like that? Feel nothing for anyone else?" She picked out another candy and nibbled on the corner before inhaling it. "Sage can really make some good stuff."

After treating so many in the ER for injuries caused by other's indifference, Edmund wished he had a solid answer for her. "I don't know. Been asking the same thing since my father died."

"It's one thing to lose your father. It's another when your brother is the one who caused the disaster."

"True." Remembering how they battled the bad guys in book three of the Harry Potter series, he handed her another piece of chocolate.

She took it without question. "Did the man who hit you go to jail?"

"Yes, but when his sentence was given, he shrugged as though he'd been sent to detention. He didn't care about us.

All he cared about was his freedom."

Resting her head on his shoulder, she sighed. "I'm sorry you had to go through that. It's not right. Fair at all."

"No, it isn't." He stroked her hair. "And it's not fair to you, either."

"How could he have done that to the Monroes? Why?" She buried her face in her hands.

Pulling her chair flush to his, he rubbed her back. "And my dad was killed by a drunk driver. The man never did seem to think he deserved such a severe punishment. If he hadn't been beat up on impact, he would have fled the scene."

She jumped to her feet and stood behind the chair. "But you weren't related to the person who killed someone. Married to the one who tried to kill you and your best friend."

"My ex-girlfriend tried to frame me for embezzlement."

"Edmund, please listen to me. I keep having this same horrible thing over and over again. It's exhausting to keep fighting this kind of chaos."

"Shitty people in our lives are shitty people." Approaching her, he rested his hand on her face, his thumb gently caressing her skin. "And through all that crap, I found you. I'd go through all that hell again if it brought me to this moment."

"Are those our only options? To go through hell to get what we want?"

Drying her eyes with his thumbs, he tilted her chin up. "No, but let us make what we've got a helluva lot better than what we had before."

"What do we have here, Edmund?"

Sandwiching her hands between his, he rested his forehead next to hers. "Happily ever after."

Her hands rested on his. "You deserve so much—"

"You're right. I have so much. With you." Having her close answered all his prayers, his hopes, his plans.

She shook her head. "I'm so tired of fighting."

"Then don't. Let me be your knight and fight for you." He pushed her hair out of her face. "I love you, Jade, and nothing your brother did will change that. I love *you*."

"I don't need you to fight for me." She moved away from his touch. "I can fight for myself. I don't need you or anyone else to do this for me."

Frustration coursed through his veins as he held his hands up in surrender. "Jade."

"I'm not some damsel in distress and I'm sure as hell not waiting to be rescued." With fire in her eyes, she turned toward the living room then reached back and grabbed another piece of chocolate. "I have been taking care of myself for a long time when no one else would."

How he hated she'd been so hurt. So purposely bruised by those she put her faith in. "Yes, you have taken care of yourself. You're a survivor and that's one of the reasons I love—"

"Please stop saying that." Running her fingers through her hair, she shook her head. "I can't do this. I can't."

"Do what?" His heart dropped like a lead weight in his

gut. "Jade, you can't mean that."

"I can't think about you, us, right now. I need you to go." She opened the front door. "Now."

Chapter Twenty-Six

IN THE THREE days since the truth had been uncovered, Jade turned down several phone calls from surrounding county newspapers and a few radio stations to encourage her to tell her side of the story.

It was well known the hosts who called her had a reputation for twisting a tale until it became sensationalist enough to sell ad spots.

As if I want your venomous interpretation out there. I already feel responsible enough.

Other calls had been from locals who were angry she hadn't done more sooner and she should have known her brother was capable of anything.

As if I would have let him walk away from that.

She'd stopped answering the phone, drawn the blinds, and binge-watched shows like *Timeless—Save Rufus*—and *Suits*.

Even Edmund's texts and heartfelt messages he'd left her wouldn't lift the dark emotional cloud that hung over her like Sadness from the movie *Inside Out*.

She couldn't pull him into her world again. Not after everything she'd been through, asked him to understand about her, and now to find out who she was related to.

A murderer.

But she missed Edmund. Desperately.

Every part of her craved to be near him again.

To talk to him.

To make him laugh.

To make love to him.

The mere idea of him hurt her heart and, yet, she couldn't stop thinking of his smile, his kisses, his awkward sexiness.

It had been the only thing that had kept her sane these past few tumultuous days. Her fingers itched to text him back this morning, but she clenched her fists and pulled her hand away from her phone.

"Don't go there. Leave him be." Curled up on the couch with nothing but the remote control, her dog, and another box of Sage's chocolates, she planned to begin season five of *Suits* when a call came in from photographer, Charlie Foster.

Jade immediately picked it up.

"Jade? This is Charlie. Can I come over? I have something for you."

-\|∽2\|-

CHARLIE HAD ALWAYS been extremely kind and honest. For the past year, she'd been dating Logan Tate and the two were a power couple.

Maybe talking to someone other than police and herself would help. "Sure. Come on over."

Brett had been nice enough to keep Fred some of the time and the hospital had been compassionate about her schedule. Still, at some point, she'd have to go back to reality and face the judgmental stares from the people around her.

I swear, as soon as that check clears from selling the property, I'm out of here.

She'd well remembered the pitying looks from her San Diego coworkers when she'd returned to the unit. The same from the social workers when they sat with her as she told her story about her stepfather.

She hated those "poor you" and "bless her heart" looks, but thankfully, Charlie didn't give her that face, because when Jade opened the door, Charlie stood there with a large coffee and two food containers from Main Street Diner.

How she loved that Charlie acted like it was simply another day.

"You look exhausted." Charlie gave Jade a quick hug and walked right in. "Honey, you've got to get out of these clothes. You look like you're homeless and they are covered in dog hair."

Fred barked.

"Nice dog hair," Charlie added after setting the food on the table. She turned and shooed Jade out of the kitchen, insisting she clean up before eating.

A good shower and teeth brushing later, Jade returned wearing clean clothes and feeling a bit more human. "Thanks."

"Better?"

"Yes."

"How long have you locked yourself away?" Charlie smiled as she handed over the coffee.

"Three days." The warmth of the drink permeated through the cup. Jade took a deep inhale and relished how the dark roast made her blood pump a little faster.

Kind of like Edmund.

She mentally growled. "Don't go there."

Charlie sat down. "Okay, now, we've got two daily specials and coffee. Time for some good, *honest* conversation."

Jade followed the smells of bacon, sourdough bread, and cinnamon to the table. "What did Gabby create today?"

Handing her one of the containers, Charlie smiled. "Mesquite bacon with pecan-cream-cheese-stuffed cinnamon bread."

Jade opened the lid and was immediately attacked by such rich aromas, she almost drooled on herself. "This smells incredible."

As Charlie settled in, she snapped her fingers and pulled an envelope from her bag. "This is for you."

"What is it?"

"Just look."

Sliding the photos out, Jade had to make a conscious effort to keep breathing. "Edmund?"

Charlie nodded as she chewed on a piece of bacon. "Yes. He joined us for a bit of lunch a couple of weeks ago. I couldn't help but take pictures of him."

The perfect curve of his lips. The chiseled line of his jaw. The broadness of his shoulders. Heat rose up her face, her body tingled. "He looks amazing."

"My camera loves him."

I love him, too. A quick sob escaped her. "These are amazing. Thank you."

Charlie searched through drawers until she found a couple of forks and returned to the table. "You know what my favorite one is?"

"What?" *Because I can't decide.*

Last year, Charlie's talent behind the lens and twelve of Marietta's hottest first responders had built a calendar to raise money for Harry's House.

The very Harry who her brother ran over.

Would the town ever forgive her for her brother's atrocity?

With a flick of her wrist, Charlie pulled out one photograph, placing it on the top of the pile. "That was the exact moment your name was mentioned."

The bliss in his eyes stole the breath from her. Jade gently touched the photo with her fingers. "My name?"

"Logan and I were talking about your rotten day and as soon as your name was out of each of our mouths, this is what Edmund looked like." Charlie raised an eyebrow. "See how he smiles? That man has it bad for you."

Her bottom lip trembled. The joy in his eyes, the curve of his mouth.

Charlie tapped the photo. "That, my friend, is a man in love."

"Yes, but—"

Wagging her finger, Charlie shook her head as she gave Fred a piece of bacon from Jade's plate. "Don't do that to yourself. I almost lost out on Logan because I let my pride get in the way."

"I can't—"

"Quit telling yourself you can't. What your brother did was abhorrent, but *he* did that. Not you." She cut off a piece of the French toast. "And you turned him in, even when your brother drew a gun on you, you still told him he deserved to go to prison."

Even though everything Charlie said was true Jade couldn't help but feel smothered by guilt. "Edmund deserves—"

"Someone who loves him."

"You're really good at this, you know."

Charlie smirked. "It's a gift."

Staring at the photo again, the corner of her mouth twitched. "I do love him, you know."

"Then go do something about it." Patting her hand, Charlie gave her a wink and stole another piece of bacon off her plate, handing it to the dog that waited patiently. "Right now."

"Right now?"

"Logan said Edmund's worked in the ER until this morning. If you're quick, you might catch him before he naps." Tapping her watch, Charlie gave her a sideways glance. "Or, you know, maybe takes a run."

Jade grabbed her keys and ran out the front steps, but before she got to her car, she saw him, jogging up the street.

With her heart in her throat, stood in the middle of the sidewalk, waiting patiently as he drew closer.

For a moment, his pace slowed, but he continued forward.

"Okay, okay." She ran her fingers through her hair, hoping to look presentable. She checked her breath when he was only a house away.

Breathe. Just breathe. The worst he can say is he doesn't want to be with you.

She choked back a sob.

That would be the worst thing ever.

Her heart pounded hard as she wrapped her brain around what she wanted to say as he stopped in front of her.

Out of the corner of her eye, a flash of gold. On the fence, a yellow warbler perched and stared at her.

Daddy's favorite.

His breathing labored, sweat on his lip. "Jade."

"I've never believed in fairy tales," she blurted and cursed herself for never taking a public speaking class. "Let me start over. Even when I was a child, those stories never made sense to me because if your happiness relied on others to save you, how would you know what happiness was?"

Silence. He rested his hands on his hips as he regained his breath.

She marveled at the width of his shoulders, the muscles in his jaw, the color of his eyes. "Look. I'm not great at this part of the, the, whatever this is."

"Okay?" A bemused look appeared on his face.

She rolled the hem of her T-shirt between her fingers as the bird hopped on the fence. "It's always challenging for me to, to, talk to someone, um, interesting."

"Go on." He tilted his head as an eyebrow raised.

"But, but, but once I'm comfortable with someone, um, interesting, the conversation is easy. I would like to get better talking with you if you'll give me the chance."

For a moment, she believed he'd walk right by her and leave her behind.

Why wouldn't he? Who in their right mind would want to deal with a thirty-something-year-old woman with a Jackie Collins heroine level backstory and a batshit crazy brother, no matter how much she loved him?

Internally, she waited for the standard rejections. "Thanks but no thanks" or "You're not worth it."

"I would like that." Pulling her into his arms, he passionately kissed her and she melted against him.

He rested his forehead against hers. "I would like to get to know you, too."

"I'm so sorry I pushed you away." Tears clouded her vision.

"I know why you did."

"That doesn't make it okay." She sucked on her bottom lip. "I can't promise I won't be nuts when my brother's case goes to trial."

Edmund nibbled the pulse point of her neck. "I'll be there every step of the way."

"And I can't promise people will be forgiving."

"I know, but a lot of people in town know you stood up to Junior even when he had a gun on you." Moving a lock of hair out of her face, he smirked. "A lot of people are angry, but they aren't angry at you."

The taste of salty tears coated her lips. "How do you know what to say?"

"I'm just honest. You smell like vanilla."

"And I know how much you love vanilla." Jade giggled.

"Enough to spend the rest of my life with it."

The bird gave another quick chirp and flew away as joy finally replaced doubt in her heart. "You like vanilla that much that you'd want to have it every day?"

"Not like. Love. I love vanilla."

"Love?"

"Yes, love."

"I see." She swallowed hard as she soaked him in. "Love?"

"Love."

Cocking her head, she playfully asked, "Don't you think you'd eventually get bored with vanilla every day?"

"No, because vanilla's great with chocolate," he whispered, the vibration of his breath tickled her skin. "Strawberry. Carmel. Pineapple. Peach."

"Cinnamon. Sprinkles. Whipped cream." She grabbed handfuls of his shirt, her body on fire from his touch.

"Yes. Vanilla's what it all starts with and, if you love vanilla, it can work with anything."

"Yes, you sure can."

Three weeks later...

"CAN I TAKE it off yet?"

"Nope, keep it on," Edmund instructed as the vehicle

bounced a few more times.

Jade always had a good sense of direction and they were for certain off the beaten path.

"Almost there." Edmund rested his hand on her thigh. "Just another minute."

She sat on her hands so she wouldn't be tempted to take off the blindfold he'd asked her to wear as soon as she sat in his car.

When he picked her up, he acted like a kid on Christmas morning. More excited than she'd ever seen him. She'd worn the sundress he'd requested and brought a good bottle of wine with a couple of plastic cups.

The car came to a slow stop and he killed the engine.

"Now?"

"Hold on, hold on." She heard the click of the automatic door locks and his door open. A whoosh of the summer scents came pouring in, igniting her senses.

When he opened her door and took her hand, she heard the sound of running water. "Edmund, are we—"

"Patience, love. Patience."

His hand rested in the small of her back as he guided her a short distance before removing the blindfold. "What do you think?"

It took a moment for her to adjust her eyes, but in front of her, the best view of the mountains, over the trees, and behind her a huge field of flowers. "Is this?"

"The property that was for sale next to yours. Yes."

"But why?"

He pulled her flush, his hand rested on her backside.

"Because I can't imagine looking at these mountains without you."

"Does that mean you're staying in Marietta?"

He shrugged. "For now, but while I'm here, this gives us a place to get away from all the chaos and the gossip in town."

She let out a long breath. "Yes, there's going to be a lot of that for a long time considering what my brother's done."

"But out here, it's just us." He kissed her without restraint until she grabbed onto him to stay standing.

The afternoon breeze drifted the scents of flowers and sunshine around them. "So, what's on your mind?"

His finger ran down the curve of her shoulder, moving the dress strap down. "Now, we've done the naked thing at night. I say we christen this place during the day."

"It's going to be a challenge to do this in your car."

"Yes, but I'm up for it if you are."

"I'm always up for a challenge with you." An excited chill ran up her spine at his brazenness. "But, goodness, Dr. Davidson. Aren't you worried someone will see us?"

Laying a path of gentle kisses against her neck, he whispered, "Out here? Not a chance."

The End

The Marietta Medical Series

About the Author

Native Texan Patricia W. Fischer is a natural born storyteller. Ever since she listened to her great-grandmother tell stories about her upbringing the early 1900's, Patricia has been hooked on hearing of great adventures and love winning in the end.

On her way to becoming an award-winning writer, she became a percussionist, actress, singer, waitress, bartender, pre-cook, and finally a trauma nurse before she realized she needed to get her butt to a journalism class.

After earning her journalism degree from Washington University, Patricia has been writing for multiple publications on numerous subjects including women's health, foster/adoption advocacy, ovarian cancer education, and entertainment features.

These days she spends her days with her family, two dogs, and a few fish while she creates a good story with a touch of reality, a dash of laughter, and a whole lot of love.

Visit her at PatriciaWFischer.com

Thank you for reading

Challenging the Doctor

If you enjoyed this book, you can find more from all our great authors at TulePublishing.com, or from your favorite online retailer.

TULE
PUBLISHING

Made in the USA
Columbia, SC
24 June 2024